MERGER

Have you been called?

Start your training at

www.soterians.com

book two THE SOTERIANS SERIES

MERGER

JACQUELYN WHEELER

Second Edition
ISBN 978-0-9825160-3-4

For Holly

But let there be spaces in your togetherness,
And let the winds of the heavens dance between you.
Love one another but make not a bond of love:
Let it rather be a moving sea between the shores of your souls.
Fill each other's cup but drink not from one cup.
Give one another of your bread but eat not from the same loaf.
Sing and dance together and be joyous, but let each one of you be alone,
Even as the strings of a lute are alone though they quiver with the same music.
Give your hearts, but not into each other's keeping.
For only the hand of Life can contain your hearts.
And stand together, yet not too near together:
For the pillars of the temple stand apart,
And the oak tree and the cypress grow not in each other's shadow.

~ from *The Prophet* by Khalil Gibran

About the Soterians

Soteria was the ancient Greek goddess of safety and deliverance. When the balance of good and evil tips too far in evil's favor, certain worthy people carrying a rare gene are called forward to restore the balance. These people are known as *Soterians*. Once they have restored the proper balance of good over evil, their powers fade, and they resume their normal lives. There are five primary types of Soterians: Scouts, Empaths, Sentries, Warriors, and Mentors.

Scouts are responsible for reconnaissance, which allows the unit to make targeted moves and minimize risk and damage on both sides. Scouts have very acute vision and hearing, can become invisible, and can fly.

Empaths are the healers and illusionists of a unit. They can read other people's feelings, cast illusions, and heal allies.

Sentries are the defenders of their unit. Their extraordinary strength allows them to be a physical barrier to harm and can stop an enemy in his tracks. They protect themselves and their allies by emanating a shield that bullets, fire, and gas cannot penetrate.

Warriors go on the offensive and take down the enemy when all else fails. Their incredible speed and strength make them highly valuable.

Mentors find and train Soterians. They have the ability to tap into universal knowledge in times of crisis.

When conditions are right, Deimos, the ancient god of fear and the greatest source of evil on earth, rises out of hibernation and spreads evil across the globe. When this happens, a Soterian with a special combination of talents can evolve into an *Alchemist*. An Alchemist draws power from both good and evil and has all of the other Soterians' powers, as well as the ability to generate fire, making Alchemists the most powerful and most dangerous of all the Soterians. Alchemists are very rare.

Lastly, *Keepers* are not Soterians but are trusted allies of a unit and help with their missions. They play an important role in doing research and assisting the entire unit.

The Soterians series consists of five books about modern-day Soterians told through the eyes of Ashlyn Woods, a Scout and an Alchemist. *Merger* is the second book in the series.

Santa Barbara Unit	*San Francisco Unit*
Mentor: John Gordon	Mentor: Theresa Silva
Scout: Ashlyn Woods	Scout: Jesse Burton
Empath: Rebecca Epstein	Empath: Claire Marks
Sentry: Christoph Voight	Sentry: Kenji Fukawa
Warrior: Michael MacNeil	Warrior: Raina Forrester
Keeper: Kai Anderson	Keeper: Paul Adams

Table of Contents

Chapter One: The Inquisition

I awoke to the sound of a gull crying as it flew past the window. I stretched my hearing toward it, then automatically took inventory of the other sounds around us. Most people in Isla Vista were still asleep, and all I could hear was the gentle crashing of the waves on the beach a few blocks away. Next to me, the sound of Kai's breathing brought a smile to my face, and I opened my eyes as I rolled over.

I stared at him in amazement, as I had so many times before, wondering what I had done to deserve having this incredible guy in my life. He stirred, then slowly opened his beautiful green eyes, blinking a few times.

"Hey," he said softly.

"Good morning. Happy spring break."

He pulled me to him, and I nuzzled into his chest, listening to the deep rhythm of his heart beating.

"I suppose we should get going," he murmured.

"We have two whole weeks. I'm not in any rush."

"I'm just looking forward to getting back on the road with you. And to getting tonight's visit out of the way."

I sighed. "I need some breakfast before we hit the road. Can't face this on an empty stomach."

"Ashlyn," he said, tilting my chin up so that I was looking directly into his eyes. "It's going to be fine. I promise."

I wanted to believe him—I really did. But I knew better.

A few hours later, we were driving north toward San Francisco when suddenly Kai pointed toward a tree. I looked up just in time to see a pair of red-tail hawks spread their wings and take off into the sky. "A good omen," he said.

I studied Kai's face. He looked happy, as excited as I was to be back on the road. We were driving up the west coast to Seattle, then east to Minnesota where I would meet his extended family (which scared the hell out of me), and then back across the middle states on Interstate 80 to California. After the crazy six months we'd just endured, we were desperately in need of a vacation, and I couldn't wait to spend two weeks on the road with him. But there was one part of the trip I was dreading.

"When you meet my dad, just be yourself," I warned him for probably the twelfth time. "He's never liked any of my boyfriends, and I don't expect it to be any different with you."

"So I shouldn't ask for his permission to marry you?"

"No! Kai, seriously, don't tease me like that. I'm already a nervous wreck."

He smiled. "Ashlyn, you're a Soterian. If you can go head-to-head with evil, you can deal with your dad."

I bit my fingernail. "I'm really worried about Deimos and what his next move will be. John wasn't very happy about us taking this trip."

"We'll be fine. Your powers are more than a match for Deimos or anyone he sends our way."

I looked out the window, watching the scenery roll by as we drove. I had promised myself I wasn't going to think about Deimos on our vacation, but knowing that the greatest source of evil on earth is after you makes it pretty hard to relax.

When we came off the Golden Gate Bridge and into Sausalito where my dad lived, my stomach began to squirm. We parked in front of his house, and I checked my hair in the rear-view mirror, taking a deep breath to steady myself. I stepped out of the car, and Kai took my hand. "Stop worrying. Your dad loves you and just wants the best for you."

I nodded sadly, certain that my dad would never think that Kai was the best thing for me.

We rang the bell, and a moment later the door flew open. "Ashlyn, you made it! And this must be Kai."

"Evelyn, this is Kai Anderson. Kai, this is my step-mom, Evelyn Woods," I said stiffly. They shook hands, and I saw her smile flicker as she glanced at his earring.

"Nice to meet you," Kai said with a bright smile. He seemed perfectly at ease and confident. At least one of us was.

"Well, come in, come in," Evelyn sang. "Would you like something to drink? How long was the drive this time?"

"About six and a half hours. Not too bad." I started biting my nails again, and Kai gently reached over and took my hand out of my mouth, an amused smile crossing his lips.

We followed Evelyn into the house. Kai paused and looked around. It was a beautiful house, its large open rooms filled with elegant furniture in creams and soft blues. The picture windows in the living room overlooked the San Francisco Bay. He gave a low whistle. "You have a beautiful view."

"Thanks. We just love watching the boats go by," Evelyn replied cheerfully.

Just then, my dad strode into the room. "Hello!" he boomed, giving me a great big bear hug. I hugged him tightly and then turned to Kai.

"Dad, this is Kai Anderson. Kai, this is my dad, Robert Woods."

Kai extended his hand. "Pleased to meet you."

My dad, who was over six feet tall and built like a tank, towered over Kai as he firmly shook his hand. "Likewise," he said, giving Kai the quick once over.

Evelyn served us lemonade, launching into questions as she poured. "So Kai, what do you do?"

I groaned. "Can't the cross-examination wait until dinner?"

Kai gave my hand a small squeeze. "I'm a guitar player. I'm working as a veterinary technician while I try to break into the music business. And I just went back to school so I can finish my degree."

"Oh, what are you studying?" Evelyn asked hopefully.

"Music."

"Uh huh." She peered at him. "And what do you hope to do with that when you graduate?"

"Well, if becoming a rock star doesn't pan out, I'll teach music. Hopefully at a university."

I felt myself wincing as Evelyn stared at him blankly. My dad's eyes were already glazing over, and he was absent-mindedly playing with his mustache. Not a good sign.

"Shall we eat?" I suggested, struggling to keep the hysteria out of my voice.

We sat down to dinner, and the conversation died down to small talk. I picked at my food while surreptitiously watching the others enjoying Evelyn's casserole. It looked and smelled delicious. The savory herbs and cheese were making my mouth water, but my stomach was in knots. After a few minutes, I was just beginning to hope that they'd stopped with the questions when Evelyn started grilling Kai again.

"What about commercials?" she asked, swirling the wine in her glass. "I hear you can make a lot of money writing jingles."

"That's not really what I'm interested in."

"Well, sure," she said with an irritated little laugh. "It would be wonderful if we could all just do whatever we want, but you have to pay the bills."

"I don't think I'd be any good at it. It's not the kind of music I write," he said simply.

4

Evelyn raised her eyebrows and glanced at my dad. "Well, I guess that's that."

"Dad, how's your job going?" I asked, desperately trying to change the subject.

"Oh, you know. The usual politics and committees. Life in academia."

"I guess Kai will find out all about that," Evelyn murmured.

"Perhaps," Dad said. I felt a wave of nausea as I realized he didn't think Kai would make it as a professor, either.

This was a fiasco. Clearly, they had decided that Kai was a complete loser. I wanted Kai to explain how music was actually a very difficult major, and that it didn't involve just sitting around listening to your iPod all day. But he just smiled and weathered their questions with incredible grace, which I had to admit was the best approach he could take. If he tried to explain it to them and talked about what good grades he was getting, he would just sound defensive. The situation was totally hopeless.

My dad picked up his glass and sat back in his chair. "So you're off to Indianapolis. What's there?"

"Minneapolis. We're going to visit Kai's family."

"It's going to be awfully cold," Dad remarked. "And bleak. Not a very exciting destination for spring break."

"Actually, it's in the mid-fifties right now, so it should be fine. Minneapolis is supposed to be awesome. I'm really excited to check it out." I looked hopefully at Kai, but he was just listening calmly.

"I was there for a conference once, about ten years ago," Evelyn said. "It was kind of a pit."

"Maybe it's just where you were. There's actually a ton going on there. Lots of cultural events, incredible restaurants."

"Not like San Francisco," she scoffed. "I mean, try to find a decent wine list in Minneapolis." She gave a little laugh again and took a sip of wine. My dad nodded in agreement.

I stared at them, bewildered. Kai just looked placidly at me, and the answer was written clearly on his face: there was nothing I could say that was going to sell them on Kai or anything having to do with him. They would get to know him at their own pace. And I was just going to have to let it go.

When dinner was finally over, and we were in the car on the way to my mom's apartment in Berkeley, Kai was upbeat.

"Well, at least they didn't kick me out." When I didn't respond, he reached for my hand. "Ashlyn, it's okay. I'm not expecting them to like me yet. They have a different idea of what kind of guy you should be with. But I'm in this for the long haul, and they'll come around eventually."

I wasn't so sure.

When we got to my mom's place, she was thrilled to see us, and I felt my spirits lift. She gave us both warm hugs and proceeded to try to feed us, even though she knew we'd just had dinner. "Have some apricot bars," she coaxed. "They're from that fabulous new bakery I told you about."

My stomach growled as I sank into one of her comfy, overstuffed chairs. I had barely touched my dinner, so I gratefully accepted an apricot bar and some tea. She asked us how it had gone with my dad. I gave her the most watered-down recap I could, resisting the urge to compare it to the Spanish Inquisition. But Mom was able to read between the lines just fine.

"Ah yes, I can imagine that was a lot of fun for both of you," she chuckled. "It's funny how you had to deal with this with Todd's family, and now Kai has to deal with it with your dad."

I winced at the mention of my ex-boyfriend. "'Funny' isn't the word I would have chosen. Besides, we don't know yet whether Kai's family is going to like me. It might be the same horror story all over again." I put the rest of the apricot bar back on my plate.

"It won't be," Kai insisted. "My family isn't like that. As long as you're pro-union and root for the Vikings, you're in. Anyway, for the next five days it's just us and the road."

I smiled. In spite of all the awful feelings that were churning inside of me, it was going to be an amazing vacation.

"Speaking of Todd, he called the other day," Mom said.

Oh God. "Why? What did he want?"

"He just wanted to chat. He's taking some classes at the junior college."

I sighed in exasperation. "Mom, you shouldn't answer his calls. He's just calling to pump you for information about me. And to tell you things he thinks might impress me."

"You're not all we talk about," she retorted. "Todd and I have our own friendship."

I could see I wasn't going to make her see reason on this point, so I stood up. "We have to go to bed. We're going to hit the road early."

"You're in luck. The weather is supposed to be very nice for the next week. No snow or rain predicted along your route for at least five days."

"You worried we're going to end up in a ditch somewhere?" I laughed.

"Don't even joke about that," she said darkly. "I'm doing everything I can to keep you protected. I've got my meditation group visualizing a safe trip for you both, and I won't be able to sleep soundly until you're back home."

I bit my lip to keep from laughing. If she only knew the kind of protections I carried with me all the time, she'd sleep just fine.

Chapter Two: Close Encounter

"Who can tell me some practical uses for the staff?" Theresa held up a long wooden pole and looked into each of our faces in turn.

It was Sunday morning, and Kai and I were training with the San Francisco unit of Soterians before we hit the road. It would be the last training session we'd have for two weeks, and we wanted to make the most of it. As the Mentor of the San Francisco unit, Theresa had a lot of the same knowledge and skills as John, but she took a very different approach to training. Today she had decided to teach us to fight with staffs.

"Let's see," said Jesse, his typical wry look on his face. "If you're shipwrecked and in a life boat, you can use an oar to fight off the other passengers when they try to take your rations."

"That's enough, Jesse," Theresa snapped. "There are many everyday objects that resemble a staff—shovels, brooms, fallen branches, even a rifle that's out of ammunition. The techniques you learn here will work with any of these."

We took the staffs and began to run through drills. She taught us to twirl them in our hands like batons, which would help deflect blows from small weapons, and to strike at our opponents. Unlike John, Theresa was a proponent of teaching offensive techniques as well as defensive skills.

Since Jesse and I were both Scouts and could fly, we practiced sparring while hovering a few feet above the ground. It was fun to swoop around and strike at each other with the staffs, although it was hard to keep up with him because he kept making ridiculous faces and howling like Bruce Lee, making me laugh so hard that I couldn't defend myself.

After a while we switched partners, and Kai and I ran through the choreographed steps on the ground, striking our staffs together overhand, underhand, and swinging them around like a bat. It felt more like we were performing a dance than sparring. As I swept my staff at his ankles, he jumped and then swung his staff down toward the top of my head. I blocked the attack by holding my staff up with both hands, the weapons making a loud crack as they connected. I fell back into a backward roll, twirled my staff overhead, and stood back in a ready stance, preparing for the next move. We were starting to get good at this.

"I don't know," Raina was muttering to herself, spinning her staff mechanically. "Seems like a waste of time to me." She was a very powerful Warrior and had incredible hand-to-hand combat skills.

"You think you could easily defeat someone even if they had a large branch in their hands?" Jesse asked as he flew over her head, brandishing his staff wildly. I laughed, and we all stopped for a moment to watch them.

Raina snorted. "You bet."

"Show us," Theresa said.

Without another word, Raina charged at me. I held my ground for a second, ready to deflect her attack, but at the last second I panicked and shot up into the air. Raina just missed me and plowed straight into Kai, knocking him flat with a loud thump.

9

"Kai!" I shouted and flew down to where he was lying on the floor, clutching his elbow.

"Whoops, sorry about that," Raina said as she climbed off of him. Jesse and Kenji, the San Francisco unit's Sentry, were doubled over on the other side of the room convulsing with laughter.

Claire rushed over to us. "Hold still, Kai. You'll feel better in a minute." She put her hands on his arm, and I could almost feel the healing energy streaming out of her. After about ten seconds, Kai sat up, color rushing to his cheeks.

"Better?" she asked.

"Yeah, much better," he said, rubbing his elbow. "Guess I need to practice falling more. You're a powerful Empath, Claire. Thank you."

"You're very welcome," she said, a proud smile spreading across her pretty face. I helped Kai to his feet.

"Maybe we should get on the road," I suggested.

"Sure. It's been fun, though. I want to spend more time on weapons."

"John doesn't like to teach them until you've mastered hand-to-hand skills," I grumbled. "But there's nothing to stop us from training with Theresa when we're here." I gave Theresa a grateful smile as we left the studio. I had a very deep respect for John, but I appreciated learning from Theresa, too. Their teaching styles complemented each other very well.

* * *

"Could you hand me the water?" Kai passed me the bottle, and I took a long drink as I gazed at the incredible scenery around us. We were hiking up a trail above Lake Quinault on Washington's Olympic Peninsula. It was in the heart of a temperate rainforest, and everything was lush and green, with moss covering the lower trunks of the tall cedar and spruce trees. A low blanket of pale grey hung in the sky, diffusing the light so that everything seemed slightly luminous. From our campsite, we heard fish jumping in the lake only a stone's throw away. It felt like paradise.

I handed the water back to Kai and smiled at him. He still looked sleepy, his hair tousled, his eyes resting peacefully on my face.

"You look beautiful this morning," he said.

I laughed. "You're very sweet, but I know I look like hell."

"Not to me, you don't." He brushed some hair out of my face. "It's cold. Are you warm enough?"

"Yes, although I've noticed that I haven't been able to generate much heat. Not a lot of evil around here, I guess." In addition to being a Scout, I had evolved into an Alchemist, a rare type of Soterian that can generate heat and fire by channeling a blend of good and evil. I'd found it to be a pretty useful skill for spring camping.

We continued hiking up the trail, enjoying the smell of the damp earth and the sound of nothing but birds and wind. The trip had been just amazing so far. The first night, we camped near Eureka at the northern tip of California, surrounded by majestic redwoods and the ocean only five minutes from our tent. Walking along the beach the next day, we fell in love with the rugged beauty of the north coast that was so different from the soft, sandy beaches we were used to in Southern California.

We spent the next night in Oregon and visited Devil's Churn, a spot where the ocean shoots up through a large hole in the rocks when conditions are just right. After nearly drowning a few months ago, I already had plenty of first-hand experience with how powerful the ocean could be, but watching the water erupt into the sky gave me an even deeper respect for it.

From there, we drove to Washington, where the blues, greens, and greys of the towering forests around us gave me a strange sense of longing. It felt like home to me, even though this was my first visit there. We ended up at Lake Quinault, which we quickly decided was our favorite spot so far. It was so peaceful and surrounded by such breathtaking views that we felt compelled to wake up early and go for a hike as soon as it was light.

We entered a clearing where we could look down over the lake and at the surrounding rainforest. Kai slipped his arm around me. "Crappy view, huh?"

"Yeah, totally sucks. I'm sure glad we don't live here."

We stood like that for a long time, admiring the landscape and inhaling the wonderfully sweet fresh air, when suddenly we heard a strange sound coming from behind us. We turned and saw a small black bear cub crossing the trail. It snuffled the ground as it lumbered along, and when it saw us, it let out a high wail.

"Ashlyn," Kai whispered, "we need to get out of here. The mother is probably right behind him."

I nodded, and we started creeping higher up the trail, moving as slowly and quietly as we could. The cub looked at us curiously and wailed again. It started walking toward us.

"Not good," I warned. "Not good at all . . . "

"Let's just keep moving," Kai suggested, and we quickened our pace. The cub broke into a lope and bounded up the trail after us. It would have been adorable if the situation weren't so dangerous.

As we rounded a corner, my stomach lurched. A huge black bear was headed straight for us. She must have weighed five hundred pounds, and her footsteps made heavy dull thuds on the path as she walked. Her bright yellow eyes flashed, and suddenly she opened her mouth and let out a loud bellow that sent adrenaline coursing through my body.

"Kai, jump on my back!" I yelled. I spun around, reached back and grabbed him, and then dived forward as the bear charged. I flew up into the air just as her massive paw took a swipe at us, making a whooshing sound as it sliced through the air just inches away. She charged after us, her paws hitting the ground like thunder, and I put on an extra burst of speed. I flew down the path about a quarter mile, clutching Kai tightly, and then dropped to the ground. Kai let go of me and looked around uneasily.

"Can you hear them?" he asked.

I stretched my hearing and found I could pinpoint their location very easily. They were crashing around in the bushes back up the trail where we left them.

"Yeah, they're still up there. Come on." I headed down the path, not looking at Kai.

"Are you okay?" Kai was trotting to keep up with me.

"Aside from being a complete idiot, you mean?" I shook my head in dismay. "Last November I thought a tape recorder was a mountain lion. Now a bear walks right up to us and I don't even hear it. I'm never going to get the hang of this."

"You're on vacation. You're supposed to be relaxing, not listening for enemies. It's not your fault."

"I'm a Soterian. As long as I have my powers, I'm supposed to be alert at all times. What if Deimos sent someone after us and I wasn't paying attention?"

"When there's evil around, you will pay attention. The bear wasn't evil, it was just a bear. And by the way, you just saved my life again, so thank you." Kai grabbed my hand and spun me around. I was about to protest, but he pulled me into his arms and kissed me. My knees went soft and my head started spinning slightly as the anger drained out of me. Kai was the only person I'd met who could change my mood just by looking at me, and the way he kissed me was enough to make me forget my own name.

But I couldn't forget that I had let us walk straight into danger, and the lesson stuck with me. During the rest of the trip, I was much more alert, and I focused on working my training into every moment. I kept a close watch on how much heat I could generate, which was always stronger when we were near larger towns. This turned out to be very useful, as I could generate enough heat to keep us warm all night as we camped. I learned to listen and watch with one part of my brain while the rest of me talked with Kai or just enjoyed looking out the window. I meditated every morning, watching the usual parade of fears, doubts, and insecurities try to pull me under. Every day, it got a little easier to just let them go by without allowing them to suck me in.

As the miles rolled by, I felt that Kai and I were growing even closer. Although we'd been living in the same apartment complex for the last three months, we'd actually spent very little time together. Between school, training, his job, and his music, we were both too busy to see each other for much more than an hour here and there. He'd started taking the regular martial arts classes at John's school while I trained exclusively with my unit, so we weren't even training together. But on the road, we finally had the luxury of time, and I relished every moment as we talked about our childhoods, our past relationships, and our plans for the future.

Sharing our stories, we discovered some differences in our personalities. I tended to be optimistic about most things, and Kai was more of a pessimist. He liked to sleep in late, and I was an early riser. His favorite book was *Moby Dick*, which he'd read about ten times, but I couldn't even get past the second chapter of that book without falling asleep.

As we learned more about each other, we realized that our differences only made us feel closer to each other. Every nuance I discovered about his personality deepened my respect for him and my admiration of what a complex person he was. It was as if we were becoming more three-dimensional to each other somehow. I still put him on a pedestal and couldn't understand what he saw in me, but I was growing more confident that his love for me wasn't just a fluke or a side effect of my powers.

On our last night before we reached Minnesota, we sat cuddled together in front of our campfire, watching sparks ride up into the air on streams of smoke. The night sky was inky black, and the stars shone like pale, silver-blue diamonds. The campground was deserted, and the only sounds we heard were the crackle of the fire, the hissing of the burning logs, and the chorus of crickets.

We had been quiet for a long while, happy just to be with each other. The heat of the fire on my face and the warmth of his body behind me were so soothing that I drifted off to sleep . . .

. . . and into my recurring nightmare about Deimos. His ebony hair was slicked back, and his immaculate black suit seemed to suck the light from everything around him. He walked slowly but deliberately toward us, a smug smile on his face that said he was certain of reaching his goal. As usual, Kai and I were trying to run from him but were completely unable to move.

The scene changed abruptly, and I was with my sister, Laurel. She was in labor, about to give birth, and there was nobody but me around to help her. She screamed as she gave one big push, and then her baby was in my hands.

"Is it a boy or a girl?" she asked breathlessly.

"It's a boy!" I looked with wonder at this tiny person. My God, I had a nephew. I was an aunt! My heart swelled with love as I gazed into his little face. I took a washcloth from a silver basin of water and began bathing him, when suddenly I noticed that he was getting heavier.

"Laurel, his cord stub has already healed. Isn't that odd?" But she was in the next room getting cleaned up and wasn't listening. I looked at him more closely. "And he's really, really big for a newborn." I peered into his eyes, which were squinted shut.

Suddenly, he turned to me, opened his eyes wide, and gave me a smile.

His black eyes shone like beetles. Just like Deimos.

I tried to scream, tried to call out to Laurel, but I had no voice. I tried again and again but no sound came out of my mouth.

"Ashlyn?"

I heard Kai's voice from far away, and suddenly I was awake again, in front of the fire, the nightmare fading.

"Kai," I murmured. "I must have drifted off."

"Were you dreaming? You sounded like you were crying."

"Yeah, a nightmare. I'm okay." But I still felt saturated by the images. Even though the San Francisco unit was keeping an eye on my family, the knowledge that Deimos could go after any of them to get to me really freaked me out. And Laurel was still in Japan, with nobody looking after her. What if he found her there? Was the dream just a product of my anxiety about my family, or was it a real warning?

"We did a lot of driving today. Why don't you go get some sleep? I'll stay up until the fire is out," Kai offered.

"I'm okay. I'd rather sit up with you." I did my best to shake off the effects of the dream and snuggled into him. We watched the fire burn down until it was nothing but ash.

Chapter Three: Ghost Town

"Ashlyn, it's so nice to meet you at last!" Kai's grandmother greeted me enthusiastically and waved me into a large easy chair in the living room. I felt my cheeks flush but managed a smile as I sat in the chair.

It was a warm and cozy room. An upright piano was centered against the far wall, a lace cloth draped across its top. It was covered by dozens of framed photographs and a couple of lush green houseplants. Several birds fluttered around a birdfeeder that hung outside the window, chasing each other and pecking at the seed. Beyond that was a large, beautiful garden, well hidden from the street of their quiet Minneapolis neighborhood.

Sarah, Kai's mom, was seated across from me. She was visiting from California, and I was meeting her for the first time, too. As I glanced around, still uneasy, she gave me a warm smile and a slight wink. She had blonde hair just like Kai, and her eyes sparkled. The heavy lump in my stomach, which had been there since dawn, started to soften a bit.

"It's nice to meet you, too," I said at last. "Kai's told me so much about all of you."

"Oh, don't you believe a word of it," his grandfather said gruffly, but there was a twinkle in his eye.

"Kai, do you still eat fish?" his grandmother asked.

"No, Grams, but don't worry. We want to cook for you." I noticed that his slight Minnesota accent had gotten much stronger after only a couple of minutes with his family. I found it totally adorable.

"Oh, there's no need for that," Sarah insisted. "We can go out."

"That Alfonso's place is good," Kai's grandfather suggested. "Mother likes the scampi."

Thirty minutes later, we were sitting at a table in a large Italian chain restaurant. It was noisy and had some questionable decorations, including trellises heavy with fake grape vines that looked as if they'd never been dusted. But we got a table right in front of a window overlooking the lake, and everyone was so friendly that I felt very much at home. Sarah, who was sitting next to me, started asking me about school.

"Kai says you're studying geology," she began.

"Geography, actually. People mix those two up all the time." It made me happy, knowing that Kai had told her about me. I wondered what else he'd said.

"Oh, that sounds interesting," she said. "What are you learning about?"

"I've been taking classes in mapping, environmental studies, meteorology . . . things like that. It's pretty cool."

She nodded. "Any idea what you'd like to do when you graduate?"

My stomach twisted. "No, I have no idea yet."

She looked kindly at me. "You'll figure it out. There's no rush. You still have over a year to go." I felt like hugging her.

"Say, did you hear about the layoffs in Cooke?" Kai's grandfather asked.

"Yes, it's awful." Sarah shook her head.

"What happened?" I asked.

"Drake Motors and Magnum merged yesterday," Sarah replied, "and today they announced that they're laying off eight thousand workers in the Drake factory in Cooke. They're outsourcing the jobs."

"But that's a catastrophe." Kai's face darkened as he turned to me. "Cooke is a small town about three hours north of here," he explained. "Their only real industry is the Drake auto factory. Most of the town works there."

"Oh God, how horrible!" I tried to imagine an entire town being laid off. "What are all the people who were laid off going to do now?"

"Best as I can tell, there's nothing they can do," Kai's grandfather said. "There aren't any other factories in the area. A lot of them will move to the Twin Cities, but there aren't eight thousand jobs lying around waiting for them. And they're not going to be able to sell their homes, because nobody's moving to Cooke after this."

"The people on the news are talking about a domino effect," Kai's grandmother broke in. "And how it might cause problems across the state and even throughout the Midwest."

"Where are they outsourcing the jobs to?" Kai asked.

"Mexico. Apparently there's a large factory down there that they're going to use instead. Labor is much cheaper there," Sarah explained.

Just then, I felt my phone vibrate. It was Rebecca calling.

"Excuse me, I really need to take this call. I'll be right back." I hurried out to the lobby of the restaurant and answered.

"Ashlyn, I'm so sorry to bother you, but have you heard about the merger between Drake and Magnum?"

"Yeah, I just found out about ten seconds ago. Why? What's going on?"

"John and Theresa are on high alert. They both think Deimos is behind it."

"Oh, lovely," I groaned. So much for my vacation.

"But don't worry, Paul is looking into it, and we all decided that you shouldn't come home early. In fact, we were wondering if you might be able to do some scouting while you're there."

"I'll talk to Kai. We only have a few days here, but I'll try."

"Are you having a nice time?" she asked.

"It's been totally incredible. We're getting along so well. And so far his family seems really nice. How is everything there?"

"Pretty good. Christoph and I have been spending a lot of time together. It's been nice to have a week off."

"That's awesome, Rebecca. You two are made for each other, you know. Enjoy the hell out of your break. Speaking of which, I need to get back to Kai. I'll call you if I find out any information on the merger."

I hung up and walked back to the table, trying to digest what I'd just heard. Kai's family looked up as I approached.

"I'm sorry about that," I said. "It was my roommate, Rebecca. She said she'd only call if it was important, so I had to take the call."

Kai looked concerned. "Everything okay at home?"

"She just had to ask me a question about something, nothing serious. But she did mention the merger, knowing that we're in the area. Kai, you're taking a business class this summer, right?"

"Yeah," he said, immediately catching on. "Maybe we should drive up there and talk to some of the people who have been laid off. I could write a research paper on it."

Sarah smiled at him. "I'm glad you're taking school so seriously this time around. I'm sure it helps to have a good influence." She winked at me.

Suddenly, I felt like crying. I was completely overwhelmed by how welcoming and accepting Kai's family was with me. I didn't realize until that moment how much my experience with Todd's family had scarred me. But I also saw the situation from their perspective for the first time. Todd and I were totally wrong for each other, fighting all the time and making ourselves miserable, so of course his family didn't like us together. It was a completely different situation with Kai. I had never been so happy, and when I was honest and looked past my insecurity, it was obvious that Kai was also a much happier person since we got together.

The next day, Kai and I got up early and drove to Cooke. It felt great to be back on the road, alone with him again. Sarah had insisted on packing some snacks for our drive before we set out that morning. She reminded me a lot of my own mom, and I wondered whether they would ever meet. I started daydreaming about moving into an apartment with Kai, cooking a Thanksgiving dinner together and having both of our families over. It sounded so cozy.

We arrived in Cooke around eleven o'clock. The small downtown was nearly deserted, and many of the stores were closed. Most of them had signs in the windows advertising huge markdowns on their merchandise. We parked in front of the Good Eats Café and went inside.

The café was a classic diner, with cheerful, pale yellow walls, small wooden tables, and a long counter with red vinyl stools in front of it. Behind the counter was an opening to the kitchen, where we could see a man in an apron moving around slowly. The aroma of grease wafted toward the front of the café. It looked like it should be a popular place, but we were the only customers.

We sat down at the counter and looked at the menu, which listed typical diner items, such as meatloaf and burgers, but it also had something I'd never heard of.

"What's walleye?" I asked Kai.

"It's a kind of pike, a white fish. It's usually pan fried. It's pretty damn good."

"I never ate much fish growing up," I said.

"Really? We ate fish all the time."

"I guess that makes sense with all the lakes around here. Do you miss eating fish?"

"Sometimes. But not enough to go back to eating meat."

A tired-looking waitress walked around the corner and automatically poured us coffee from her pot. "Morning folks, what'll it be?"

I closed my menu. "I think I'll have the grilled cheese with fries and a side salad with Italian dressing."

"I'll take the waffles," Kai said. He glanced at me and smirked. "Yes, we can split them."

"You got it," the waitress said. She turned to the kitchen window to call our orders to the cook.

I sipped the coffee and swallowed hard, trying not to make a face. "Hand me the half and half," I hissed. Kai laughed. We were both very picky about coffee, and Cooke wasn't exactly Seattle. We dumped a lot of cream into our cups and made the best of it.

The waitress came back with my salad. "It's kind of empty today. Where is everyone?" I asked her innocently.

"At home, I guess. You folks passing through?"

"We're on our way to the Twin Cities," Kai said.

"Good idea. You're not going to see much action here after the layoffs."

Kai nodded. "I heard something about that. What happened?"

"Those fat cats decided people's lives didn't matter," she answered bitterly. "Doesn't matter to them that these people already live paycheck to paycheck. Now they're sending their jobs south of the border."

I felt terrible for her. It was such a small town, and it had to be awful to watch so many people you know lose their jobs. "What are they going to do now?" I asked.

"No idea. But people are going to start getting desperate real quick." She stuffed more straws into the dispenser even though it was already nearly full. "I hear people talking about all kinds of plans. Some people are moving, others are talking about getting training for other kinds of jobs. Some are talking about doing illegal stuff." She wiped the counter absent-mindedly with a rag.

"What kinds of stuff?" I asked.

"Drugs, Internet scams, that kind of thing. They're careful what they say in public, but you can read between the lines."

"What's going to happen to the café?" Kai asked.

"If people stop coming in, we'll have to close our doors. I have a friend in St. Paul I can stay with until I find work, but I'm not in any hurry to leave. I've lived here over twenty years."

"Order up!" the cook shouted as he rang a bell. The waitress turned back to the window, grabbed two plates, and placed them in front of us. The smell of the fries mingled with her strong perfume.

"There you go. You let me know if I can get you anything else."

"Thanks, it looks really good," I said. "I hope everything works out so you can stay."

"We'll keep praying, anyway." She wiped her hands on her apron and wandered back into the kitchen.

Kai and I ate in silence. When we got the bill, Kai paid it, and I noticed he left the waitress a huge tip. I reached into my pocket and gave him a ten-dollar bill.

"It's okay, I got it," he said.

"No," I insisted, pressing it into his hand. "I love how generous you are, but you need to watch your money, too."

We drove out to the Drake factory, where the gates were shut tight. We paused in front, and I noticed several cars in the parking lot. "Who do you think is here today?" I asked.

"Probably security guards," Kai answered. "I wouldn't be surprised if people were trying to break in to steal equipment." He kept driving and pulled around a corner.

I rolled down my window. "I'd like to take a look around. Can you stay out of sight?"

"No problem. I'm well-equipped." He held up his copy of *Moby Dick*.

"Hopefully you won't have time to read much. I should be back in half an hour, tops." I looked around, listening hard for any movement nearby. It was all clear, so I disappeared. "I love you," I said and kissed him. He got a strange expression on his face, and I realized I'd never kissed him when I was invisible before. I giggled as I flew out the window.

I soared over the gates and headed toward the buildings beyond the parking lot. The property was massive, and it looked like it housed not only the auto manufacturing plant but also the corporate headquarters for Drake Motors. It was easy to see how they had employed nearly the entire town of Cooke. The sheer scale of the place gave me a better sense of just how many people had been laid off.

I flew along the front wall of the factory, looking in the windows, but it appeared to be completely deserted. I headed toward some smaller buildings that I guessed were the corporate offices, and suddenly I heard voices. They were coming from a room with no windows, so I hovered close to the outer wall, listening.

". . . can't tell me that this is the right thing for the company. What about the down time?"

"There won't be any. The factory is already operational and ready to fulfill orders," replied a man's voice. He sounded vaguely familiar, but I couldn't place him.

"This is in direct violation of our contract!" a woman shouted.

"If you'll recall, the contract expired two days before the layoffs. While you were busy trying to negotiate higher salaries for yourselves, you let the existing contract expire. We were no longer bound by its terms, and therefore we were under no obligation to retain any of the workers. And might I remind you that we did keep the corporate staff?"

"But you cut their pay twenty percent!"

"Sadly, the economic downturn has had consequences for everyone." The man's voice was tinged with poorly feigned concern. "No one regrets it more than I. But our first responsibility is to our customers and our shareholders, and the measures we have taken will ensure our ongoing success for generations—"

"Spare me the pitch," another man interrupted. "We both know that this is purely a self-serving move on your part."

"I can't see how you can think that when the executive staff has also taken pay cuts."

"Yes, I'm sure that five percent is quite a blow." His voice became quieter. "I don't know exactly how you're planning to turn this to your advantage, but I look forward to being there when it comes crashing down around you." I heard the sound of chairs scraping and then footsteps, followed by a door closing.

After a moment, the familiar voice spoke again. "Linda, get James Bennicort on the line, please."

"Yes, Mr. Prescott."

A jolt shot through me. Bennicort? Prescott? Wait a minute, could this be Gary Prescott? Bennicort was one of the people behind the riots last fall, and Gary Prescott was an associate of Bennicort's that I'd spied on in San Francisco. At the time, he'd seemed like nothing more than a business man who was working on closing a deal. Could the merger have been that deal?

I heard him walk into another room, and I followed the sound of his footsteps to another office with a window. I peeked in, and sure enough, it was Gary Prescott. It was so jarring to see him here, almost like seeing a ghost. I watched him pick up the phone.

"Hi, Jim. Yes, I just met with them . . . well, what could they say? They know they don't have a leg to stand on. We should keep an eye on Kirkpatrick, though. Okay, I'll keep you posted." He hung up and rested his chin on his hands, looking deep in thought.

Kirkpatrick . . . I wondered if that was the man who had just left. I flew back to the parking lot, where a man and a woman were walking toward a blue sedan. The man's face was etched with deep creases, and he looked very tired. The woman was furious and talked rapidly.

" . . . and if he thinks he can get away with this, he has another think coming! The union will—"

"Enough," the man cut in. "The union blew it. It's over, Ellie. He's right: we let the contract expire and left the workers with no protection at all. This whole mess was caused by greed on all sides, not just theirs."

"On *our* side?" she yelled. "Tony, how can you say that?!"

"We're the union's attorneys, and we had a responsibility to protect the members. With the economy being what it is, we should have settled for a simple renewal and looked ahead to the next term."

"You can't be serious!"

He sighed. "Ellie, I don't want to talk about it anymore. We have a lot of explaining to do when we get back to San Francisco, and I need time to think."

They got in the car and drove away. I could hear Ellie continuing to rail about Prescott as the car raced through the gates and down the street.

I flew back to our car, trying to make sense of everything I'd just heard. The union couldn't sue the company over the layoffs because their labor contract had expired. How could the lawyers have let that happen? Maybe the company had made some verbal promises agreeing to more favorable terms, lulling them into a false sense of security. Or maybe the union leaders had simply been greedy and underestimated the company's ability to outsource the jobs once they had merged with Magnum. Tony Kirkpatrick seemed to think the executives of the company were up to something. I wondered how much he actually knew.

I gave a low whistle as I slid in through the window so I wouldn't surprise Kai, who was absorbed in his book. When I was certain nobody was looking our way, I reappeared in the passenger seat.

"Well?" he asked.

"Let's drive. I have loads to tell you."

On our way back to Minneapolis, I told Kai everything I'd heard, and then I called John and gave him the full report. He thanked me and said he'd have Paul look into Tony Kirkpatrick and reopen the file on Prescott. With Prescott in Minnesota, it would be a perfect time for Jesse to scout his house in San

Francisco and see if he could find more information. I didn't think much would come of it, but it was the only real lead we had.

Having done some productive scouting made me feel a lot better. The gnawing feeling that something bad was coming had been bothering me the whole trip, but since I'd finally done something useful, I found it much easier to relax. Kai and I settled into our road-trip rhythm and started bantering about music. I was surprised to find out that he didn't like opera.

"Opera is absurd," he insisted.

"Why do you say that?"

"Because it's a hybrid art form that does mortal damage to each of its constituent parts. Neither the play nor the music actually work."

"You've got to be kidding me," I argued. "Just look at *La Bohème* . . ."

"Perfect example. While Mimi is lying in bed dying, one of the onlookers decides it's the right time to sing lovingly to his overcoat. You'd never see such an implausible scenario in a play, but they put it in there to give the character something to sing about. And then there's the problem of Mimi singing a very challenging aria as she's supposedly dying of consumption. Do you know what consumption is? It's tuberculosis. People who are dying of TB can barely breathe, let alone sing an aria."

I was amused by this crankier side of Kai. He was generally so easy going, but he had some very strong opinions, and certain topics got him really worked up. I couldn't help pushing his buttons a bit.

"Come on, Puccini's music is so beautiful. It's absolutely transcendent," I gushed.

"I disagree. It's all fluff. It's like eating an entire meal of whipped cream."

"Well, I think *La Bohème* is incredible. The music and the setting are so romantic, and the love story—"

"Love story? He leaves her because he can't stand watching her die, and then they decide to stay together through the winter because it's too cold to break up. That's not love."

"So you wouldn't leave me if I were dying?" I teased.

"I certainly hope you're kidding."

"I am. I know how you feel about me, Kai." I cuddled into him, and he put his arm around me.

"I'm glad to hear it. Because I would die for you, Ashlyn. I mean it." I felt the full weight of his sincerity, and once again I was blown away by his devotion to me.

We arrived at his grandparent's house to find his mom getting dinner ready. The kitchen smelled absolutely wonderful. She'd made roasted potatoes, sautéed greens with mushrooms, garlic bread, and chicken breasts for the meat-eaters. After dinner, we sat around talking and playing cards, and by the time we went to bed, I felt like I was already part of the family.

But the memory of Prescott's phone call to Bennicort haunted me. Perhaps it was just a legitimate business deal and the union lawyers had screwed up. I didn't know much about Gary Prescott, but James Bennicort was a cold-hearted bastard, and I had a feeling that whatever he was involved with was bound to be bad.

Chapter Four: A Spy

The next morning, while the family went to church, Kai dragged me away from the computer, where I had been half the night searching for information on Prescott, and took me to explore Minneapolis. He was a great tour guide, pointing out landmarks as we drove through the different neighborhoods. I fell in love with the Lake District, a beautiful neighborhood with magnificent old homes surrounding a chain of small lakes. The pathways around the lakes were filled with people running, walking, and skating. Kai explained that Rollerblades were invented in Minneapolis, and that skating was very popular there. I decided right then that if we ever moved to Minnesota, that was the neighborhood where I wanted to live, although the price of real estate there was almost as inflated as back home in the Bay Area.

At lunch time, we met up with Kai's Uncle Nick and Aunt Leslie at an Ethiopian restaurant. Nick was several years younger than Kai's dad. He had spiky brown hair and a warm, cheerful smile that lit up his whole face. Leslie was a pretty blonde with porcelain skin and a musical laugh. I liked them both immediately.

I had never had Ethiopian cuisine before, and I was a bit perplexed by the unusual names on the menu. Sensing my concern, Nick assured me I would love the meal.

"It's like a lot of different curries and stews, and it's served on top of a spongy flatbread called *injera*," Nick explained. "You tear up pieces of the bread and use it to eat the stews."

"Where are the forks?" I asked.

"Don't need them . . . that's what the bread is for," Kai said. "You'll see."

When the platter arrived, I first tried a bit of the injera. "It tastes kind of like sourdough," I said happily. I tore off a larger piece and scooped up some tomato stew with it. It was incredibly flavorful.

"That one's called *timatim fitfit*," Leslie pointed out.

"What a great name!" I laughed. "Kai, you should consider that name for your band."

He shook his head. "I bet it's already taken. Original band names are almost impossible to find."

Nick and Leslie, who were also musicians, nodded knowingly. "When your dad was in a band in high school, they were always having a hard time trying to come up with a name," Nick said. "I think Ruptured Spleen was my favorite for a while. And hey, weren't you in a band called Chewing Guam?" he asked Kai. "That was pretty good."

We continued discussing music and the best and worst band names. Nick and Leslie were hilarious, and it was hard to eat through all the laughing. I caught a glimpse of a man staring at us, and I tried to tone it down a bit, worried that we were going to get kicked out of the restaurant.

When lunch was over, I gave Nick and Leslie big hugs. As we said good-bye, they promised to come visit us in California.

"I really do hope they come visit soon," I said as we walked to the car. "They're so cool!"

"I know. I wish we lived closer."

"Well, maybe we can arrange that." I smiled at him. "Come on, I'm looking forward to seeing the Walker."

Soon we were strolling through the impressive sculpture garden of the Walker Art Museum. On the front lawn was a huge sculpture of a gigantic spoon with a cherry on it. I squinted as I gazed up at the handle, which must have been thirty feet high. The clouds moving across the sky made me dizzy, and I nearly toppled over. I tried to imagine how the artist had managed to build something so tall without being able to fly.

Kai looked appraisingly at everything we saw, as if he were cataloging the details in his mind. I had noticed before that he had a remarkable memory. As we entered the conservatory and started looking at the flowers, I asked him whether he'd always had that ability. Kai was my unit's Keeper, which meant that he was our ally and supporter, but he wasn't a true Soterian and wasn't supposed to have any special powers. But it occurred to me that an improved memory might be a side effect of becoming a Keeper.

"I don't know that I have such a particularly good memory," he said with his typical humility.

"Really? What's the name of the artist who did that rabbit jumping over the bell?"

"Barry Flanagan," he answered.

"Mmm hmm. And the name of that crazy orchid we both liked back in the last section?"

"Dendrobium."

"I rest my case."

"But that doesn't mean anything," he argued. "We just saw those names a few minutes ago."

"And I've already forgotten them, as I think most people would have. You have an amazing memory, Kai. It's going to help you a lot in school. And it's going to be very useful for *us*, too," I said significantly, careful not to say the word "Soterians" in public.

"I wish that were true." He looked down, a serious expression clouding his face.

"What do you mean?"

"I mean so far I haven't done anything. Paul is doing most of the research. I'm mostly sitting around in the car reading while you put yourself in danger."

I put my arms around him. "Kai, even if you didn't spend one more minute on research for us, you are the key to my powers. You're doing us a huge service just by being with me."

"That's not exactly work."

An ominous feeling crept up my spine, and I turned to see a man standing several feet away. He caught my eye, then hurried out of the conservatory. My heart started hammering as I realized it was the same man I had seen earlier in the restaurant.

"We've got a problem," I whispered. I looked around, but there was nowhere I could disappear without someone noticing. I had no choice but to remain visible. "Come on, we need to follow that guy."

We walked after him, trying to act casual, pretending to point out flowers and sculptures to each other. He moved quickly across the lawn toward a black car parked on the street. I looked desperately for a place to disappear, but we were out in the open. I watched in dismay as he got into the passenger side of the car and sped away.

I read off the letters and numbers on the license plate to Kai just before the car was out of sight. It had a Minnesota plate, which could mean that it belonged to someone local who was working for Bennicort, or it could be a rental car. I called John and gave him the license plate number, which Kai recited back to me.

"Got it," John said. "I'll check it out. But what makes you think he was following you?"

"I noticed him staring at us in the restaurant, and then I saw him again at the museum, which is all the way across town. He was listening to our conversation."

"Did you say anything incriminating?"

"Well, um, yeah, I guess I did. I sort of said something about Kai being . . . well, about him being the key to my powers." I cringed. I could not believe I had been so careless. How could we have had that conversation in a public place?

John didn't say anything for a moment, making my heart sink. Sometimes I really wished he were a shouter instead of the silently disapproving type. "Okay, I'll check it out," he said quietly. "I suppose I don't need to tell you to be more careful in the future."

"I'm really sorry, John. It was incredibly stupid of me."

"I'll let you know what I find out." He hung up, and my cheeks burned as if I'd just been slapped.

We spent the rest of the afternoon visiting with Kai's grandparents back at their house, but I found it difficult to concentrate. Once again, I'd made a careless rookie mistake, and this time it might endanger Kai and his family. I wondered yet again if I just wasn't cut out for this Soterian business.

"Is everything alright, dear? Are you waiting for a phone call?" Kai's grandmother asked. I looked down at my lap and realized I was still clutching my phone.

"Oh, sorry about that," I said, flustered. "I'm just waiting to hear back from my friend. About, um, a guy."

"Ah, boy troubles. I hope Kai isn't giving you too much grief in that department."

I smiled. "Not at all. Your grandson is a prince."

Kai's grandfather scoffed. "Kai, how did you manage to talk this nice girl into believing such a bunch of hooey? You've got to watch out for this one, Ashlyn, I'm telling you." He chuckled, and Kai smirked his adorable half smile at him. It was so endearing to see Kai with his family, but inside I was in agony. They were such a nice family, and the thought that I might be putting any of them in danger made me feel ill.

Chapter Five: Burned

As Minneapolis disappeared from view behind us, I immediately felt myself start to unwind. I had really enjoyed meeting Kai's family, and I found myself feeling very sad to say good-bye to them. But it was such a relief to just kick back with Kai and watch the miles roll by, with no pressure to try to impress anyone or figure out what Deimos was up to, even though part of me never stopped thinking about him.

John had finally called to let us know that the car we'd seen was a rental car. This was actually good news, because it meant it probably wasn't someone who would stick around and bother Kai's family. The bad news, of course, was that we had no idea who they were, but I was sure they were connected to Bennicort.

We also learned that Tony Kirkpatrick had been a union lawyer for several years and had a reputation for resolving particularly difficult negotiations. I wondered how he'd dropped the ball this time. Something about the way he'd been talking gave me the feeling that there was a lot more to his part in this than we knew.

Jesse had tried to scout out Prescott's house, but he came up empty-handed. Just like when I'd scouted there, their dog had barked at Jesse while he hovered overhead, clearly aware of his presence even though he was invisible. I was beginning to hate that stupid dog.

We followed Interstate 35 to Des Moines, Iowa, where we got onto Interstate 80. From this point, it was 1,800 miles almost due west to San Francisco. We had decided to do a long first day, so after stopping for lunch and seeing a little bit of downtown Des Moines, we drove straight through Iowa and Nebraska to Cheyenne, Wyoming, where we pulled into a campground for the night.

As we cooked pasta over the camp stove, I marveled at how totally at peace I felt. I was so at home on the road with Kai, pitching our tent together every night and spending our evenings around a campfire. It was also very cool to travel through so much of the states, although there wasn't a whole lot to see at that time of year. A lot of it was open farmland, and since it was early spring, nothing had been planted yet, and everything was grayish brown and somewhat dreary. I tried to imagine what it would look like once the crops were mature, when it must seem like a large green sea of corn and grains. Whenever the scenery became a little too monotonous, we would find ourselves getting punchy, singing ridiculous songs, playing word games, or just listening to music in silence.

"Let's do this trip again in the summer," I suggested as we cuddled in front of the fire. "It would be nice to spend more time with your family next time."

Kai gave me a strange look. "You'd want to do that?"

"Of course. They're really sweet people." He was quiet for a moment, staring into the fire. "What is it?" I asked.

"It's just nice," he said finally. "Kelly didn't want to meet my extended family at all, let alone spend time with them. She refused to come with me to Minnesota the whole time we were going out."

"Really? Why?"

"She didn't see the point. She said if she were going to spend time and money on a vacation, it would be someplace fun, not Minneapolis." He tossed a small twig into the fire.

"But Minneapolis is great," I said. "Didn't you explain how cool a city it is?"

"She wouldn't listen. She said she'd only go to New York. She's always wanted to go there, but we never had the money to do it."

"Well, it was her loss, then. Your family is awesome. They really made me feel at home."

"They loved you, too. My mom told me so."

"She did?" I felt a glow inside. I'd liked her a lot, too, and I thought we had hit it off. But I had a hard time reading her feelings because I was so paranoid and was second-guessing everything I felt.

"Definitely. She never liked Kelly much . . . I believe the expression she used for her was 'horror of the universe,' and she wasn't at all sorry to see us break up. But she took to you instantly."

"Mmm, that is really, really nice to hear. My mom loves you, too. It makes things a lot easier."

He looked into the fire, a very serious look on his face. "I've never believed in fate, Ashlyn. But every day I'm with you makes me reconsider it." His eyes burned with that intensity that always made my stomach go all fluttery. I took his face in my hands and gently kissed him.

"It is fate," I said. "I'm one hundred percent certain." I watched the firelight flicker in his eyes as he stared back at me with a penetrating gaze. I'd seen that same look on his face twice before: once on the bluffs in Isla Vista, right before he'd told me that he'd dreamed about me when he was a kid. The other time was in Sedona, when we had stopped for a short break on our crazy two-day drive from Minnesota to California the previous December. Each of these times, it felt like there was something he wanted to tell me but couldn't, and there was an intensity emanating from him that made my heart race.

I was just about to ask him what he was thinking when my phone rang. I pulled away from him and saw that it was Rebecca calling.

I flipped open the phone. "Hey Bec, what's up?"

"Ashlyn, I have some news. We just got word that Andrews took the blame for the conspiracy to blow up the Golden Gate bridge, since he hired Bennicort's men and coordinated their efforts. But they somehow pulled some strings with the judge, and he only got sentenced to twenty years in prison with the possibility of parole after five."

"No way! How could they let him out after only five years for an act of terrorism?"

"There's more. Bennicort pleaded no contest to aiding and abetting, claiming he didn't know anything about it. He got a sixteen-month sentence in a minimum-security prison."

"You have GOT to be joking!" I yelled. A log exploded in the fire and shot sparks in all direction. "Oops, sorry!" I said as Kai jumped to his feet and beat out the sparks that had reached the ground. "What did John and Theresa say?"

"They're upset, but not surprised. Bennicort's reach is pretty long. They're positive now that he's working for Deimos."

"This is a nightmare. Although I suppose if he's behind bars, it will at least make it harder for him to stir up trouble."

"That's the hope, but I wouldn't count on it. Theresa thinks he can run his operation just fine from the inside." Rebecca sounded very tense.

"We'll be in San Francisco in a couple of days, and we'll meet up with Theresa and her unit then. I want Paul and Kai to have a chance to collaborate on the information that's coming in, and I need to help Jesse scout Prescott's place."

"Oh, that reminds me, we have an inroad there," Rebecca said more cheerfully. "It turns out Prescott's wife, Helen, is a customer at Theresa's gallery. Theresa is going to invite Helen to a special show Saturday night to see if she can pump her for information."

"Perfect! Theresa is so resourceful. Well, at least there's that good news. I think I'll go to the show and see if I can hear anything."

I said good-bye to Rebecca and told Kai what I'd learned. He wasn't nearly as surprised as I had been. "That's about what I figured would happen," he said. "I wonder how much Bennicort paid him to take the fall and go to prison for five years. It must have been in the millions."

"Or a combination of money and threats. I wouldn't put it past him to simply blackmail him into it. Bennicort is a very smart man."

"And an extremely dangerous one. You need to be careful. I don't want anything to happen to you." He ran his fingers through my hair, and I felt my heart melt. I pulled him to me and kissed him as the firelight danced all around us.

The next couple of days were much more relaxed. On Tuesday, we stayed in a tiny one-room cabin at a campground in Salt Lake City, which proved to be a nice break from tent camping. The property had a hot tub, pool, showers, and a video arcade. Kai loved air hockey as much as I did and had a competitive streak I hadn't seen in him before. We played late into the night, and when we realized that neither of us could hold onto the lead, we finally agreed to call it a draw.

The following day we camped at Lake Tahoe. I absolutely loved the Tahoe area, with its sea of pine trees and vast blue lake. The surrounding mountains were still covered in snow, but it was a particularly warm spring, and the weather was almost balmy. We went for a long hike in the afternoon and then talked for hours in front of the campfire, eating chips and salsa and sipping hot cocoa. It was amazing to me how we never ran out of things to talk about, and how in those lulls in the conversation, one look from him could still make me turn to jelly inside.

Thursday morning we awoke early and went for a hike again. The air was very cold and fresh, the scent of snow and pine trees filling our noses as we stepped onto the trail. As the sun climbed in the sky and we hiked higher up the mountain, the temperature rose considerably, and the boulders glistened with melted snow. After a couple of hours, we reached a pool of crystal clear water in the rock.

"That looks pretty enticing right about now," Kai said, removing the bandana he'd tied around his forehead and mopping his face with it.

"It really does. What do you say to a swim?"

He looked around anxiously. "You sure? There's nobody around?"

I reached out with my hearing, but I couldn't hear a single hiker. "It's all clear."

We grinned at each other and started stripping down. "I'll race you!" I said, kicking off my boots. I quickly pulled off the rest of my clothes, tossed them onto a large rock, and jumped into the water.

The cold was unlike anything I'd ever experienced. It felt like frozen ice picks stabbing me all over my body. The air escaped my lungs in a rush, and as my muscles froze, I felt paralyzed. I couldn't move, let alone swim.

"Yoooooow!" I screamed as I shot into the air. As I hovered above the water, shivering with cold, Kai stared at me for a moment with his mouth hanging open and then fell to the ground, howling with laughter. I looked down at my skin, which had turned beet red from the cold. From his perspective, it must have been pretty hilarious to see me rocket out of the water, stark naked and red, screaming at the top of my lungs. But it didn't seem quite so amusing to me.

"Oh, you think that's funny, do you?" I flew down and picked him up off the ground, and before he knew what was happening, I flew him out over the middle of the pond and started dipping him in the water.

"No!" he screamed, still out of breath from laughing as he tried to pull himself higher to get away from the freezing water. I laughed as I dipped him repeatedly, his legs flailing wildly. I dropped him near the edge, and we started an epic water fight, splashing huge waves of ridiculously cold water at each other. Finally, I flew back to shore and threw my arms around him.

"Truce?" I asked, my teeth chattering.

"Truce," he agreed, also shaking from cold. "I don't suppose you could generate some heat for us, could you?"

"Not much evil around here to draw from."

"Guess we'll just have to make the best of it," he said with a smile. We lay back on the rocks and watched the little wispy clouds drift by as the brilliant sunlight warmed our skin.

Several hours later, we knocked on the door of Claire's dorm room on the UC Berkeley campus.

"Thanks for letting us stop by," I said as she greeted us. "I did what I could, but my healing power has never been very strong. Guess I didn't realize that it's so easy to sunburn this early in the year." I bit my lip to keep from laughing.

Kai walked stiffly over to Claire's bed and sat down gingerly. She carefully lifted his shirt. "Oh no, you look like a lobster. Is it all over?"

Kai cringed. "Yeah, you could say that."

"Don't worry, this will only take a second." She put her hands on his shoulders, and I saw his body relax as the healing spread through him. The redness in his face faded to a blush, then a soft pink, and finally back to his normal color. He breathed a sigh of relief.

"Thanks, Claire. Where were you when I was a kid?"

"Did you get bad sunburns?" she asked.

"Yeah, it's this Norwegian skin. I'm somewhat melanin-challenged, as you might have noticed."

"I'll be sure to remember that next time we're out hiking naked," I said.

"Okay, overshare!" Claire covered her ears. "I don't need to hear the details, thank you very much."

I laughed. "Speaking of details, has there been any more information on Prescott or the merger?"

Claire shook her head. "Jesse and Paul are working on it, but from everything they've read, Prescott is a legitimate businessman. Bennicort owns a lot of amount of stock in Magnum and Drake, but that's it."

"We're obviously missing something." I chewed on a nail and then glanced at my watch. "Shoot, we have to go. My mom will be getting worried. Claire, thanks again."

As we pulled up to my mom's place, I let out a sigh and unbuckled my seatbelt. I was sad that our vacation was coming to an end, but I was excited about the prospect of meeting Helen Prescott tomorrow night and possibly learning something about her husband's business. There was no doubt in my mind that he was up to something big, and I was determined to figure out what it was.

Chapter Six: Beautiful Things

I gave a low whistle as we walked into Raina's store. We'd heard it was the most popular skate shop in the city, but it was way beyond our expectations. There was a thick crowd of customers milling around, checking out the clothing on the racks and the colorful skateboards that lined the walls. A heavy metal song was blasting through the speakers, and everyone in the store seemed to have that same blend of relaxed tension that Raina and Michael had. I wondered if some of the customers were Warriors in the making.

Raina was working behind the counter and talking to a very large guy about why he needed to choose a different type of board.

"That deck is all wrong for you, Trent," she insisted.

"How do you mean?" he asked.

Raina flipped the board over and pointed to the edge. "See that? It's only six-ply. I've seen you skate, and you're a bruiser. How many decks have you broken in the last six months?"

"Um, maybe four."

"Exactly. Go for the eight-ply with the fiberglass layer. It'll be a stiffer ride, but you'll get much longer life out of it. Let's look at trucks."

Raina put the deck aside and was starting to walk toward a case of shiny metal parts when she caught sight of us. "Hey, Ashlyn! Kai!" she yelled, waving. "Dirk, take over here,

44

wouldja? Dirk will take care of you, Trent." She clapped the customer on the shoulder and walked over to us.

Raina seemed completely in her element. She was dressed in her usual long baggy shorts and fitted T-shirt, her blonde hair messy and pulled back under her cap. It was so inspiring to see someone who was doing exactly what she wanted with her life, and I felt a tinge of envy.

"How's it going?" she asked, her eyes gleaming. I'd never seen her look so happy.

"Great!" I said. "The trip was awesome. We're not heading back to Santa Barbara until tomorrow, so we wanted to come see your shop."

"Here it is, in all its glory." She spread her arms wide.

"It's totally busy in here. You must be doing really well."

"Can't complain." She shrugged modestly, but I could feel the pride spilling out of her. "So, you guys ever skate?"

Kai nodded, but I shook my head. "My sister broke her ankle once skateboarding, and I've been too chicken to try ever since."

"Ah hell, you have to give it a try. Come on, let's go. I'll set you up."

"You mean right now?" I looked at Kai, whose eyes lit up. He obviously really wanted to do it. After all, how often did you get a chance to skate with a real pro?

"Sure. Hey Dirk!" she yelled. "I'm taking my buddies to the skate park for an hour. Don't burn the place down while I'm gone, cool?"

He rolled his eyes. "Wouldn't dream of it, boss."

Raina grabbed helmets, elbow pads, knee pads, wrist guards, and skateboards from the rental bin, and we headed down the street. When we entered the skate park, Raina was greeted by several people who said hello or stopped to give her a high five. I was instantly intimidated. It was like being with a rock star who was about to teach us to play guitar in front of a crowd.

I looked around at the park. We were standing on a wide, flat section next to a large bowl with lots of dips and ledges. Raina helped us put on our gear, then gave us a quick lesson on how to stand on the board, how to push off, and how to find your balance.

"And that's basically it," she said. "Try just going back and forth for a bit."

It felt weird to stand on this wiggly board that seemed intent on shooting out from under my feet. I felt very self-conscious, sure that I was going to fall, and scared that I might hover if I did.

Kai rolled easily around the flat area and turned in a wide arc. After a few wobbly tries, I found myself relaxing a bit and enjoying the sensation of rolling. I sank into it more, starting to feel more connected with the board. I was beginning to see why people liked this so much, and I realized that once again, I was in danger of starting another hobby that I didn't have time for. I stopped and picked up the board.

"Raina, would you mind giving us a demo? I'd like to see what you can do." Kai stopped and hurried over, eager to watch her in action.

Raina glanced around the park. "Sure. It's a bit crowded today, but I think I can carve out a space." In one smooth motion, she stepped onto her board as she dropped it, landing in a crouch as she rolled forward into the bowl.

Raina made skating look effortless, her body completely relaxed as she picked up speed. She headed up an embankment, turned and glided along the edge, then swooped back down and across the bowl to a tall, steeply sloped wall. She shot up the wall, spun around in the air several times, then landed perfectly and raced across the bowl again, popping up over the side and landing on the ledge on the tail of her board. For a brief moment she was perfectly still, and I was struck by how much she looked like she wasn't quite real, more like a work of art than a human being. Her skating was a thing of absolute beauty.

She dropped back down in the bowl, and when she reached the other side, she grabbed the ledge and did a one-armed handstand, holding the skateboard to her feet with the other hand. I heard murmurs of appreciation from the people standing around watching.

She dropped back in again, did some more fast runs through the bowl, and then launched up onto the flat section. She sped across, jumped up onto a rail and skidded along it, and then dropped off and did a series of jumps that caused her board to flip under her feet, each time landing perfectly again. All the other skaters had stopped to watch her by this point, and everyone was just as mesmerized as I was.

Finally, she stepped on the tail of her board and came to a dead stop. She picked up the board and walked casually back over to us while people applauded and clapped her on the back.

Kai shook his head. "That was insane! You tore it up."

She shrugged. "It's what I do. I'm stoked they finally built this skate park," she said, looking around happily. "I took a gamble when I opened my shop where I did. It wasn't clear that the plans for the park would make it through the city's red tape. But now I'm the closest shop to the most popular skate park around."

I was nearly speechless. "I'm so impressed, Raina. You're so lucky that you have this to go back to when our 'special project' is wrapped up."

She gave me a rare smile. "Yeah, it's cool being strong and fast and all that, but as long as I can still skate, I'm not attached to it." I hoped I could come to that kind of peace with letting my powers go when the time came.

It was a beautiful spring day in the Mission district, which has some of the nicest weather in the city, so after saying good-bye to Raina, we picked up burritos from a taqueria she had recommended and went to a little park to eat. At times like this, it was hard to worry about Deimos, Prescott, Bennicort, my dad's opinion of Kai, school, my future, or any of the rest of the things that kept me awake at night.

After lunch, I dropped Kai off at Paul's and drove to Theresa's penthouse, where she and John were waiting for me. After we quickly went over everything we knew about Prescott, I got cleaned up and changed my clothes, and we headed down to the gallery for the art show. Theresa was wearing a flowing dark-blue outfit that made her look beautiful and mysterious. I noticed that John looked particularly nice that night, wearing a black dress shirt that fit as if it had been tailored just for him and a pair of black pants. As the gallery began to fill up, I focused on watching each person who came through the door, trying to pick up on their feelings.

Finally, a tall woman with honey-colored hair walked in, and I recognized her from the day I had scouted out the Prescott's house last fall. Theresa greeted her, and I crossed the room quickly to be introduced.

"Ashlyn Woods, this is Helen Prescott," Theresa said. As I shook her hand, I tried not to stare at her. She was wearing a shimmering gold sleeveless blouse that hung in draped folds from her shoulders and showed off her cleavage. Her black silk pants hugged her thin, muscular legs. She was perched on some of the highest heels I'd ever seen but looked perfectly balanced. I was always astonished by women who could walk in shoes like that. If she weren't so tall, I wouldn't have been surprised if she'd been an Olympic gymnast when she was young.

Helen gave me a cheerful smile. "It's a pleasure," she said. "Do you like folk art?"

"Yes. My mother was in the Peace Corps in Central America, so I thought I'd find her something for her birthday." John walked up and stood next to me, a glass of champagne in his hand.

"Theresa has a fabulous collection," she purred. "I'm a devoted fan. My husband and I take trips to Mexico a lot, and I just can't help but buy up everything I see." She had a vapid look in her eyes, and the only emotion I picked up from her was a basic sort of child-like enthusiasm. She didn't seem too bright.

"In fact," she said turning to Theresa in excitement, "I should be a buyer for you! We're always going down there. And I speak pretty good Spanish. I bet I could get some fantastic bargains!"

Theresa smiled rigidly. "Interesting idea. I already have several channels I use, but I'll let you know if something opens up."

"Wonderful!" Helen beamed. "Now, I must go and talk to Emily. I want to hear about her trip to Greece. Nice to meet you all!" I noticed her eyes lingered on John for a moment, who returned her gaze. I could feel a definite spark between them.

Theresa rolled her eyes at John. "She's married to Prescott!" she hissed.

"I'm aware of that," he said, looking slightly amused. "It's a gallery. I'm here to appreciate beautiful things."

I was glad Theresa wasn't an Alchemist, because at that moment I was sure she would have hurled a fireball at him if she could. It made me wonder: was there something more between Theresa and John than just collaborating as Mentors?

I couldn't believe I hadn't thought of it before. I could feel a lot of tension between them, and definitely some attraction.

"Anyway, it was nice of her to offer to be a buyer for you," John continued, watching Helen as she walked away.

"It would be, if she knew the first thing about art," Theresa said acidly.

I decided this would be a good time to check out the rest of the gallery. I wandered the room looking at the paintings, pottery, and crafts. There was nothing in my price range, but Theresa pointed me to a bin of prints, and I found a gorgeous reproduction of a vase of sunflowers that would be perfect for Mom. I kept my eye on Helen and saw Theresa talk to her a couple more times. I tuned my ear to Helen's voice and listened to her conversations, but she never said anything about her husband.

Finally, I approached her again. "It must be great to see so much of this art right at the source. What does your husband do that takes you to Mexico so often?"

"Oh, he's in business," she said vaguely. "He serves on several boards of directors, that kind of thing. But the most exciting one is Magnum, you know, the auto maker? They just merged with Drake, and now they're opening this wonderful new factory in Mexico. They're employing lots of people down there who otherwise wouldn't have jobs, and it's going to save the company a lot of money."

I couldn't believe how clueless she was. Did she have no idea that eight thousand workers in Minnesota had just lost their livelihoods? I played dumb to keep her talking.

"That sounds great!" I gushed. "Where in Mexico is the factory?"

"It's just south of Tijuana. I've been there a couple of times and have found some wonderful pottery."

"I've never been to Mexico. Is it nice there?"

"You've never been? But you simply must go! Tijuana is a tourist trap, but go just a little bit south and it's beautiful. The beaches are magnificent, and the food is to die for." She spoke for a long time about how wonderful Mexico was, and I started to envision a tropical paradise. Maybe that was where Kai and I should go on our next vacation.

Helen finally moved on to talk to someone else, and eventually I said good-bye to Theresa and John. I'd actually had a nice time, but I hadn't gotten any useful information. Helen Prescott seemed to know very little about her husband's business except for where she got to travel as a result. She wasn't the smartest woman in the world, but she was harmless. Her husband, on the other hand, still had me very worried.

As Kai and I drove back to Berkeley, I told him about the evening. "All Helen could do was talk about Mexico. Which reminds me: what do you think about going there on vacation some time?"

"I'm not too into the idea. I've been there once and it was pretty depressing. It looked like the crappy parts of L.A."

"I guess that depends on where you go. She said some parts are really beautiful."

"I'd much rather go to Hawaii," Kai said. "But if you want to go to Mexico, we can do that."

"No, you're probably right. Hawaii is fantastic. I went to Oahu right after my high school graduation, but I'd love to see the other islands. And it would be nice to be there with you instead of a bunch of friends and Todd."

"Must have been very romantic," he said with a slight smile.

"It would have been, if we hadn't been drunk and fighting the whole time."

"Sounds like it's a good thing you don't drink anymore."

I shook my head sadly. "You have no idea." I was quiet for a moment, pushing back the memories that lurked at the edge of my thoughts.

Kai suddenly spoke. "Hey, I forgot to tell you: my dad and Angie want us to come to dinner on Tuesday. They're really looking forward to meeting you."

Instantly, my stomach felt like it was full of lead, but I smiled. "Okay, sounds good. It'll be nice to meet them, too."

"You're not still worried, are you?"

"A little. But I'll be okay." After all, he had survived meeting my dad, and I loved the rest of his family, so I felt confident I could make it through one more dinner. How bad could it be?

Chapter Seven: Hidden Talent

After getting a late start because I couldn't decide what to wear, Kai and I headed out to his dad's house. Kai looked relaxed and happy, and I tried to calm my nerves. I looked out at the ocean as Kai drove, enjoying the sight of the setting sun casting diamonds of golden light on the ripples of water. As we drove through La Conchita, about ten miles south of Santa Barbara, the highway wrapped around a wide bay where there were several surfers in the water. Suddenly, Kai pointed out at the ocean.

"I hoped they might be out there right now," he said with a smile. "Look." I looked past the palm trees at the water and gasped. Swimming among the surfers about thirty feet from shore was a pod of dolphins. I watched their dorsal fins break the surface as they caught the waves. They appeared playful and animated as they streamed through the water.

"Oh man, that is amazing!" I said, straining my neck to see them as we drove past. "Let's go jump in!"

"Another time, definitely. We probably don't want to show up at my dad's soaking wet."

"Oh, all right," I conceded as the bay disappeared behind us. I would have much rather been out swimming with dolphins than meeting Kai's dad. I bit on the corner of my fingernail and tried to ignore the squirmy feeling in my stomach.

When we arrived, Kai took my hand as we approached the front door. He knocked lightly as we entered. "Dad? Angie?"

"In here," called a voice from the next room. We walked into the large, bright kitchen where Jerry and Angie were preparing dinner.

"Kai!" Angie gave him an enthusiastic embrace. Jerry hugged him warmly and then shook my hand. "Ashlyn, it's so nice to meet you." He smiled widely, and I saw that he had the same oval face as Kai.

As I shook Angie's hand, I noticed her dark brown eyes twinkling. "Kai's told us a lot about you. What took you so long to come meet us?"

"I—I'm sorry," I began, feeling the anxiety building at the thought that I'd already offended them.

"I'm only teasing," she said brightly. "I just couldn't wait to meet the girl who stole Kai's heart."

All of a sudden I felt famished. "It smells great in here. Can I help you with anything?"

"The enchiladas are almost done, and I'm just making the salad. You can help me chop the vegetables if you like."

As we finished preparing dinner, they asked us about school, and they told me about their jobs. They were perfectly friendly and didn't seem to be grilling me at all. I stole a glance at Kai, who had an I-told-you-so expression on his face. I decided I could breathe a little easier.

During dinner, we talked about the upcoming election for the California governor. The last governor had been elected as a result of rigged voting machines, and new candidates were campaigning for the special election in June.

"How long is it going to take to convict Senator McIntyre, anyway?" Angie asked. "I still can't figure out why he stole the election for his opponent instead of for himself."

"He wanted to pull the strings without being on the front lines," Jerry explained.

"Well, I don't understand any of it, but I do know he should be in jail."

"It's going to take a while to build a case against him," Kai said. "What I hear is that the prosecutors are having a tough time proving that he was responsible for the voting machine fraud instead of just peripherally involved."

I suddenly felt queasy. For some ridiculous reason, it had never occurred to me that McIntyre might not be convicted. It seemed so obvious that he was guilty, but what if they were unable to prove that he was actually responsible? He was incredibly smart and had covered his tracks very cleanly. I couldn't bear the thought of the prosecution blowing it after we had worked so hard to expose him. I scooped more guacamole onto my enchiladas and tried to forget about it for the moment. It was just too upsetting.

After dinner, Kai insisted I relax and talk with his dad while he and Angie cleared the dishes and got dessert. Jerry had the same soft-spoken manner that Kai had, and the same dry sense of humor that I loved so much.

"How did you like Minneapolis?" he asked.

"It was great! And I really enjoyed meeting Nick and Leslie."

"The feeling was mutual." He chuckled. "They knew when Kai first moved back there that he wouldn't stay long."

"How so?"

"One of the first things he told them about was an extraordinary young woman named Ashlyn that he met in Santa Barbara," Jerry said with a hint of a smile. "It was pretty clear that he was a goner."

My heart sank. "I hope nobody thinks I'm taking him away from his family, because that's the last thing I'd want to do."

"No, not at all. Kai is at the age when he should be leaving the nest. I let him move back in with us after he and Kelly split up, but I didn't like the way he sat alone in his room night after night playing his guitar. It wasn't healthy. I'm glad he met you and is moving on with his life."

I smiled at him gratefully, but the thought of Kai spending so much time alone caused me a stab of pain. How could someone so brilliant and gorgeous and funny and amazing not be snatched up right away? I would have thought there would be girls lined up around the block waiting for him to be available. I shook my head, thinking again how bizarre it was that Kai chose me when he could have had anyone he wanted.

"I do hope he's getting a better handle on his finances," Jerry said, jarring me out of my reverie.

I was taken aback. "Has that been a problem?"

"Still is, unless by some miracle he's managed to pay off his credit cards. I keep trying to explain to him how dangerous it is to get in debt, and how it takes years to climb out of the hole you end up in, but he doesn't really seem to get it."

Just as I was about to reply, Kai and Angie walked back in. I sat in silence, ruminating over this bit of news. I knew Kai probably didn't make much money as a vet tech, and he did seem to spend somewhat freely. I had never thought to ask him about his finances. I was taking out student loans, but my dad also gave me some money each month, making it possible for me to go to school without having to work. I wondered if Kai's situation really was as bad as Jerry said, or if he was just being a worried father.

After dinner, as we were walking to the car, Kai took my hand. "See? Nothing to worry about."

"You were right. They're wonderful. I guess I can finally relax. Unless . . . there aren't any relatives you haven't told me about that are going to pop up out of the woodwork and hate me, are there?"

He just smiled and kissed me, then opened my door. We drove in silence as I thought about what his dad had said. Kai was one of the smartest people I knew. He used credit cards now and then, but nothing out of the ordinary. Maybe he'd made some stupid choices when he was younger, but I felt sure he had gotten a handle on it.

Kai interrupted my thoughts. "You're sort of quiet. Is everything okay?"

"Yeah. I'm just wondering . . . "

"About?"

"It's nothing. Never mind."

He looked at me. "What? Tell me."

"Um, can we stop and swim if the dolphins are still there? You won't get a sunburn this time, since it's dark out."

He smiled and looked back at the road. "They're usually gone by this time of night, but sure, if there are any out there, we can stop. I'll always be happy to take you up on naked swimming."

I cuddled into him and felt his warmth spreading through me. I made a mental note to leave a book on personal finance where he'd find it. Just in case.

* * *

"Any news on the job front?" I asked Candace. She shook her head and poured salt on her fries. It was the end of April, and with only a little over a month left until graduation, she still hadn't found anything. Ryan, who was sitting next to her, immediately stole three of her fries and popped them into his mouth. Candace was so distracted she didn't react at all.

"I don't want to go to grad school, but I don't know what else to do." There was a hard edge to her voice. "There are only so many research library clerk positions in the world."

"What about coaching? You could teach children to play volleyball," Christoph suggested in his thick German accent.

I burst out laughing at the thought of Candace teaching a bunch of kids to hit the ball. She glared at me, and I quickly shut up.

"Not everyone loves kids the way you do," Rebecca reminded Christoph gently. He had a very sweet temper and was planning to open a preschool after graduation, something you never would have guessed from icy blue eyes, spiky blond hair, and tall, hulking physique. He looked better suited to bounce drunks out of bars than to bounce balls on a playground.

Candace stared at her half-eaten dinner. "No, I'm just going to keep applying everywhere and sign up with a temp agency until I find something."

"That can be a really good way to go," I pointed out. "My sister works temp jobs in the summers sometimes, and they always end up wanting to hire her on permanently."

"Speaking of which, when does she get back from Japan?" Rebecca asked.

"Not until September, sadly. I can't wait to—"

"But getting back to me," Candace interrupted, looking extremely agitated. "You've been out there in the working world, Ashlyn. Is it horrible?"

"It depends entirely on what you do. I didn't like retail. But I could see you really enjoying being in an office where you get to work with other people on projects, give presentations, that kind of thing."

"Yeah," she said, a glimmer of hope in her eyes. "Getting coffee in the morning, trying new restaurants at lunch, going out for beers after work. . ."

"There's some actual work in between all that," I laughed. "Don't worry, Candace. If you take a temp job, they'll hire you on permanently in no time."

Candace perked up. "You're right. They'll be lucky to have me."

"I wonder who our new roommate will be," Rebecca mused. "I can't imagine anyone as cool as you, Candace."

"You should find out the second week in May. That's usually when they organize the big shuffle and schedule the dates for everyone's move."

I turned to Kai. "So you won't know for another couple of weeks if you'll even still be in the complex." I hoped desperately that he would get to stay. Even though we were both so busy and saw very little of each other during the week, it felt good just knowing he lived right across the courtyard.

Just then, Kelly walked into the café. She was flanked by three friends, who looked bored as they scanned the room for an open table. Ever since I confronted her last fall, we kept our distance from each other, and after Kai moved into the complex, she seemed less inclined than ever to be around us. The only open table was next to ours, though, so they sauntered over and sat down, their backs to us.

Kai put down his napkin. "I have to get going. Max and I are auditioning a bass player."

"I hope it works out," I said. "This is what, the fourth guy you've auditioned?"

"Yeah, something like that. But it's not as bad as trying to find a singer. I'll see you tomorrow, okay?"

"Okay. I love you." I leaned over and kissed him, and immediately I heard a retching sound coming from the next table, followed by the sound of Kelly's friends giggling stupidly. We ignored them, and Kai looked into my eyes for a moment before turning and heading out the door.

Ryan stood up abruptly, a strange expression on his face. "I, um, think I better go, too. See you all later." He hurried out of the café.

"What's with him?" Candace asked. Rebecca and I exchanged glances and shrugged. I'd felt a lot of tension suddenly coming from Ryan. What was he up to?

"I guess we should get back to our homework," I groaned, pushing my chair away from the table. As we made our way upstairs, I thought about the paper I had to write for my Geography of Europe class and the assignment I hadn't finished for Water Quality. Geography had turned out to be such a great major. My teachers were amazing, much better than I had ever imagined. They treated students almost like peers, not like a bunch of kids. And the classes were fascinating. But, like Candace, I still had no idea what I was going to do once I graduated. It was getting harder and harder not to let that thought keep me awake at night.

Later that night, I was in bed reading when I heard a small tap at the window. Startled, I pulled the curtain back, and there was Kai. I opened the window.

"Hey, what are you doing?" I asked.

"I have some news," he said with a small smile. "Do you have a minute?"

"Of course!" I flung back my covers and ran to the front door. When I opened it, he took me into his arms. He held me closely for a moment and kissed me, making me feel all melty inside.

"Hi," he said, grinning at me.

"Hi," I said, smiling back. "So, what's your news?"

"Did you know that Ryan plays bass?"

"What? Ryan Evans, our Ryan?"

"That's the one. He followed me out of the café and said he'd been wanting to audition. He hasn't played in a while and was worried he'd suck, but when he heard how much trouble we'd had finding a bass player, he got his courage up and asked if he could give it a try. So he dug his bass out from under his bed where it's been collecting dust for the last two years and met me at Max's place."

"And? Was he any good? Better than the other guy?"

"The other guy never showed up. And yeah, Ryan was good. Definitely a little rusty, but he and Max locked into a tight groove right away, which is what matters most."

"Kai, that's awesome! Is Max stoked?"

"He's really happy about it. Ryan's not a complete drug addict, and he's not a flake, which is about the best you can ask for in a band member these days."

"So he's in?"

"He's in."

"Hooray!" I threw my arms around him again. "Now you just have to find a singer. But at least you guys can jam as a trio in the meantime."

"Exactly. It'll give us a chance to get some solid tunes in place before we throw a singer's gigantic ego into the mix."

"Oh, like guitar players don't have gigantic egos," I teased. "Thanks for sharing the news with me. I'm really happy for you."

"Yeah, well, it gave me a chance to see you in your pajamas." He grabbed me around the waist. "God, you look good."

I kissed him again and then pushed him away. "Off to bed with you. You have work in the morning."

I watched him walk to his apartment. We smiled at each other across the courtyard as we closed our front doors.

One of the advantages of our crazy training schedule was that Rebecca had made great strides in her fitness. She had even become a decent runner, so we started our sessions with a three-mile run through Goleta. It was fun to run together, talking about training and comparing opinions on what we would face next with Deimos. Even Michael, our Warrior, had loosened up and was friendlier toward us. It was clear that he was very slow to let people in, but once he considered you a friend, it was probably forever. The only exception to his slow-to-friendship rule was Christoph, whom he'd befriended almost immediately in his kickboxing class, but the fact that they both had such incredible athletic ability had likely helped them bond more quickly.

"How are your classes going?" I asked Michael one day during our run.

"Okay," he said. "It's harder to concentrate these days. I want to be tracking down Deimos so I can kick his ass, not stuck inside studying."

"I know. It's really frustrating, this waiting around for him to appear, not knowing where he is or what he looks like. Wondering where he's going to attack next."

"If at all," Rebecca said.

I glanced at her in surprise. "What do you mean?"

"I mean look at his track record. So far, all he's done is back other people. And even though he sent his men to find out about you, don't you think it's odd that he hasn't done anything about it?"

"You mean like how he hasn't bothered Kai again, or taken any of my family hostage?"

"Right. I've been thinking about this a lot," she continued, breathing hard. "And I don't think he's going to attack. At least not openly."

"How do you figure that?" Michael asked.

"Because he wants Ashlyn and her powers on his side. He knows that love is the key to her powers. If he were to harm Kai or someone in her family, her powers would fade, and then she would be of no use to him. He can't just blackmail her into using her powers. Otherwise, he would have kidnapped Kai by now."

"Are you saying that I don't have to worry that he's going to hurt anyone?" After months of being sick with worry, I felt like a huge weight was lifting off my shoulders even as I said the words.

"I'm saying that it's not likely he's going to try to get to you through someone else." She bit her lip. "I think he's going to be a lot more subtle than that."

Christoph looked at her with admiration. "You are very smart, Rebecca. I see precisely what you mean. He will probably try to trick Ashlyn, and maybe the rest of us, to work for him. But he'll be sneaky about it."

"So we all have to be on our guard for something we're not expecting," Michael muttered. "Well, that's specific."

"Actually, I think it's going to be very specific," Rebecca said, dodging a pothole in the sidewalk. "If I were him, I would play on our greatest weaknesses. So it's up to us to know our weak spots as well as he does, if not better."

"Which means more meditation and mindfulness training," I said with a sigh. I really disliked meditation. Sitting and watching my thoughts made me a little stir crazy. But it had been incredibly helpful in my personal life. I had gotten much better at noticing when my insecurity came up around Kai and was usually able to nip it in the bud before I did something stupid.

Michael was quiet. This was probably harder for him than for the rest of us. He definitely had a problem with anger, compounded by a tendency to drink too much. I doubted he wanted to sit around and look at that any more than I wanted to look at my insecurity and fears of Kai leaving me.

We turned onto John's street and raced up to the dojo. We bowed as we entered and started stretching. After a moment, John walked silently into the room wearing his usual black martial arts uniform and his calm, inscrutable expression. We told him what we'd been talking about on our run.

"A very astute observation, Rebecca," John said. "I agree, although I think Jesse should continue to keep an eye on Ashlyn's family to be on the safe side. And our training with the San Francisco unit has made us twice as powerful. We're continuing to operate with them successfully as a single team, which will be critical if we need to jump into action."

"Jumping into action sounds good to me." Michael slid one leg forward and sank into the splits.

"Any news from Paul and Kai?" John asked.

I shook my head. "Not much. Prescott has been made CEO of the new merged company. And they've confirmed that Kirkpatrick is a lawyer and negotiator for the union as we expected. He's kind of fallen off the radar lately, though. Apparently, he hasn't been showing up for work."

"I hear the situation in Cooke is getting desperate," Rebecca said as she reached forward. She could now touch her toes, a big improvement over when we had started training the previous fall. "Most of the town has left. Those who are still there are struggling to stay afloat. And there's been a dramatic increase in crime."

I nodded. "Kai's grandfather said that it's having an impact on the housing market in the Twin Cities and driving up rents, plus putting a real strain on social services."

"I agree that it's very bad there," Christoph said. "But what can be done?"

"There must be a way to get the factory running again," Rebecca answered. "Maybe another auto maker will be interested in buying it."

"Not likely," John said. "The trend seems to be toward outsourcing."

We stretched a bit more in silence and then started drills. We ran through our kicks and punches, and Christoph and Michael worked on sparring with staffs. Rebecca and I moved on to practicing joint locks and falling. Even though I'd been training diligently for seven months and had made a lot of progress, it seemed like the longer I trained, the more I had to learn.

John had promoted us from white belts to yellow belts and then up to blue belts. The next rank was red, and then brown, and finally black. He explained that the belts were just an indication of the techniques we'd learned and gave students a sense of accomplishment, and that the belts themselves weren't the goal. But I couldn't wait to get my black belt. There was a certain glamour to having a black belt, and when my days as a Soterian ended, it would make me feel like I still had some special powers, however they might pale in comparison.

While Rebecca continued working on falling, I practiced handstands. They scared the hell out of me, and I was taking it slowly, kicking up into a handstand against the wall, trying to get used to the idea of being upside down. The next step would be handsprings, but I didn't know how I'd ever be ready for that. I kicked up and pressed my feet against the wall, feeling the blood rush to my head and the adrenaline course through me as I faced the fear of falling on my face. My arms shook, but I fought the urge to hover, holding myself steady until I couldn't hold myself up any longer. I kicked away from the wall and touched my feet to the floor as I glanced at the clock. Five seconds longer than the last time . . . yes!

John called us to the middle of the room, and we moved on to agility training, which involved jumping over an increasingly taller stack of mats, running backwards and sideways, and throwing balls at each other and dodging them. Michael, who usually wore a slightly bored expression on his face, looked vibrantly happy during this part of the training. He reminded me of one of those working dogs that's only content when it's out on the ranch herding sheep all day. Michael was definitely a man of action.

Exhausted but happy from a great day of training, Rebecca and I headed back to the apartment, stopping first at the mailboxes to pick up our mail. Usually, there was mostly junk, but this time there was a letter from the housing office, addressed to both Rebecca and me.

"Our roommate assignment!" she gasped. "Quick, open it!"

I tore open the letter. It simply said that a girl named Tracy Maxwell, currently a sophomore at UCSB, would be moving in on July first.

"Never heard of her," I said. "I wonder what she's like?"

"Let's go ask Candace," Rebecca suggested, and we raced up the stairs to the apartment. Candace was sitting on the couch studying.

"Hey, Candace, we got our new roommate assignment. Do you know Tracy Maxwell, a sophomore?"

Candace looked thoughtful for a moment. "Tracy . . . Tracy . . . why does that name ring a bell? I'm sure I do, but I can't think of her right now."

"Well, we'll just have to wait and see, I guess. It's going to be such a drag losing you, Candace," I said.

"Yeah, but it's time for me to get out of here. I'm starting to get kind of excited about it now. If I can ever get through finals, that is." She tossed her book on the coffee table. "I have senioritis in the worst way. I just can't bring myself to care right now."

"You're almost done." Rebecca put a hand on her shoulder. "Hang in there, and before you know it, you'll be walking across the stage accepting your degree." After a moment, Candace looked calm and focused, and she picked up the book again.

"You're right. I'm going to go out with a bang. Besides, if I can't find a job, I'm going to need to have good enough grades to get into grad school."

Just then, Kai knocked lightly on the open door. "Hey, is this a good time?" he asked.

"Don't be silly." I rushed over and put my arms around him. "It's *always* a good time. You know that." I noticed he had a gleam in his eyes. "What's up?"

"I've got some news. About my housing assignment." I felt my stomach lurch. Of course! If we'd gotten our roommate assignment, he would have gotten his today as well.

"Well? What does it say?"

"It says I'm moving." My heart sank, and I was about to protest when he quickly added: "But don't worry, it's good news. Toby and Ryan and I are moving into the large three-bedroom unit on the corner."

"Wow!" Candace said. "Those corner units are awesome! But they're for five people, not three. What's up with that?"

"We've been assigned two more roommates." He paused, and Rebecca and I looked at him in anticipation. We could both feel that something hilarious had happened and that he was about to deliver the punch line. "It's Christoph and Michael."

"What?!" I shouted. "You can't mean—are you serious?"

"Yes I am. They applied to live here and put us down as references. And since we're a nice quiet bunch and have been good with paying our rent, they felt we'd be a good group for that apartment."

"Rebecca, this is awesome!" I gushed. "Christoph will be living here in the complex!"

"Yeah," she said, looking unsure. I felt a mixture of glee and concern brewing inside of her.

"Oh Rebecca, get over it. He's not going to monopolize your study time. He's been great about giving you space for that. It just means you won't have to waste time driving to each other's places."

She brightened. "That's true. This is good! I wonder how Michael will like having all of you for roommates."

"More to the point, I wonder how you guys will like having Michael as a roommate," I laughed. "There goes your reputation as a nice quiet bunch."

Kai smiled. "Michael's okay. I think we'll all get along well. So, are you happy?"

"Are you kidding? I'm thrilled! I can't wait to see your new place. Can you point it out to me?" Rebecca, Kai, and I walked outside, and I noticed there were a lot of students milling around, pointing at doors. Everyone was curious to see what their next place would be like.

We walked to the corner. It was on the same side of the building as ours, only three units away. The front door was open, and we peeked inside. It had a huge living room with large windows.

I gasped. "It's enormous! Looks like you'll have your work cut out for you to keep it clean. Do you move in on July first as well?"

"No, June eighteenth. I think they do staggered moves so they have time to repair stuff before people move in."

"That makes sense. I'll help you move, although with Christoph, I doubt you'll need a lot of help."

As we strolled back to our apartment, I heard a perky voice behind me call out: "Well, here they are!" I turned around and saw Kelly walking up to us. Next to her was a very pretty girl with brown hair and large blue eyes. "Tracy, this is Ashlyn and Rebecca, and Kai." She said Kai's name with a marked sneer in her voice. "The girls are your new roommates. Kai's just an ornament." She gave him a sarcastic smile.

"Oh hi, it's great to meet you!" Tracy chirped. "I just heard that I'm going to be your roommate. Kelly said this place is great." She looked at Kai appraisingly, smiling sweetly at him. I felt my jealousy rise, and he took my hand reassuringly.

"Nice to meet you, Tracy," Rebecca said, looking completely bewildered. "Where were you living before?"

"I was sharing an apartment with a couple of girls. I'm a little sister to a fraternity, the Omegas." She pointed to a pin on her shirt. "But of course I don't get to *live* there."

"Little sister?" I asked.

"We like, help them out with fundraisers and community days and stuff like that. Support the guys, you know? We get to go to all of their parties."

"Mmm, sounds like fun," I said with as much enthusiasm as I could muster. I could feel the horror emanating from Rebecca and knew she could feel mine as well. But I tried to keep my face friendly. Kelly had a nasty smirk on her face, and I didn't want to give her the satisfaction of seeing us upset. "Well, Tracy, we look forward to seeing you in July."

"Yeah, nice to meet you," Rebecca said.

"Okay, see you soon!" Tracy sang, and they walked away.

We walked slowly into our apartment to find Candace shaking with laughter.

"What's so funny?" I asked.

"*Now* I remember who Tracy is!" she howled.

Chapter Eight: Unexpected Visitor

As the end of the school year approached, it seemed like I spent every waking moment training and studying for finals. Kai had it even worse, squeezing in his job and working on the band. He and Ryan had turned out to be very compatible song writers, and they spent endless hours working out arrangements. They were still having trouble finding a singer, though. Early on, I had secretly hoped that Kai would ask me to audition, but I knew I wasn't the best person to front their band if they wanted to get past the garage-band phase, and they were pretty set on finding a male singer. I still had fantasies sometimes of being in his band, going on tour with him, and sharing a career in music with him. It was so hard to watch him go off to band practice night after night. But I knew this was just part of dating a musician. It wasn't that his music was like a mistress taking him away from me . . . it was like *I* was the mistress taking him away from his music. I was supportive of him most of the time, but sometimes it really got me down. I thought a lot about our time on the road and was dying to escape with him again to get away from our busy schedules and all our responsibilities.

Adding to my anxiety was the fallout from the merger. Crime was soaring in Cooke and the surrounding areas. The unemployment levels were at their highest since the seventies, and the housing market was out of control. Cooke had become nearly a ghost town, and some economists were worried that a ripple effect would destabilize the whole region. I talked to John about it almost every day, but there didn't seem to be anything we could do. I started having nightmares several times a week and regularly woke up in a cold sweat.

On the day after my last final exam of the year, I awoke early. This time, it wasn't because of a nightmare—I just had a strange feeling I couldn't shake, like something from my past was lurking right around the corner. As I sat in bed, trying to figure out what it was, I heard a knock at the door. I got up quickly and went into the living room as quietly as I could so I wouldn't wake Rebecca or Candace. I opened the door and nearly fainted.

It was Todd.

"Hey," he said. "How's it going?"

I was flabbergasted. "Todd, what . . . it's six o'clock in the morning . . . what in the hell are you *doing* here?"

"I came to see you," he said, smiling.

"At six in the morning?"

"I couldn't sleep, so I drove down. Can I come in?"

"Um, yeah, okay, but be quiet. My roommates are asleep." He walked in and glanced around the room.

"So, do I get a hug?" He gave me his sad puppy dog look. My emotions bounced between wanting to laugh and to hit him. I decided to play it cool.

"Sure," I said in as casual a tone as I could manage. I hugged him quickly and then pulled away.

"You look great, Ash," he said in a smarmy voice, making me bristle. I hated that nickname, but he had persisted in using it no matter how many times I told him not to. "Really great."

"Thanks. Um, you too. Listen, let me get dressed and we can go down to the café where we can talk, okay?"

"Sure thing. I'll wait here." He sat down on the couch, his eyes never leaving me.

I cringed. "I'll just be a minute."

I walked into the bedroom, my mind racing. What was he thinking, driving all night to come see me? What was going on? I quickly threw on some clothes and hurried back into the living room. He was lying back with his eyes closed but quickly opened them when I walked in.

"Come on, we'll get you some coffee," I offered. We walked out of the apartment, and I closed the door quietly behind me.

"Nice place you've got here. I bet you're happy to have the pool."

"Yeah, it's great," I murmured. It was so unsettling to see him there, like the past and present had collided. "Todd, what are you doing here?"

"I told you, I came to see you."

"How did you get my address?"

"Your mom," he answered with a smirk. "She still adores me, you know."

I gritted my teeth. "That's wonderful." I was going to have to have a serious talk with Mom once I got rid of Todd. But he'd just driven three hundred miles in the middle of the night, so I felt obligated to at least get him some breakfast before I made him go away.

We were the first ones in the café, and to my relief, we had the place all to ourselves. I loaded up a plate for him and quickly paid with my resident card. I hoped he would eat fast. The last thing I wanted was for someone to see me with him.

I chose a table in one of the far corners of the dining room. He waited until I sat down, then sat right next to me and moved his chair close to mine. I immediately scooted my chair a foot away, but he just smiled.

"So, um, how are things at home?" I asked, trying to keep the conversation light.

"Not bad. School and work are keeping me off the streets. Who'd have thought I'd turn into a college boy, huh? Bet you didn't think I had it in me."

"That's great." I was only half listening. I was too busy looking out the window to make sure nobody I knew came along.

"How are things going with that guy you're dating . . . what's his name, Ty?"

"Kai," I corrected him. "Fine. It's going really well."

"Well, which is it? Fine or really well?"

"Todd, what do you want?" I asked, drumming my fingers on the table.

He took a long sip of coffee, his eyes lowered as he looked at me over his cup. "You look beautiful, sweetie," he said in a low voice.

"Don't call me that."

"Sorry, old habit." He took a bite of potatoes. "Mmm, these are good."

"Todd, you know me well enough to know that I'm about thirty seconds from walking out of here, so why don't you cut to the chase?"

He put down his fork. "Okay, I'm sorry. It's just so good to see you." His deep grey eyes bored a hole into mine, giving me a very bad feeling. "I was talking with your mom and reminiscing about old times. I've missed you a lot, swee—Ash, I mean. I was lying awake thinking about you, and finally I just decided to get in the car and come see you."

"Why didn't you call first?"

"I was afraid you might tell me not to come."

"Very perceptive of you."

"Are you sorry I came?" he asked.

"That depends. I still don't understand why you're here. If it's to tell me that you've fallen in love with the woman of your dreams, then yes, I'm glad you came so I can wish you joy."

"Ash, you know *you're* the woman of my dreams."

I put my head in my hands, hoping this was just another nightmare and that I would soon wake up, but he kept right on talking. "I know you're dating some guy that you're all excited about right now, but come on. He doesn't know you like I do. Me and you have a history together. I know we don't always get along, but you have to admit that we love each other. I still have all the letters you wrote me, and you weren't making those things up."

"I meant them at the time," I conceded, "but things are different now. I'm in love with Kai."

"Yeah, *right*." He laughed bitterly. "What's he doing with his life? Playing guitar? I don't see a ring on your finger. Are you engaged, or are you just assuming he's going to stick around?"

"That is none of your business." I felt my face get hot.

"I thought so," he said triumphantly, then lowered his voice. "Sweetie, think about it. We belong together. It's good that we've had some time apart so we could go out and see that there's nothing out there that's better than what we have. But we'll be back together. I guarantee it." Before I knew what he was doing, he took my hand and kissed it. I was about to slap him when I heard footsteps behind me.

It was Kai.

He looked stricken. "Oh. Sorry." He wheeled around and walked out.

"Kai, wait—oh for . . . Todd, wait here," I barked. I got up and ran after Kai.

"I can wait as long as it takes," I heard Todd call after me. I was amazed that I had the self-control not to hurl a fireball at him right then.

"Kai, please wait," I said, catching up to him. He paused, his body half turned, his face like stone. I could feel his pain from where I stood. "That wasn't what it looked like."

"I'm listening," he said coldly.

"That's Todd," I began, and his eyes turned hard. I'd never seen him look like that at me before, and I fought to keep my panic from rising.

"What's he doing here?"

"I was just asking him the same thing. He drove down to see me. I don't know what he's up to, but I was just getting to the part where I was sending him home."

"Holding hands with him is kind of a funny way of telling him to get lost." He bit the side of his lower lip, something I'd only seen him do when he was irritated with someone else. It made me want to cry.

"Todd, I mean Kai—damn it!" I pulled at my hair as his eyes grew even colder. "This is way too much for me to handle this early on a Saturday morning. Kai, I love you, and you know that. I don't know what Todd's problem is, but I don't want to be with him. He's probably having trouble meeting someone who will put up with his crap and decided he'd try me again. But, as I told him, it's over."

"Are you sure?" His voice was flat. "You seem conflicted."

"How can you say that?"

"Because you just called me Todd."

"Cut me some slack, will you? It's been kind of a shock seeing him turn up here on my doorstep when I haven't seen him in a year, and I haven't had my coffee yet. Speaking of which, what are you doing awake so early?"

Kai got a strange look on his face, and I felt a churn of inner turmoil coming from him. "Kelly called me and woke me up. She said you were in the café and that I should come find you."

"Kelly?!" I nearly yelled. "And you listened to her?"

"Well, she was right, you were in the café."

"That freaking . . . argh!" I bit back the string of expletives I wanted to scream.

"Hi, you must be Ty." I turned and saw Todd standing there, looking condescendingly at Kai.

"Hey," Kai said, not correcting him. "I'll see you later, Ashlyn."

"Wait," I said, but Todd put his arm around me, and Kai gave me one last icy look before he turned and walked away.

I whirled around. "What the hell do you think you're doing?"

"Sorry. Old habit again. He doesn't seem to trust you too much. Must not be all that serious."

I closed my eyes and sucked in my breath. I felt rage building up in my core, and I needed to stifle it before—

"That's better," Todd cooed, and before I could say another word, he was kissing me.

My eyes snapped open. The world had taken on a strange red hue, and I felt heat shimmering off my body. Before I knew what was happening, I had pulled my fist back, and I watched in amazement as my arm moved in a right hook and slammed across Todd's jaw. In slow motion, his eyes widened and then rolled back in his head as he fell to the ground.

Ten minutes later, Rebecca was standing over Todd as he lay on our couch, his hand on his jaw. "Where the hell did you learn to hit like that?" he asked through clenched teeth.

"Shut up and let Rebecca look at you."

"She doesn't look like a doctor," he said, sizing up Rebecca. She looked especially young and un-doctorlike in her pajamas.

"She's studying to be one. And I told you to shut up." I turned to Rebecca. "Rebecca, this would be a great opportunity to practice those pressure points you've been studying," I said significantly.

"Um, right, yes, I agree. Todd, I'm going to press gently on your masseter muscle. Just hold still and let me know if anything hurts." Rebecca put her hands gently on either side of Todd's jaw and started healing him. I saw his face relax, and soon he moved his jaw around easily.

"Mmm, that's incredible. You learned to do that in school?"

"Just something I picked up along the way," she said, glancing at me.

"Well, you're good at what you do. You're going to make a great doctor." He sat up and smiled at her. "Thank you."

"Oh, for the love of God, now you're hitting on my roommate?! What is wrong with you!"

"I'm not hitting on her!" he insisted, but Rebecca and I had both felt his attraction to her.

Rebecca turned toward the bedroom. "I'm going back to bed. It was, um, nice to meet you, Todd," she said dubiously and left the room.

"Just so you know," I hissed, "Her boyfriend could do more damage to you with his little finger than I could do if I were *really* trying to hit you, and he's extremely protective of her. So I'd be very, very careful if I were you."

"You sound jealous," he said, smiling.

"You wish. Now, I think you'd better go."

"What? I just got here. And considering you just decked me, you could at least let me crash on your couch for a few hours before I drive back."

"You deserved to be decked. How could you possibly think I'd want you to kiss me? And what were you thinking, acting like that in front of Kai?"

"Oh come on, you saw him bail on you at the first sign of competition. You know he's just using you. But I'm in love with you, Ashlyn."

"No!" I yelled, fighting back the rage that was threatening to explode again. "You don't get to do this! You do not get to come down here after all this time because you're having trouble finding a girlfriend and expect me to uproot my life for you! Don't you get it? It's *over*. We were terrible for each other and always will be. Kai and I are meant to be together. We have something so beyond anything I've ever experienced—way, way beyond what you and I had. Once you find the right person, you'll know what I mean. But I guarantee it: I am *not* the right woman for you."

Todd looked furious. "You really think he loves you more than I do? Well, you're wrong, honey. Nobody will ever love you the way I do."

"Yeah, you already said that a year ago, and you were just as wrong then as you are now. Kai is my soulmate. I have found the greatest happiness with him that I have ever known, and I am going to spend the rest of my life with him."

Todd looked stunned. "You're telling me you're going to *marry* that guy?"

"We haven't talked about marriage," I said coolly. "But yes, I would marry him if he asked me to. In a heartbeat."

"You're the one who's dead set against marriage, remember?"

"That was before I met Kai."

Todd looked furious, and I saw his fists clench. I stood my ground and stared unblinkingly right back in his eyes. *Just give me a reason, you bastard*, said a little voice in the back of my brain. How dare he treat me like crap all those years and then come down here and try to win me back when it suited him? I fantasized for a moment about throwing him across the room and hurling a fireball at him, and I felt the heat rising in my core.

But suddenly, I snapped back to reality and saw what I was doing. I was giving in to the worst part of myself, the part of me that wanted to wield my powers over my enemies, not to overcome evil, but to use it for myself. The realization shocked me. I lowered my hands, which I saw were balled into fists, ready to strike. I closed my eyes and took a deep breath before I spoke.

"Todd, I apologize," I said at last. "I shouldn't have spoken to you like that just now. And I'm sorry for hitting you. That was way, way out of line. You shouldn't have come down here unannounced—it totally threw me off guard. But I know that some part of you did it out of love, however misguided that might have been, and you don't deserve my anger. I'm sorry I can't give you what you want, but trust me, you'll thank me when you meet the right person."

"I don't need your sympathy," he spat. "Whatever drugs you're on these days have obviously fried your brain. You better shape up or you can forget it."

"I'll keep that in mind."

He looked ready to explode. "You've just made the biggest mistake of your life. This is your last chance. Don't expect me to be waiting around for you when that guy dumps you."

"That's a risk I'm just going to have to take." I moved toward the door. "There's a rest stop up the highway on the ocean side. I recommend you stop there and catch a nap for a few hours before you head home."

"No, I think I'll go to L.A. and drop in on an old friend. I used to see her sometimes when me and you were fighting." He had a victorious look on his face, but it was clear that he was lying.

"Suit yourself. I hope you have better luck with her."

He gave me one last withering glare and stormed out the door. I stood at the threshold to watch him go, when suddenly I caught a glimpse of something out of the corner of my eye. I whirled to my left and saw Kai standing against the wall outside my apartment, looking at me with a perplexed expression.

"Kai, what are you doing there?"

"I'm sorry. I couldn't help overhearing." He looked searchingly at me for a moment. "Can we go somewhere and talk?"

Chapter Nine: Swimming with Demons

We walked along the beach for a while in silence. Kai occasionally picked up a shell and tossed it into the waves. I could feel a huge amount of turmoil and confusion within him. I was dying to hear what he had to say, but I didn't press him, sensing that he needed to collect his thoughts. Finally, he spoke, still not looking at me.

"I'm sorry I got so upset with you this morning. I woke up from a deep sleep to Kelly telling me to go find you, and then I saw Todd holding your hand, and then when you called me Todd . . ."

"I know what it must have looked like. But I promise you, things are totally over with Todd and have been for a year. I didn't invite him to come visit."

"I know. He's a manipulative prick. I wanted to kill him."

"That makes two of us." I was still so angry with myself for losing control and hitting him. The whole focus of our martial arts training was to *avoid* physical altercations whenever possible, and to use martial arts only in self-defense, never in anger. I had broken all the rules today. Kai seemed to know what I was feeling.

"I, um, saw you hit him. I have to admit that I was pretty glad to see it in the moment, but I'm sure you're not feeling too happy about it right now."

"Yeah, you could say that." Oh God, what was John going to say?

"Don't be too hard on yourself. You're still learning. It takes time to master your weaknesses. Sometimes a lifetime."

"Unfortunately, I don't have that long." I sighed and looked out at the water. Why did everything have to be so complicated? Why did that stupid Todd have to come down there and make such a mess?

"There's another thing," Kai began and then stopped, biting his lip, as if he were angry at himself for having said the words out loud.

"What is it?" I asked. He had that same pained expression I'd seen a few times before. "Kai, there's something you're not telling me. You have this look on your face, and for the life of me I can't figure out what it means. All I feel coming from you is turmoil."

He looked down at the sand for a moment and then back into my eyes with such a serious expression it made my heart ache. "When we first met, we talked about how we were both against marriage."

"Yes," I said. "I remember."

"I meant it. My parents' divorce really messed with my head, and I swore I'd never repeat their mistake."

I breathed a sigh of relief. "Kai, if you think I'm expecting you to change your mind about that, please don't worry. I know I said that I want to spend the rest of my life with you, but I'm not expecting you to change your values for me. I love you, and I'll be with you in whatever way works for both of us."

He looked confused again. "Is that what you think? That I'm worried that you're going to want to marry me and that I don't want to?"

"Isn't that what you're saying?"

"No, not at all. Ashlyn, I've been struggling with this ever since that night in the hospital. When you told me we couldn't see each other because Deimos would come after me, everything became very, very clear to me. That the only thing that really mattered in my life was that I was with you. For the rest of my life. And at that moment, I knew exactly what that meant."

My heart stopped beating. I couldn't be hearing him correctly. I just couldn't.

"But I knew how you felt about marriage," he continued, "and we're still way too young and all that, so I just tried to forget about it. But when I overheard you telling Todd that you would marry me if I asked you, I knew I had to tell you how I feel about this. But then I thought maybe you were just saying that to get rid of him . . . " His eyes were full of anxiety, his heart racing as fast as mine was.

I managed to find my voice, even as I lost myself in that gaze that threatened to pull me in and never let me go.

"Kai, I meant every word I said. I am yours forever. And I feel the same way you do: I *was* dead set against marriage, until I met you. It turns out I wasn't really against marriage itself. I was just against marrying anyone other than you."

His eyes burned with intensity, relief and happiness spilling out of him. He took a deep breath and was about to speak again, when suddenly I heard a sound that made my heart race. I turned my head toward the ocean and listened carefully.

"What is it?" he asked, but I motioned for him to wait as I listened again. In between the sound of the breaking waves, there was a feeble voice crying out for help. Without another thought, I peeled off my jacket and ran toward the ocean, vaguely aware of Kai yelling behind me.

I dived into the body of a wave just before it broke, coming up safely on the other side. I started pulling hard, straining to hear over the sound of the splashing my strokes made. I was swimming faster than I ever had, streaming through the water like a torpedo. I could hear the voice getting nearer but more feeble. I put on a burst of speed and shot across the ocean.

A few moments later, I came upon a boy flailing in the water. He was about twelve years old, and he looked terrified. His face was pale, and he seemed to be having trouble holding his eyes open. That's when I saw something that nearly made me fly out of the water in terror.

His upper arm was missing a large chunk of flesh, and he was bleeding badly.

Struggling to conquer the panic that was rising as a scream in my throat, I swam behind the boy and grabbed him around the chest as I'd seen lifeguards do, and I started swimming to shore with everything I had. Part of my brain became very calm and logical, as it always did in a crisis. *If he'd been bitten by a shark, the arm would be missing altogether*, the voice in my head reasoned. Obviously, a seal or something mistook him for a large fish, and it was scared away when it realized its mistake. But the other part of me knew that the scent of blood in the water was like a dinner bell, and even though there were rarely any sharks in these waters, all it took was one.

I could feel the boy's heartbeat slowing, and I split my energy between swimming as fast as I could and pouring healing into him to keep him alive. It was a tough battle, and I soon felt light-headed. The boy was going into shock, and I had to do something. Just as I was about to disappear and fly, a wave swelled beneath us, carrying us up and shooting us forward. When we were almost at shore, I used a little bit of flight to help us ride the wave in so it wouldn't break on us. As the wave retreated, my feet touched the sand, and I picked up the boy in my arms and leaped through the water to the beach, where Kai was waiting for us, his cell phone in his hand.

"Can you hear me?" I shouted to the boy as I lay him down on the sand. He moaned but didn't speak. He was shivering. Kai quickly took off his shirt and handed it to me, and I tied it around the boy's shoulder.

"I called 9-1-1," Kai said. "The paramedics will be here in a minute."

I wrapped my jacket around the boy and sent heat from my core into his body until his shivering subsided. "He looks like he's lost a lot of blood," Kai whispered. I poured more healing into him until I started seeing spots. As we heard sirens approaching, the boy opened his eyes and looked at me.

"You're safe now," I said. "What's your name?"

"Travis," he replied, his voice breaking.

"Travis what?"

"Rogers."

"Hi, Travis, I'm Ashlyn. How are you feeling?"

"My arm is killing me."

"We need Rebecca," I whispered to Kai. "Go run and get her."

But Kai shook his head slightly, and I stared at him, dumbfounded. The ambulance pulled up, and two paramedics ran down onto the beach carrying something that looked like a yellow sled. I waved to them, and they hurried over to us.

"This boy was bitten in the water and has lost a lot of blood. I think he was going into shock but seems to have stabilized. His name is Travis Rogers."

"Travis, are your parents here?" a paramedic asked as he looked into his eyes and briefly inspected the wound. Travis shook his head.

"I rode my bike. It's locked up over by the stairs."

"We'll call your parents on the way to the hospital, okay?" Travis nodded. The paramedics put him on the yellow sled, strapped him in, and then carried him off. I stood watching them go.

"Good thing you heard him," Kai said, putting his arm around me. "I don't like to think what would have happened if you hadn't been here today."

I pulled back and looked at him. "Why wouldn't you get Rebecca?"

"Because it would have blown our cover," he said. "You gave him exactly what he needed to get him safely to the hospital, no more. Although hopefully nobody could actually see you swimming," he said, glancing around anxiously. The small crowd that had gathered was slowly dispersing. I hadn't noticed them at all before. As I watched them walk away, I looked up at the top of the stairs and saw the last person in the world I wanted to see right then: Kelly.

She had the strangest look on her face I'd ever seen, a mixture of confusion, intimidation, and victory all at once. She gave me a crooked sneer and walked away.

"That's not good. That's not good at all," Kai said. "I know that look."

I laughed half-heartedly. "Why, what's she going to do? Tell people I'm a fast swimmer and that I saved a boy's life? That's hardly going to score her any points."

"I don't know what she's planning, but she's undoubtedly noticed that there was something unusual going on, and from here on out she's going to be watching you very closely. The point is, now we have to be extra careful around her. Although I suppose that was always a good idea."

"Kai, what would you have had me do? That kid was going to drown! Are you saying I should have just let him?"

"Of course not," he said, putting his arms around me. "I just wish there could have been a way to do it with a lower profile. I never want you to be in a situation where you have to choose between exposing your powers and letting someone die."

"Well, that choice is obvious. Even if I end up in a lab being studied for the rest of my life, it's worth it if I can save someone else's."

"I know, and I'd do the same thing. Especially if it were you." He kissed my forehead. "That must have been rough out there. I'm proud of you."

The memory of being in the water with something lurking below, able to attack at any moment, filled me with panic. I didn't know how I'd ever go out there again.

"I have an idea," Kai continued. "Why don't we go get a big breakfast and then veg out at my place and watch movies. Candace's graduation isn't until four o'clock."

"I have training this morning," I said, my voice trembling.

"Just skip it today." He stroked my hair gently. "You've already been through enough for one day."

The idea of just chilling out and escaping into a stupid movie sounded wonderful. But just as I was about to agree, a small voice in the back of my head said no, that it would be running away and letting fear win. I felt panic rising up again as I realized what that voice was suggesting I do. I wanted to scream.

I took a couple of slow, calming breaths and looked out at the ocean. "There's something I have to do first."

"What?" Kai asked.

"I have to go for a swim."

Ten minutes later, I was standing at the edge of the water. I still hadn't moved. The wise voice in my head was telling me that this was the right thing to do, and I would start to lean forward to walk into the surf, but then a voice of panic would shriek in my head and I'd jolt to a halt. I felt like there was an epic battle going on inside my brain, and either way, I was losing. Kai sat on the beach, watching me. I wondered how he could be so patient. He must have learned it during those insanely long winters he endured as a kid in Minnesota.

The voices continued arguing, the panicked voice getting louder, until I couldn't take it anymore. "Stop it!" I shouted out loud. I decided I wasn't going to let the fear stop me for one more second, no matter how strong it was. I ignored the screaming in my head as I marched into the surf and dived in. I felt driven, angry that I'd let it get so far out of hand. I swam through a wave and popped up on the other side. So far, so good. I swam a few strokes and started settling into a rhythm.

But as soon as I was past the waves and could sense the depth of the water, I started panicking. A shark could be down there at that very moment, swimming below me, ready to attack. I felt the fear rising up as I treaded water and had trouble catching my breath. I found myself pulling my legs up into my chest, afraid that if I extended them they'd attract a predator. *Easy, Ashlyn*, I said to myself. *It's not real. It's just fear.*

"That bite was real enough!" I said out loud, glad that nobody was around to see me talking to myself and generally acting like a lunatic. I felt the fear driving me up out of the water, but I thought about Kai's reaction, about Rebecca, and about John. I had to fight this and not let them down. I thought about all the people who swam out there every day and nothing happened. About all the times I'd been out there and been fine. What happened to that boy was a freak accident—that's all. I knew I needed to get my head back on straight so I could get back to my job as a Soterian, defeat Deimos, and start my life with Kai.

At that moment, I remembered what Kai was saying to me before I'd heard the boy in the water. About how he wanted to spend the rest of his life with me. As I remembered the look in his eyes, the fear drained away as if I'd simply pulled the plug. I breathed calmly again, feeling the water lapping over my arms, tasting the salt in my mouth. I floated on my back and flashed back to several months ago, when I had almost died in the ocean beneath the Golden Gate Bridge, and how focusing on Kai had kept me fighting for my life. It seemed like however strong my fears were, they were no match for the feelings I had for him. His love really was the key to my powers, Soterian and otherwise.

As I swam back to shore, feeling totally at peace, I thought about what John had taught us: that learning to move past your fears was the most important skill of all. They might never go away completely, but that didn't have to stop me. I let a wave carry me onto the sand and then walked straight over to Kai.

"Well?" he asked.

"*Now* let's go get breakfast." I took his hand, and we made our way up the beach.

* * *

On the way to the dojo, I told Rebecca what had happened. She was surprised that we hadn't called her, but when I gave her Kai's rationale, she nodded. "He was right. You were able to do just what you needed to without exposing us."

"What do you think about Kelly?"

"I can't see what she has on you. So she saw you swimming fast . . . so what?"

"That's exactly what I said. But Kai was sure she was planning something."

"We'll just deal with it when it comes, then. I can't see any reason to worry about it now."

When we arrived at the dojo, Michael and Christoph were already warming up with John. Michael came over as soon as we walked in and gave me a high five.

"Way to go, Ashlyn!" he said. I was confused. How could he know about the rescue already?

"That's not something to be congratulated," John said, his voice flat. I whirled around and looked at him, even more confused than before. Out of the corner of my eye, I saw Rebecca twirling a lock of hair around her finger.

"Er, I think they're talking about what happened with Todd," she explained.

"Oh." I'd completely forgotten about him. It already seemed like weeks ago. Michael was grinning widely, and Christoph was smiling in spite of himself. "How do they know about that?"

"Christoph called this morning, and I kind of told him," Rebecca admitted, sounding sheepish. "And he must have told Michael."

"And Michael told John," I added, filling in the gaps. "I see. Well, I'm glad I was able to furnish you all with such juicy gossip."

Michael shook his head. "I just wish I'd been there! So Little Miss Perfect is human after all."

"I never said I was perfect," I retorted. "I let my anger get in the way of my judgment and did something I immediately regretted. Well, *almost* immediately. The point being that I realized soon after that I had made a bad mistake, and I apologized to Todd for it."

"You apologized?!" Michael groaned. "Oh man, don't go and ruin it! Don't tell me any more."

"You were right to apologize," John said. "Using your skills in anger is completely at odds with everything you are learning here."

"I know. I'm really sorry." I felt deeply ashamed of myself.

Michael rolled his eyes but still had a small smile on his face. From that point forward, he was much more open with me, as if I'd passed an initiation to join his secret club. It made me feel worse about what I'd done, but I was happy to have broken through a barrier with him. I guessed he was just glad that he wasn't the only one with a temper that got out of control.

That evening, after making my way back to the apartment after Candace's long but admittedly moving graduation ceremony, I called my mom to chew her out.

"Guess who showed up on my doorstep at six o'clock this morning?" I began.

Mom sighed. "Yeah, I know. He called me from the road on his way home. Sounds like it wasn't the happy reunion he was hoping for."

"How can you be surprised? Did you expect me to drop everything and welcome him back into my life?"

"Not in the slightest. I just hoped that seeing you would help him move on with his own life. He's had a rough time of it, honey."

"It's his own damn fault, and you should *not* feel sorry for him. If his highest priority is going out and getting wasted, not to mention trying to stroke his own pathetic ego by flirting with whatever girl drifts by, then he can't expect women to be throwing themselves at his feet. You should try explaining that to him in one of your little heart-to-heart sessions."

"Don't get angry with me, Ashlyn. I didn't tell him to drive down there in the middle of the night. I told him you were happy with Kai and had moved on. I guess he needed to see it for himself."

I took a deep breath, trying to stay calm. "I know, Mom, but you shouldn't have given him my address. It was just a really bad scene. Kai saw us together, and it hurt his feelings."

"Kai should know better than to be jealous of Todd, for heaven's sake. Unless you gave him something to be jealous of?"

"No, but Todd put his arm around me and did his best to make it look like there was something Kai should be jealous of. Oof, it was awful. I don't even want to think about it."

"Is everything okay with Kai now?"

"It's better than okay." A warm glow spread through my body. "He told me that he wants to spend the rest of his life with me. He said he's been wanting to tell me for months, but he knows we're too young, and he thought I was against marriage."

"So did I." She sounded shocked. "Are you telling me you're engaged?"

"Not exactly. It's more like we're promised to each other. I want to make sure we go into this with our eyes open. Believe me, I never want to look back and blame our problems on the fact that we got married too young. But Mom, I can't tell you how happy this makes me."

"Well, I'm very glad to hear that you're going to wait a while. But I do think you and Kai are just great together, and I'm really happy for you. Have you told your sister yet?"

"No, this just happened today. I'll send her an email tonight."

Mom chuckled. "She's going to be furious that she hasn't even met him yet, but that's what she gets for moving so far away. I can't wait for her to come home."

"Me too. Anyway, I'm glad you're not weirded out by the whole thing. I know Kai and I haven't been together all that long."

"But you've known each other for many lifetimes, it would seem. You don't have the easiest road ahead of you, honey, but you two have an incredible connection, and that's going to carry you through the hard times. Like when you tell your father."

My stomach lurched at the thought. "Yeah, well, I'm not going to be telling him anytime soon. No point in doing that until we're actually engaged."

Her voice softened. "He'll come around at some point. Try not to worry."

"That's what Kai said. I'm still skeptical. But I'm not going to let it get to me. This is *my* life, *my* future. And even though I'm only twenty, I've had enough experience to know what I want."

"Are you trying to convince me or yourself?" she asked with a laugh.

"Just planning out what I'm going to say to Dad. It's going to take a couple of years to prepare for that conversation."

"Put it out of your mind for now, Ashlyn. There's no point in borrowing trouble from the future." That was certainly the truth. I had enough to think about without worrying about a conversation with my father that might not happen for months or even years.

I said good-bye to my mom and lay back on my bed, staring at the ceiling. I found it fascinating that while part of me was worried about my dad's reaction to Kai, another part was worried that I wouldn't have a future at all and that Deimos would win in the end. John and Theresa were convinced that Magnum-Drake was the next move in his plan, but the layoffs were perfectly legal. What the people in Cooke needed was work, and so far nobody was stepping in to buy the factory. I just didn't see what we could do about it, which was driving me crazy. I rolled over and picked up a book, determined to stay on top of my studies so I could graduate with good grades. *That is, if I even live long enough to graduate.*

Tuesday was election day, and we decided to throw a party to watch the results come in and to send Candace off in style. We invited Adam and Carla, who were also graduating, as well as Max, Ryan, Toby, and several of Candace's friends.

Christoph and Michael came over early to help us set up. Michael was carrying a huge bag of tortilla chips, a large container of salsa, and a bucket of guacamole. Christoph was casually toting a keg as if it were a small parcel. I never quite got used to seeing how strong he really was.

Ryan and Toby had ordered a huge chocolate cake. They brought it in and set it down on the kitchen counter.

"Go ahead," Ryan told Candace, beaming with pride. "Open it up!"

"It's a cake. What exactly does she need to open?" Michael asked.

"Just open it," Ryan urged. Toby winked at me, piquing my curiosity.

"Okay . . . ," Candace said, sounding dubious. She grabbed a knife and slit open the tape that held the sides of the pink cardboard box closed. She lifted the lid and burst out laughing.

I stepped forward and saw that "Congraduations!" was written across the top of the white frosting in large blue letters. I groaned, but Candace looked thrilled.

"I love it!" she said and hugged Ryan, who looked very pleased with himself. Despite the stupid message, the cake looked beautiful, with delicate blue and white flowers around the edges. I jotted down the name of the bakery. Kai and I were turning twenty-one later that year, and since our birthdays were only two days apart, we were going to have a joint birthday party. I was already starting to plan it, even though it was over three months away.

The graduation party got into full swing around eight o'clock, and every now and then someone would shout out the latest election results as they appeared on the television. Unlike the last election, I wasn't all that interested this time around. Both of the candidates were fairly middle-of-the-road and seemed to be reasonable people, but I'd lost my faith in politicians. Adam and Carla were very politically active, so they kept a close eye on the results and were rooting heavily for one of the candidates.

By nine o'clock, most of the people at the party were well on their way to being drunk, and Michael was hammered. He was telling loud and rambling stories about his Scottish relatives. He had several people laughing hysterically, but I was worried that it was only a matter of time before his mood turned. I'd seen enough of his brand of drunk to know that The Rage always cropped up toward the end of the night.

Candace had streamers wrapped around her head and was singing a sea shanty with Ryan, their arms around each other's shoulders. Predictably, it wasn't long before they ended up in a heap on the couch, making out. I wondered why they had never hooked up before, but on second thought, maybe it wasn't the first time.

Kai, Rebecca, Christoph, Toby, and I hung out in the tiny kitchen, eating chips and drinking sodas. Kai and Christoph talked about industrial bands in Germany, while Toby and Rebecca and I planned a camping trip near Lake Cachuma, which was up in the mountains above Santa Barbara.

"We've got a tent, camp stove, lantern—everything we need," I said. "All you have to do is get a tent and a sleeping bag and you're all set."

"I don't need a tent," Toby insisted. "I like sleeping under the stars."

"But what if there are bears?" Rebecca asked.

"You think a thin layer of nylon is going to protect you from a bear?" Toby laughed. "As long as we're careful about not leaving food out, the bears aren't going to bother us."

"You sound like you've done this before," I said.

"My dad and I used to go backpacking in the mountains," he explained. "One time, we were doing this twenty-mile hike—"

But his words were interrupted by Adam shouting.

"It's over! They've called it for Taylor!" A cheer erupted from the room, and we all rushed over to the TV. Sure enough, they'd counted enough of the votes to call the election for Taylor with a four-point margin. Everyone hugged, and Candace pulled out a bottle of champagne and popped the cork. Michael tore off his shirt and let out a long whoop.

"Here's to Governor Taylor!" Candace shouted, holding the bottle high in the air. "And," she said, grabbing a handful of cake, "to never growing up!" She threw the cake at Michael. It hit him squarely in his bare chest and bounced onto the floor, leaving a smear of white frosting and bits of chocolate cake stuck to his skin. He looked stunned for a second and then got a gleam in his eye. In a flash, he darted over to her and mashed a handful of cake into her hair. She shrieked with laughter, and suddenly the room was in chaos. Cake was flying everywhere, brown chunks and clumps of white sticky frosting going in all directions. A large piece hit me in the side of the face, and I burst out laughing.

I glanced at Rebecca, who looked horrified. She was hiding behind Christoph, who stood protectively in front of her but was laughing in delight at the absurd scene before us, his shirt a mess of frosting and cake. Kai and Toby had ducked behind the kitchen wall, but when Kai saw that I'd gotten pegged, he came over and nibbled some off my cheek.

"Let's not do this at our wedding," he said.

"No, but let's *definitely* do it at our birthday party." I snatched a chunk of flying cake out of the air and broke it in two, giving one half to him and shoving the other half happily into my mouth.

Chapter Ten: The Manor

"'Magnum-Drake announced their earnings today for the second quarter,'" Rebecca read aloud. "'Sales rose eight percent to one-point-five billion, but due to higher-than-expected expenses, the company posted a loss of three hundred million dollars. The stock dropped twenty percent to close at fourteen dollars a share.' What's up with the higher-than-expected expenses? The entire point of moving the factory out of the country was to save money."

"I don't get it at all," I said, stretching out on my bed. It was the middle of July, and we were sitting in our room with the window open, attempting to keep cool while we tried to make sense of the latest news about Magnum-Drake. We clicked through more headlines on our laptops and kept looking for answers. All of the reports indicated that the shareholders and the board of directors were edgy. Prescott had given a rosy speech about these being temporary setbacks and that they were on track to be profitable again in the third quarter, but rumors were circulating that there was something fishy with the books, and that costs had actually gone up since the layoffs, not down.

"I wish I understood this better," Rebecca said. "I don't know the first thing about business finance."

"Me neither. But," I added, suddenly getting a flash of inspiration, "we know someone who does! I can't believe I didn't think of it before. Come on!" I hopped off the bed, and Rebecca followed me. She looked confused for a moment before the light dawned.

"Toby!" she said. "Of course!" Toby was majoring in business administration, so he might be able to help us sort it all out.

We headed into the living room, locking our bedroom door behind us. We briefly surveyed the scene before us as we moved quickly toward the front door. Tracy and Kelly were sitting on the couch watching the huge television Tracy had brought with her when she moved in. Tracy's dishes were stacked in the sink, as always, and her magazines were everywhere. I tried to remember what John had said about people who drive you crazy being a gift that help you to grow and to practice mental discipline. But right then, all I felt was irritation.

"Hey girls, where are you off to?" Tracy asked.

"Going to see the guys. We'll see you later," I replied as we hurried toward the door.

"Hope we didn't disturb your studying," Kelly said, giving me a sarcastic smile. "Seems like that's all you two ever do."

In fact, we did spend most of our time holed up in our room. Even though Tracy had her own room, she was always in the living room, and she often had Kelly over to hang out and watch such riveting entertainment as soap operas and reality TV shows.

Needless to say, we missed Candace a lot. She'd landed a job working as a marketing assistant in San Luis Obispo, which sounded like a great job for her, and so far she was enjoying it. I was happy she found something she liked, but our lives felt so different without her. I missed her witty comments, but most of all, I realized just how great a roommate she had been. Tracy came home drunk a lot, often accompanied by one of a string of guys she was dating, and she always made so much noise that she woke us up. She left her dishes to mold in the sink and never wanted to do the weekly cleaning. And after we'd noticed that our toilet paper kept disappearing, and I caught her going through my closet for something to "borrow," Rebecca and I finally ended up installing a lock on our bedroom door.

Our saving grace was the guys' apartment—The Manor, as they called it—where we spent all our spare time. There was always something entertaining going on there, whether it was Christoph, Michael, and Toby yelling at the TV as they watched soccer, Kai and Ryan jamming and writing music, or all five of them playing poker. It was a wonderful place to hang out, but not an ideal place for studying. Since Rebecca, Kai, and I were all taking summer classes, we often locked ourselves in our room to study and kept our voices down so Tracy wouldn't come and bug us. It was a real drag.

As usual, the door to The Manor was wide open. Ryan and Toby were in the living room reading, and Kai was sitting on the floor changing the strings on his guitar.

"Hey guys," I said, knocking lightly on the door before walking in. All three of them looked up and smiled. They always seemed so happy to see us, and it occurred to me that Rebecca and I were kind of like little sisters to The Manor. I went over and sat next to Kai, and Rebecca sat in the chair next to Toby.

"Christoph and Michael are surfing," Toby told Rebecca. "I heard Christoph dragging him out the door early this morning. Michael didn't sound too happy about it. I think he was a little hung over. Again."

I snorted at the mental image of Christoph literally dragging Michael and two surf boards out of the apartment.

"What are you up to this morning?" Kai asked, giving me a quick kiss before turning back to his guitar.

"Actually, we were just talking about Magnum-Drake, and we wanted to ask Toby about it." I turned to Toby, choosing my words carefully. "I've been following their news since the layoffs happened while we were in Minnesota. And I don't understand how they can have record sales but still lose money."

"And why there are questions about their books," Rebecca added. "Don't they have to make all of that public?"

"Yes, and they're audited quarterly, but they don't walk through every single transaction," Toby explained. "The questions coming up are about why the expenses are so high across the board. There are always one-time costs associated with a merger, but the layoffs and salary reductions were supposed to cut many of the costs, and instead those numbers have actually gone up. So now they're going through a special audit to find out what's going on."

"Is it possible for the executives to just lie about those things and use a corrupt auditor to back them up?"

"It is, but it's much harder since the Sarbanes-Oxley Act was passed. If the executives get caught, they can't just plead ignorance anymore. They're personally responsible for fraud and can go to prison for up to twenty years. So it's generally not worth it."

"But if enough people are conspiring together, they could potentially get away with it?" Kai asked.

"Sure. But that would be hard to do with a company as large and visible as Magnum-Drake. It's more likely that there's been some error, or that there were higher costs associated with the merger than people anticipated."

Kai looked deep in thought as he fed his strings through the tuning pegs and tightened them up. I could feel something stirring in him, a kind of revelation. He looked at me and nodded slightly, letting me know that he'd fill me in later.

Just then, Christoph and Michael returned. When Christoph saw Rebecca, his face lit up, looking like a kid on Christmas morning. He went over and kissed her softly. Michael looked cranky.

"How was surfing?" I asked.

"Beautiful," Christoph said just as Michael muttered "Sucked." Christoph ignored him. "We caught some excellent waves."

"Mmm, sounds terrible." I gave Michael a sarcastic smile, and he shot me a nasty look in reply. "Come on," I said, standing up. "Let's all get breakfast. Michael, we'll get you some coffee and an omelet." He opened his mouth, undoubtedly to tell me where I could shove my omelet, but right at that moment his stomach growled loudly. He closed his mouth and settled on just looking irritable as we headed down to the café.

After breakfast, Kai came with us to our place so we could talk. "So what are you thinking about all of this?" Rebecca asked him.

"I think the factory in Mexico has to be the key. If it's really that hard to cook the books, their best shot would be to inflate expenses at the foreign plant."

I nodded. "That makes sense. Do you think we should head down there and investigate?"

"I think it's the only way we're going to get any answers," Kai replied. "If they're pulling off a massive fraud, they're going to be covering their tracks carefully. It'll take some scouting to uncover the truth."

"Good point. And it's perfect timing, since our classes end in two weeks. It'll be nice to go on vacation again." I smiled at

Kai, happily picturing another road trip with him, but he frowned.

"I can't take any more time off of work. I'm going to have to sit this one out."

I tried to hide my disappointment. It totally sucked that Kai had to work while he was in school. I remembered all too well how hard it was to balance work and classes, and it didn't seem fair that I got the luxury of being just a student while he had to do both.

"Okay," I sighed, "I'll ask John and Theresa to organize a trip down there. Maybe Jesse and I should go first to get more information. God knows what type of situation we're going to be dealing with."

"That's probably the best strategy," Rebecca agreed. "And you'll attract less attention if it's just the two of you."

Kai nodded. "Especially if you're invisible." He looked gravely at me. "Just please be careful."

When we'd let both units know about our idea, John and Theresa agreed that Jesse and I should head down first and do some scouting. That night, I called Jesse to discuss our strategy, and he was very excited about the trip.

"Mexico! We're going to have a blast. Have you tried real one hundred percent blue agave tequila?"

"I don't drink, and we're not going there to party," I reminded him.

"Not at all like the swill they put in margaritas," he continued. "You can't have margaritas down there anyway. You have to be very careful to avoid any drinks with ice in them. Montezuma's Revenge is no joke."

I cleared my throat impatiently. "You want to give me a call back when you've finished your monologue?"

"Oh, lighten up. I'm just looking forward to it, that's all. I'm ready to celebrate because I graduate on Saturday."

"You're done with cosmetology school? Jesse, that's awesome! Congratulations!"

"Thanks! But I've got a lot of thinking to do about the next step." There was a hint of anxiety in his voice.

"I thought you were opening a salon."

"Yes, but I'm not sure if I should try to open my own place right away, or if I should rent a station at another salon so I can get more experience first. You know, learn more about running a business. I've been putting off thinking about it, and now here I am at the end of school with no plan. Paul is just a wee bit annoyed with me."

"I can imagine. But hey, a road trip might be just the thing to help sort out what you want to do next. You need a break."

"That's just what I told him. So, I'll drive down to Santa Barbara on Friday the thirty-first, and then we can drive to TJ the next morning. I'll start compiling a playlist of road-trip music on my iPod."

"Sounds good. In the meantime, Paul and Kai are going to get us as much information on the factory as they can so we can be fully prepared."

He snorted. "If that's some kind of hint, don't worry. I'll be just as ready as you are."

"I'm sure you will be," I laughed. Jesse was one of the most perceptive people I knew. He tended to hide his intellect behind a casual, almost flaky attitude, but it was all an act. Nothing got past him. We had really hit it off, and I was looking forward to spending some time with him on the road. I'd learned over the last year that travelling with someone was definitely the best way to get to know them.

I hung up and headed over to The Manor. It was one of those rare occasions when Kai and I had both finished our homework and he didn't have band practice. There never seemed to be enough time to spend together, and just being around him made me feel so happy, so peaceful. But having an entire evening together was bliss.

I found him in his room, playing guitar, his hair hanging into his face as he looked down in deep concentration. I stepped in the room, closed the door quietly, and leaned back against it, just watching him and listening. There was nothing in the world cooler or sexier than Kai playing guitar. He looked up at me with that intense gaze that always made me so weak, set his guitar down, and walked over to me. He slipped one hand behind my head, his fingers lacing into my hair, and with his other hand pulled me to him. His eyes wandered slowly around my face before he finally kissed me. And as always, he completely took my breath away, my knees giving way as he lifted me into his arms and laid me down on his bed. I didn't understand how being with him could still feel so new after all these months, but I didn't really care. I just hoped it would never change.

Later, as we lay on his bed listening to music, we talked about our future and where we wanted to live after graduation. He loved San Francisco, but a lot would depend on what happened with the band. If they found a singer in Santa Barbara or L.A., he'd have to stay in Southern California for a while. I was fine with that, although I hoped we'd end up in San Francisco some day. I had always dreamed of living in the city, and I had spent many hours as a kid looking out my bedroom window at the San Francisco skyline across the bay.

We never talked much about getting married or even when we would get engaged. We definitely wanted to wait until after graduation, and he wanted to save up enough money to buy me a ring. We both felt that there was no rush, and we wanted to be sure we spent enough time together first so that we went into it with our eyes open. Neither of us wanted to repeat the mistakes our parents made. It was enough for me just knowing that he actually wanted to spend the day with me, let alone the rest of our lives.

As we lay there, his arms wrapped around me, I thought about that day on the beach when he'd spoken those words that I still couldn't believe were for me. It was especially crazy that he'd been feeling that way for such a long time.

"Kai?"

"Hmm?" he murmured, his breath warm on my neck.

"When you told me that you wanted to spend the rest of your life with me . . . why hadn't you told me that before?"

"I wanted to, but something always got in the way, or I just felt there wasn't any point."

"Right," I said, rolling over and looking at him. "That's the part that's bothering me. Why would you hold something like that inside?"

He looked pensive. "If you were dead set against marriage, there wasn't any reason for me to tell you how I was feeling."

"Wrong. You should feel like you can tell me anything. It's extremely important to me that you're always honest with me."

"I didn't think of it as being dishonest. I just didn't see the point in talking about it."

"The point," I said, stroking his hair, "is that I never want us to have secrets from each other. From the very beginning, I knew I could never keep anything from you, and I took a big risk telling you about The Soterians. If I could trust you with that information, don't you think you can trust me with just about anything? No matter what it is, no matter how badly you think I'm going to react, I need you to be open with me."

He kissed me softly and then looked into my eyes. "I'm sorry," he said. "I promise not to keep things from you."

"Good. Because if there's one thing I can't handle, it's surprises."

"Not even good ones?"

"There's no such thing, in my opinion. So no, no surprises, no secrets, definitely no lies, no matter how small. Deal?"

"Deal. And that goes both ways, of course. I don't want you to keep secrets from me, either."

I immediately felt guilty that I hadn't mentioned what his dad had said about Kai's financial situation. But that was different, I decided—it really wasn't my business, so there was nothing to discuss. I rolled over again and felt his arms wrapped tightly around me, the sound of his breathing and the music drowning out the sounds of Isla Vista and the rest of the world.

Chapter Eleven: Tijuana

"Time's up, everyone. Pencils down, papers over, please. Make sure that your name and your TA's name are on your paper."

I put my pencil down and rubbed my temples. It had been next to impossible to study that week, because all I could think about was the upcoming trip to Mexico. I spent a lot of time learning about the factory and its location, which was just across the border, south of Tijuana. I had studied French in high school, not Spanish, so I wasn't going to be able to understand much, but Jesse was nearly fluent and would be able to get us around.

I'd also been spending as much time with Kai as he could spare while he wrapped up his summer classes at the junior college. Despite the more intense class schedule during the summer semester, he'd still managed to pull off a 4.0 grade point average for the second semester in a row. It amazed me that he was able to take a full load, work at the vet clinic, practice guitar, and still do so well in school. Best of all, he got a letter confirming that pending his final grades from summer, he was all set to transfer to UCSB in the fall. I was ecstatic for him.

But I could tell that the schedule was wearing him down. He was obviously torn between spending time with me, working, studying, and playing music. He liked to give everything he did his full attention, and it bothered him to have to split his time among things that mattered so much to him. I tried to make it easier by studying with him or just going to his band practices and watching so that we could be together, but we also had to carve out time for just the two of us. It was an insane amount of juggling.

I took one last look at my test and then handed it to the teaching assistant who was collecting them. As I walked out of the classroom into the glorious sunshine, a weight lifted almost palpably from my shoulders. I was free for another seven weeks! And the next day I was going to Mexico. It was so exciting to finally be starting a mission again.

When I got home, I found Rebecca in our bedroom, as usual. She was reading her email on her laptop and looked distressed.

"Hey Bec. What's up? You seem upset."

Her fingers started twisting a lock of her hair. "My parents want to meet Christoph."

"But that's great!"

"No, it isn't! I haven't told them . . . everything about him yet."

"What do you mean?"

She bit her lip. "I haven't told them that he's not Jewish."

I stared at her in surprise. "Does that matter to them? You've never mentioned that your family was very religious."

"To tell you the truth, we've never talked about it. It's just always sort of been implied. Strongly implied. Things like: 'When you get married at the temple' and 'Are there a lot of nice Jewish boys in your classes?'"

"Hmm. Well, I didn't grow up in a religious household, so I can't imagine what that's like. Although telling my dad that I plan to marry a guitar player instead of an investment banker is probably somewhat similar." I started to feel gloomy and quickly shoved the thought away.

She looked at me in despair. "Ashlyn, what am I going to do?"

I sat next to her. "Nobody who sees the way Christoph is around you can doubt that he's madly in love with you and worships the ground you walk on. And it's equally clear that you're crazy about him. So that has to count for a lot right there. Secondly, he loves children and wants a family, so that should make them happy, right?"

"Yes, that will definitely help, as long as he doesn't mind raising them Jewish."

"Have you talked about that with him?"

"No!" she said. "It seems awfully early for that."

"Okay, well that's your first problem right there. You need to talk about what you want in the future. It might change, but at least know what each other's basic values are to make sure you're starting out on the same page."

Her finger worked more quickly, twisting and untwisting her hair. "I think that part of me just doesn't want to know. What if I find out that we want completely different things out of our lives?"

"Then it's better to know that up front so you can start seeing where you need to compromise. Besides, you must already know a lot of these things about him. I mean, you can read his feelings, right?"

She shook her head. "I've made a point of blocking them out. I don't know, it just feels wrong somehow to have that advantage over him. I don't want to be in his head without his permission."

"It sounds like you guys have a lot of talking to do. Sweeping all this under the rug isn't going to make things better. It's just going to hold you back, which I'm sure is the last thing you want. Are your parents going to come here to meet him, or do they want you to bring him to New York?"

"They're coming here in a few weeks."

"Oh, good! I'm glad I'll be here when they visit. I can't wait to meet them."

She looked hopefully at me. "You really want to meet them?"

"Of course! You're my best friend, silly. Why wouldn't I want to meet your parents?"

She smiled. "You're my best friend, too. I just wasn't sure if you felt the same way."

I laughed. "Rebecca, for such a talented Empath, you're doing a pretty lousy job of applying it in your personal life. I'm the one with the insecurity problems, remember?"

"I guess there's plenty of that to go around." She took a deep breath. "Okay, I'm going to talk to Christoph. You're right, we need to start having these conversations."

"Has he told you he loves you yet?" I asked. I was burning with curiosity about their relationship, but I had learned early on that Rebecca was a very private person, so I never pried.

"No. But I don't think I've really given him the chance."

"Let him in, Bec. It's only going to make you happier." I squeezed her on the arm and got up to finish packing. "And take full advantage of next week, since Tracy and I will both be gone." To our relief, Tracy was going home for a month. I doubted we'd miss her for even a second.

Jesse arrived right at six o'clock. He was wearing a pair of long red and black shorts, a black T-shirt, and red high-top shoes. I stared in disbelief at the five bags he had with him.

"Jesse, we're only going for a week. What on earth did you pack?"

"Just a few different things," he said in a breezy voice. "Just in case."

"In case what, we need to stay for a year?"

"Hilarious. What did you pack? A pair of jeans and a sweatshirt?"

I smiled. "Something like that. Come on, let's stash your arsenal in my room and go get dinner. Everyone is in the café."

We went downstairs, where Kai, Rebecca, Michael, and Christoph were waiting for us. We talked about our units and laughed about some of the crazier moments during the last year, all the while choosing our words carefully in case we were overheard. I sat next to Kai and held his hand tightly. I was so sad that he wasn't coming with us.

"Try to get lots of songwriting done while I'm gone," I suggested. "It's amazing that you almost have enough material for a gig."

"All but the vocals," he corrected. "We have to find a singer soon."

"You're smart to hold out, though. If you get some hack in there, you'll just have to start all over again in six months."

He looked seriously at me. "I hope you get some good information on your trip. I'm not happy about you going, you know."

"I know. But you were right: it's the only way to find out what's really going on. Jesse and I will be okay. There will be plenty of evil to draw on, and as long as I have your love, I'm going to be fine."

"You always have my love. You know that."

"I do," I said. I smiled, trying to reassure him as I felt the worry and concern spilling out of him.

Early the next morning, Jesse and I were heading south on Highway 101, the windows rolled down and the music thumping. It turned out we had the same taste in music, and we were having a blast rocking out and getting to know each other. He told me about cosmetology school and his ideas for the salon.

"Paul was trying to get me to open the salon in Walnut Creek, but I think there's an untapped market in Oakland."

"Sounds like a great idea," I said. "But why don't you want to open it right away?"

"I feel like I have more to learn where I am now, and I'd rather learn from someone else's mistakes first. It takes a lot more than talent to have a successful salon. Besides, I want to save up more money. I hate the idea of taking a loan from my parents."

"Won't Paul loan you the money?"

"That's even worse!"

"Why?" I asked, perplexed.

He shook his head. "I don't know, I just need to do this on my own. My whole life I had things handed to me. My dad made a lot of money, and he never wanted us to know what it was like to be deprived, the way he was when he was a kid. I want to open a successful salon and know that I did it myself."

"But you will still be doing it yourself. It's not having something handed to you—most business owners start with some sort of a loan. You could set up a contract with Paul or your dad and agree to pay them interest, or give them a share in the business. That way, it's not a gift but an investment."

"I don't know, it still sounds like I'd be just working there. I want it to be *my* place."

"And it will be. Seriously, Jesse. Don't be so focused on doing it yourself that you make bad business decisions."

He looked pensive as we drove in silence for a while, watching Los Angeles stretch out before us. We pointed out signs for Malibu and Hollywood, squinting at the houses glittering in the sunlight, trying to guess how much they cost. When we drove past a sign for Anaheim, Jesse suddenly gasped.

"Let's stop at Disneyland!" he shouted, a crazed gleam in his eye.

"What?"

"Oh come on, we could go in over the gates so we wouldn't have to pay, and we could fly inside the rides and look around! And oh holy night, we could even sit on top of the Matterhorn!"

"Jesse, you have lost your goddamn mind! We are *so* not stopping at Disneyland. And we're definitely not using our powers to get out of paying and to go where we're not supposed to be." But even as I slammed the idea, I had to admit to myself that it sounded awesome. I loved Disneyland, and I had always wanted to explore the caves in the Pirates of the Caribbean. I imagined sitting on those huge piles of fake gold, and I was sorely tempted to give in.

Jesse was bouncing in his seat like a kid. "Come on, Ashlyn! Oh, please!"

"Not going to happen," I insisted. "And don't treat me like your mom. We have serious business ahead of us. Imagine what Theresa would do to you if she knew you'd delayed your job as a Soterian to gain illegal entry into the Magic Kingdom." This thought sobered him a bit, but then his eyes lit up again.

"Okay, so let's use it as a reward. If we get good information from this trip, we party with Mickey afterwards to celebrate."

I considered this for a moment. After all the work we'd been doing, it sounded like so much fun to go and be stupid and spend a day playing at Disneyland. Finally, I came up with a compromise. "Okay, but only if we pay to get in *and* we don't use our powers while we're there."

"Agreed," he said. He looked happily out of the window and started singing "It's a Small World."

"And no singing that song!" I shouted and turned up the music. He cackled with laughter, and we continued down the highway, bantering happily all the way to the border.

We arrived at our hotel without too much hassle. We had decided that crossing the border and dealing with traffic in Mexico would be too hectic, so we parked at a long-term parking lot near the border and took a trolley into Tijuana. It had been a long day, and we were relieved to arrive at last.

Our hotel was a dingy little building that looked much shabbier on the outside than it had in the pictures on the Internet, but the rooms were clean, and the beds were comfortable enough. Best of all, we were on the second floor and had a reasonably large window in our bathroom, which meant that we could easily fly in and out of the hotel room while invisible if we wanted to come and go without being spotted. I doubted that Deimos and his henchmen knew where we were, but I was getting more and more cautious as time went on.

It was early afternoon, and we'd already had lunch on the road, so we decided to go explore the factory site without delay. We weren't expecting a lot of action on a Saturday, but as it turned out, there was plenty.

"Remind me never to work in a factory," I whispered as we approached the site. "Don't they know about weekends?" The factory's huge parking lot was full of cars and bicycles. Across the road was the ocean, where a new dock stretched far out into the water.

"They built that dock just for this factory," Jesse pointed out. "That way they can ship cars by boat and clear customs here, avoiding the wait at the border crossing." He spoke in a barely audible whisper, but I could hear him perfectly.

"Thank you, Professor Burton. You're not the only one who read Paul and Kai's report, you know."

"Shut your pie hole," he said, and I stifled a giggle. We flew over the parking lot and around the main building, checking out the property. We peeked in window after window, seeing only offices.

Finally, we found a side door that was propped open, and we slipped inside. We found ourselves in a large room where cars were moving slowly along an assembly line. Workers dressed in blue coveralls were using various types of machinery and tools that whined and banged, and the noise was nearly deafening. The workers moved swiftly, deftly performing their tasks as the cars rolled by. We flew all around the room, being careful to avoid the cables, sparks, and heavy machinery. So far, everything looked like I'd imagined a factory would look.

We moved up a corridor and came upon several office rooms. Men and women sat at desks typing on computers or talking rapidly in Spanish on the phones. Like the assembly room, the offices looked clean and fairly new.

We explored more hallways and found a warehouse with cases and cases of parts, which were stacked on shelves that stretched all the way to the ceiling. Forklifts moved among the aisles, pulling boxes from the shelves and moving them through a large double door that led back to the assembly room.

After thoroughly exploring the building, we made our way out a side door in a deserted hallway. We circled the property, looking for anything unusual, but there was nothing. Finally, we headed back to the hotel.

"Well, that was a complete waste of time," I said.

Jesse clucked his tongue. "Hello, where were you? I learned something very interesting."

"What? I didn't see anything."

"Didn't you notice how many cars came off the assembly line while we were there?"

"No, I was too busy trying not to get crushed by heavy machinery."

"Three cars in about ten minutes. That's a rate of only eighteen per hour."

"And Kai and Paul said . . . "

"That the factory produces thirty per hour," he said. "Now, it's possible they have a slower line on Saturdays, but it's something we need to check."

"Why would they say they're making more cars than they actually do?"

He shrugged. "Hard to say. Maybe those numbers came from what the plant claimed they could produce, but they actually make fewer than that."

"But that would have an impact on sales," I argued. "If they can't meet demand, they'll lose business. So I don't see what they gain by it."

"Maybe demand has simply gone down. But I think we need to count how many employees they have, how many cars they produce, and what their hours are."

"It would probably also be helpful to see how much they're actually getting paid, in case there's something fishy there."

"They get paid every Friday, so we can spy on them then. And speaking of fish," he said, suddenly sounding cheerful, "we have a long boring week ahead of us, so let's go get some dinner and enjoy ourselves for tonight at least."

We stopped off at the hotel to change our clothes, then walked up Avenida Revolucion, or "La Revo", which was bustling with activity. We wandered up the street for a while, looking at all the colorful storefronts, dodging the shop keepers and waiters who were trying to get us to come inside.

Finally, we chose a restaurant that had a huge neon sign and a statue of a burro in front. We sat at a table on the second-floor balcony overlooking the street, which became busier as night approached. We perused our menus as we munched on chips and salsa and carefully chose only cooked food and canned drinks, despite the menu's claims that the water was filtered. Jesse had warned me that you can't ever trust the water south of the border, and that in addition to avoiding drinks with ice, you have to be careful when showering not to get any water in your mouth. He even advised using bottled water to brush your teeth. I thought he was being a little overly cautious, but I wasn't willing to risk it. My healing powers probably weren't strong enough to counteract dysentery.

When the waiter came, Jesse ordered for us in Spanish, even though the waiter spoke English, and made sure that my food would be vegetarian. I was very glad he was there. The more I got to know Jesse, the more I adored him. He was definitely the brother I never had. We had a great time together, bantering and laughing as we stuffed ourselves on delicious enchiladas and watched the sun sink over the horizon.

After dinner, we walked up La Revo and were amazed by the sheer number of people there. It was getting darker, and the vibe on the street was definitely changing for the worse. We headed off into a little park, where we found some historical monuments. As we checked them out, Jesse translated the signs for me, enjoying his role as tour guide and throwing in his own commentary along the way.

"Here we have the world's ugliest man, and, as you can see, they decided to immortalize him in bronze."

"And his donkey," I said, pointing to a nearby sculpture.

"That's his wife. Don't you know anything about art?"

We walked slowly amongst the lush trees and fragrant blooming shrubs. Aside from the crazy main drag, Tijuana was really quite nice. Jesse consulted his pocket guide to find something fun to do.

"We could catch a movie at the theater in the mall," he suggested. "Or go bowling."

"What about dancing?" I asked. "Would you be up for that?"

"Are you kidding? I was trying to tone it down for you! Wait, you don't mean ballroom dancing, do you?"

"Hey, just because I don't drink doesn't mean I'm a stick in the mud. I love dancing, and Kai isn't really into it . . . "

"And since I'm gay, you assumed I must love to go dancing," he said with a smirk.

"No, I assumed that based on the massive quantities of dance music on your iPod."

"Okay, fair enough. Let's get changed."

I looked down. "Er, I already did change."

"What?!" He looked appalled. "You can't go to a club looking like that! It's a good thing I brought extra provisions. Come on."

As we walked back toward the street, a group of young men strolled into the park. They looked us up and down and made some comments in Spanish. I got a somewhat hostile vibe from them, but nothing dangerous. I looked at Jesse, but he just stared straight ahead and kept walking.

"What did they say?" I whispered to Jesse after they passed.

"Let's just say they didn't have anything very complimentary to say about either of us."

I felt anger rise in my chest. I was used to guys being idiots and making stupid comments to me, but it infuriated me that they would pick on Jesse.

"It's a good thing I didn't understand them or I probably would have done something stupid," I said. "I'm proud of you for not reacting."

"Hon," he said with a sigh, "I've known I was gay since I was eight years old. I've had a lot of time to learn to let people's comments roll off of me. Doesn't mean I never react, especially when it's a comment from someone I know. That really pisses me off."

"It must be such a drag to have to deal with that kind of discrimination hanging over your head all the time."

He raised an eyebrow at me. "It's not that different from what you have to deal with. Just wait until you're up for a promotion and you have to prove you're twice as competent as the guy next to you because you don't have a penis. At least you're attractive, which helps. You just need to learn to use it to your advantage more."

"Jesse! I'm not going to use my looks to get ahead in life!"

"Certainly not with that outfit," he said, rolling his eyes. "Come on!"

An hour later, I didn't recognize myself. Jesse had fixed my hair and makeup and had done the best he could with my clothes. He added a stylish black belt to my jeans and loaned me a beautiful shirt that I wore open over a black tank top. He'd blown my hair into ringlets that stood up a bit at the roots and draped around my face. I didn't have much makeup with me, but he heated my eyeliner under hot water until it was soft, and then smudged it into a shadowy ring around my eyes. It made me look kind of mysterious and, frankly, very cool. I hugged him tightly.

"Jesse, consider me a customer for life. Will you do my hair at my wedding?"

"I'll have to check my calendar," he said haughtily before smacking me on the back of the head. "Of *course* I will do your hair! Otherwise you'd probably do it yourself, and we simply can't have that." We grabbed our wallets, did one last check in the mirror, and headed out the door.

Saturday night on La Revo reminded me a little bit of Halloween in Isla Vista. We wandered up the street until the sound of dance music lead us to a club that looked promising. We paid the entrance fee, fully aware that we were also paying the gringo surcharge, and walked in. Crowds of people were already filling the dance floor, and we quickly found a spot.

Jesse was a fantastic dancer, and I felt like a bit of a clod with him, but I didn't care. We were in Mexico! It was so much fun to take a night off from everything. I wished Kai could be with us, but honestly, this just wasn't his scene. Jesse, on the other hand, was fully in his element, and we had a blast, making up all kinds of ridiculous dance moves. We did the Clam Dig, pretending to rhythmically poke a shovel into the sand and then toss its contents over our shoulders, and the Flight Attendant, pointing to imaginary fore and aft exit rows in time with the music. Despite all the cautionary tales I'd heard about Tijuana, nobody bothered us in the club, maybe because we were acting like idiots.

We laughed and danced until the wee hours of the morning. Ears ringing, we left the club and made our way up the street.

"Jesse?"

"Yeah, hon?"

"I'm really glad I met you."

He put his arm around me. "Me too. You're pretty okay, for a fashion criminal."

"Don't make me kick your ass."

He snorted. "As if."

We talked happily all the way back to the hotel, pretending that morning and the dismal chore of recon would never come.

Chapter Twelve: A Terrible Discovery

"Twenty again," I said dully. For the past three days, we'd been staking out the factory, counting the number of cars that came off the line and the number of employees that worked each shift. It was getting toward evening on Tuesday, and the pattern was clear. They were producing only twenty cars an hour, with almost no variation. They worked in two overlapping shifts a day for a total of fourteen hours a day, and there were about five hundred workers at the plant.

We'd also seen groups of people coming through, mostly English and Chinese-speaking men, who toured the plant and talked with the factory's administrative staff. Occasionally there were tourists as well, although why you'd want to tour an auto factory when there were so many other things to do in Mexico, I really couldn't fathom. After three excruciatingly boring days, I'd had enough of factories for one lifetime.

As the day wore on, we decided to explore the plant again and drifted up the hallway past the administrative offices. Suddenly, there was a loud bang behind us, and we turned to see the assembly line screech to a halt.

I started to fly back toward the assembly room to see what had happened, but Jesse caught me by my shirt and pulled me up higher just as three people from the office dashed down the hallway. He pointed emphatically at the now-empty office and shot into it. I followed, and we immediately started searching the desks. There were papers lying around and piles of envelopes, but everything was in Spanish.

All of a sudden, the words on a computer screen made sense to me. It was showing a payroll report. I hit Print, and a copy of the report slowly rolled out of the laser printer.

As the pages printed, I saw a stack of paychecks sitting on the desk. I shuffled through them, noting the names and amounts. Very interesting. Now we were getting somewhere.

Jesse tapped me on the shoulder, and I grabbed the pages from the printer. We rose into the air just as the office workers returned. We flew carefully over their heads and headed out of the factory.

"What did you find?" he asked when we got outside.

"I printed a payroll report, and those were the paychecks I was looking at. Look at the date on this report . . . it shows that it's for this Friday's payroll, right? So I compared some of the paychecks I found on the desk with the amounts on the report, and the actual checks are for lower amounts."

"Are you sure that's not just because of payroll taxes?"

"No, look, this report shows the actual payout amounts. Withheld taxes are transferred into a liability account and accounted for separately. "

"Since when do you know anything about accounting?"

"About the same time I was suddenly able to read Spanish. Shut up and let me finish before it wears off. The other thing I noticed is that this report shows that there are one thousand employees, but as we've noticed, there are only about five hundred people working in this factory. So who are the extra five hundred? I highly doubt that half the factory is on vacation."

Jesse looked serious for a few moments. "I think we'd better grab dinner quickly and head back here. I have an idea."

I sighed. "Why do I get the feeling we're about to double our shift?"

At two o'clock in the morning, we were sitting on top of the factory building, staring out into the blackness that surrounded us. We had decided to take turns napping while the other watched, but neither of us could sleep. If Jesse was right, this could be a big breakthrough, but if not, it would mean an entire night wasted.

As we waited, we talked more about our childhoods, favorite movies and books, and all the places we wanted to visit. In quiet moments, we could hear the waves crashing in the distance. In the dark, with the warm night breeze, I could easily imagine myself back in Isla Vista, and it made me very homesick. I missed Kai so much. I wasn't used to being without him for this long anymore, and it was wearing on me.

"Are you missing Paul?" I asked Jesse.

"Yeah," he admitted. "A lot, actually."

"I wish he and Kai were here with us."

"We're pathetic."

"No, we're just in love with our guys. I think it's great."

"Don't you ever worry, though?" Jesse's voice sounded strained. "I mean, doesn't it bother you to have signed away your freedom forever, to have decided that you're sticking yourself with the same guy 'til death do you part?"

"I used to see it that way, before I met Kai. But now I feel like committing to him actually gives me a kind of freedom. I'm free from dating, and worrying about meeting guys, and wondering what their damage is and what kind of annoying habits they'll have. I feel so incredibly lucky to have met Kai now, while we're still young and have our whole lives together. I wouldn't want to spend one more minute without him."

Jesse was silent for a moment. "But how do you know Kai is the right guy?"

I shrugged. "I've dated enough assholes to know. Kai and I have a lot of respect for each other, we love each other so deeply, and we love being together. And, most importantly, we're both totally committed to each other. I think with all that, we'll survive whatever life throws at us. I really like having time by myself, but I'm always sad to see him leave, always happy when he returns. That's very different from my previous relationships, where I felt nothing but relief when I got space from them."

"See, that's what worries me," Jesse said. "Paul and I have the respect and the love and all that. I'm absolutely crazy about him, and he's crazy about me. But after I've spent too much time with him, I start getting really edgy, and then I have to escape to my apartment. I start feeling like I'm losing my identity."

"You can't lose your identity unless you give it away, Jesse, and I simply don't see how you of all people could ever do that. You're way too independent. Have you tried just sticking it out through the edgy moments and telling him what you're feeling?"

"No!" Jesse said in alarm. "He'd be so hurt."

"Why do I keep having this conversation with people?" I muttered. "Look, you have to give him a chance to go through this with you. You'll probably be surprised at how well he handles it. Paul is awesome, and you guys are just totally right for each other. Don't let fear stop you from experiencing the greatest happiness you can."

Suddenly, the darkness was pierced by a faint light in the distance. Jesse and I both sat upright and watched as the light moved up the road and then split into several pinpricks. Moments later, we could hear a convoy of large trucks.

"Bingo," Jesse said. "Our patience paid off. Let's go get a closer look." We flew down to the front gate and waited for the first truck to pull up. Sure enough, it slowed as it approached the gate and then stopped in front. The truck's horn blew twice, and the gate rolled slowly open. In the glare of the headlights, I couldn't see its cargo, but I already knew what it was carrying.

The truck was full of cars, all the same models as those produced by the factory. I flew higher and saw that there were over a dozen trucks lined up, all carrying the same cargo, waiting to drive through the gates. Jesse gave me a thumbs-up and smiled broadly. His theory was correct: the factory could be short by over a hundred cars each day because they were being built somewhere else and brought here. Which meant there were still two big questions remaining: where were the cars being built, and *why* were they being built elsewhere?

We watched the trucks roll onto the factory grounds and park next to dozens of other similar trucks, all of which were loaded with cars ready for transport. The drivers got out, locked up, and then walked to their own vehicles and drove away into the night.

Jesse and I flew back to the hotel, tired but excited. This was big news, and it sucked to have to wait until morning to share it with the others, but even Theresa wouldn't appreciate being awakened in the middle of the night unless it was an emergency. Exhausted, we crawled into our beds and promptly fell asleep.

The next morning, after a quick breakfast, we headed back to the factory. It was already ten o'clock, and we wanted to do more scouting. But the trucks full of cars were gone, replaced by a line of empty trucks that workers were gradually filling with cars that had just come off the line.

"Damn it, we missed it!" Jesse seethed.

I looked toward the ocean, where I could see a large freighter in port. "Maybe they're being loaded onto that ship."

We shot through the sky to the dock. Sure enough, the cars were being unloaded from the carriers and driven into the belly of the ship.

Jesse rubbed his hands together. "Perfect! Now all we have to do is follow the trucks, and I bet they'll lead us straight to the other factory."

We hung out and waited for all the cars to be unloaded. As they pulled away, we flew to the truck that was in the lead and landed on its lower platform, where we could sit right behind the cab and be sheltered from the wind. We stayed invisible but at least got a break from flying, which would help us preserve our energy. As the truck picked up speed on the highway, the wind roared too loudly for us to talk, so we sat quietly, watching the scenery go by. It was a hot day, and the dry wind combined with the arid landscape made us very thirsty. We had a couple of water bottles and energy bars with us, but we rationed it all carefully, since we had no idea how far we were going.

After two hours of driving, we slowed down and turned onto a narrow two-lane highway that wound its way up into the hills. It seemed odd that a factory would be in a hilly area. Jesse consulted a map in his guidebook occasionally to keep track of our path. After another hour, we finally came to a stop. We stood up and stretched, stiff from the long ride, and then flew away from the truck and looked around.

We were on a dusty plateau, surrounded by scrubby trees, and right in the middle was a large compound of several buildings. In the center was a huge, dilapidated building. It had no windows and was covered with metal siding. I saw several men walking around with rifles, and to my dismay, I noticed that a couple of them had dogs. I nudged Jesse, who frowned and nodded when he saw them. Damn it. The dogs were going to make it much more difficult to get around unnoticed.

We flew in a wide arc around the property, checking out the boundaries first. The buildings were surrounded by fences topped with barbed wire, and on the far side was a forest. Near the large metal-sided building were several smaller wooden buildings, also without windows. The largest of the wooden buildings had a small hole in the side, and Jesse and I took turns peering through it.

It was a barracks. There were thin blankets laid out haphazardly on the floor with a few pillows scattered here and there. Balls of wadded-up clothes were strewn about. In one corner was a disgusting toilet and a small sink that was dripping rusty water. Spread throughout the room were about fifty people sleeping on the ground. They were all filthy and very thin. The stench that wafted through the hole was so bad that I gagged.

We turned away and approached another building. This one had dirty windows, through which we could just see tables and benches lined up inside with a large counter at one end. We crept through a door and went into a kitchen, where a fat man in a dirty apron was measuring sugar from a plastic bin into a large container, which he stirred slowly using a long metal spoon. We drifted closer and saw that the container was filled with a red liquid that looked like fruit punch. On the stove, a huge vat of something that looked like oatmeal bubbled slowly. There was a tall trash can in one corner that was overflowing with garbage. As I flew over to take a closer look at what was in the trash, several pineapple rinds fell off the top of the pile and onto the floor.

The cook dropped his spoon and whipped out a hand gun, pointing it toward the corner where I was frozen in mid-air. He looked around wildly for a moment and then relaxed and put his gun back in his belt, taking up his spoon and resuming his stirring. Jesse raised an eyebrow at me and took off for the door.

"What?" I mouthed as we sneaked back out of the kitchen. "How was I supposed to know the cooks here are armed?"

"I would think the fact that it's clearly a prison might have tipped you off," he hissed.

We continued our tour, using our phones to take pictures of everything as we went. There was a large warehouse that was full of parts just like the other factory. We found four small buildings that looked like nicer quarters, undoubtedly for the people who ran the place, and a little building that housed a handful of showers.

Lastly, we came upon a large field where all the new cars were parked. Jesse pointed to the dust-colored canopy covering the area, which was the same color as the field.

"Probably prevents people in helicopters from seeing the cars," I mused.

He nodded. "Definitely not a legal operation. They must load the cars on the trucks after dark, which would explain why it took until two in the morning for them to arrive at the Tijuana factory."

We ended up back at the main building, searching for a way to get inside. We stayed as far away from the dogs as we could, certain that they'd give our presence away. There was a slight breeze, so we tried to stay downwind of them. It was like trying to fly through an obstacle course.

Finally, we found an air shaft in the side of the building. It housed a large fan that looked like it hadn't worked in years. We squeezed through as carefully as we could, afraid to make the blades move at all in case it came back to life, and finally found ourselves inside the main room.

About a hundred prisoners toiled on the assembly line, their clothes and hair matted with sweat and dirt. The cars were moving much more quickly than they were at the Tijuana factory. There was a lot of heavy machinery, but whereas the Tijuana plant was neat and clean, this plant looked downright dangerous. There was broken machinery lying in the corners, and people were stepping over extra parts. Guards sat on stools against the walls, lazily holding rifles. It was stiflingly hot, and I was tempted to try to get the fan moving so that these poor people could breathe more easily.

We flew around, being extra careful not to get too close to any of the ancient machinery. We looked into the dull eyes of the prisoners, who looked lifeless even as they worked. It was the saddest thing I had ever seen, and I felt myself getting more and more upset as their despair washed over me.

I tapped Jesse on the shoulder and motioned to the air vent. I had seen enough and desperately needed to get out of there. He nodded, and we were just turning to fly away when suddenly I saw something that nearly made me gasp out loud.

There, laboring on the assembly line, was Tony Kirkpatrick, the lawyer for the union. He was a shadow of his former self, only vaguely resembling the man I had seen leaving the factory in Minnesota, but it was definitely him. He had the same dull look in his eyes as the other workers and looked gaunt and sickly pale. How on earth had he ended up in such a hell hole? What were any of those poor souls doing there? I choked back a sob as I snapped a picture of him and then shot toward the vent. We squeezed back through and soared into the sky, heading north toward Tijuana.

Chapter Thirteen: Capture

"Those bastards! Those evil bastards!" I cried as we flew, fighting the urge to throw up. I checked my cell phone repeatedly, but there was no signal. I felt like I'd go mad waiting to get back to civilization so I could call John.

"Ashlyn, hold up a second," Jesse said, coming to a stop. I turned and looked at him in surprise.

"What are you waiting for? We have to get back! We need to get the rest of the unit down here now!"

He looked thoughtful for a moment. "I think we need to do more scouting first."

"What else do we need to know? They're holding people in an illegal prison. And they've got Kirkpatrick! That's why he hasn't been showing up for work. He's been captured!"

"Are we entirely sure about that?" Jesse asked. "First of all, how do we know that's not a legitimate prison? I don't know anything about Mexico's prison system. Do you?" Before I could answer, he continued. "Secondly, how do we know that Kirkpatrick isn't in there undercover? Granted, I think going undercover in an illegal prison in a foreign country is taking things a bit far, but you never know."

"Jesse, we need to get our units down here now so we can rescue those poor people! We can ask questions later!"

"Look, I'm not happy about this, either," he insisted. "That was the most disgusting thing I've ever seen. But we have to make sure we have all our facts straight before we bring in the units. All we know right now is what we've seen so far. We need to scout the perimeter, see what would be the best routes for breaking into the compound. We need to know their schedules, how many guards there are . . . "

"To hell with that!" I shouted. "It's taking all the restraint I have to fly away to call in reinforcements, when what I really want to do is charge back in there and start blowing things up. And you want me to stop and watch some more?"

Jesse narrowed his eyes at me. "It's our job, Ashlyn. We're Scouts, not Warriors. Remember? And the best way we can protect our units is to give them as much information as possible. You wouldn't want to send Rebecca in there without knowing what they're up against, would you?"

He'd found my weak spot. The thought of Rebecca in that place made me feel sick again. I closed my eyes and took a deep breath.

"Okay. You're right. Oh my God, Jesse!" I burst into tears. He put his arms around me and held me as we hovered in mid-air, letting me cry until I was finally calm again.

"I know," he whispered, stroking my hair. "This is the shitty part of this job. But we're the only ones who can do it. They need us."

I nodded and wiped the tears off my face. I was determined to do my absolute best and promised myself not to let my emotions get in the way again.

"I agree that we need more information," I conceded. "But it's going to have to wait until tomorrow. If we're going to stake out that awful place, we need to have provisions with us. Let's go back to our hotel and get supplies for a couple of days. And let's call John and Theresa and let them know what's up so they can start making plans while we're scouting."

He smiled at me. "That's more like it. Back to your rational self. Let's go."

We flew north with renewed energy and planned our strategy for the next couple of days. When we were finally within range of a cell signal, we called John and Theresa and told them everything we knew. Jesse had pinpointed the illegal factory on the map, so we were able to give them the location, and we also sent them the photos we'd taken.

"Don't go back there until tomorrow," John said. "I want to see what information we can come up with on this end first. Take today to rest. You're going to need it."

John was right. When we got back to the hotel, we were completely exhausted. We'd never flown that long or that far before, and we had barely enough energy left to fly in through the bathroom window. We collapsed on our beds and passed out in our clothes, sleeping through the rest of the afternoon and all night without waking.

At six in the morning, I finally awoke, my body stiff and aching all over. I groaned as I sat up and pulled out a bottle of water, draining it in a few gulps. Jesse was still sleeping soundly, and I didn't want to wake him, but I was suddenly ravenous. When was the last time we'd eaten? It must have been the energy bars we'd had on the truck as we rode south. My stomach growled noisily, and I slipped into the bathroom to brush my teeth.

When I came back out, Jesse was beginning to slowly open his eyes. "Oh my God, was I hit by a truck?" he moaned.

"Flying and disappearing takes a lot more out of you than I would have thought. Here," I said, handing him a bottle of water. "This will help." He sat up and swigged down the whole bottle.

"I'm starving!" he said, his eyes suddenly wide. "We need to eat right now."

"Agreed. Get cleaned up and we'll go find food."

"To hell with getting cleaned up. I want to eat."

"You? Going outside without making yourself look fabulous first? You *are* hungry."

"I always look fabulous," he growled as he staggered to the door.

At the restaurant, I dived into my huevos rancheros. I couldn't seem to eat fast enough to curb my hunger and was wolfing down the eggs and beans in what must have undoubtedly been a very unattractive manner.

"Doh' choke," Jesse said through a mouthful of chorizo omelet and potatoes, eating just as fast as I was. I laughed as a chunk of potato fell out of his mouth and back onto his plate, but he didn't seem to notice. I took a large drink of orange juice and felt the sugar starting to hit my blood stream. I couldn't remember ever being so hungry.

After breakfast, we headed back to the room and took turns taking long hot showers. It seemed like I'd never get the grimy feel of the prison off of me, and I dreaded going back there. But if I could do anything to help my unit so that they in turn could help the prisoners, I was going to give it my all.

We sat in our room and waited to hear back from John and Theresa. We studied Jesse's map yet again, forming a strategy for staking out the compound, and making contingency plans in case one of us became trapped in a building or was detected by a dog.

Satisfied that we were ready, we lay back on our beds and turned on the television, which turned out to be very entertaining. There were some hilariously wacky game shows and overly dramatic soap operas, both of which involved a lot of yelling. I couldn't understand a word of it, having lost my ability to understand Spanish shortly after we'd left the Tijuana factory, but I didn't need Spanish to find it amusing. Our fun was suddenly squashed, though, by a news report that came on about the latest killings in the area that were attributed to the drug wars.

"It's gotten bad here," Jesse said as he translated. "People are being murdered all the time. It's just sickening."

"What's up with that?"

"It's the drug cartels," he explained. "They're all killing each other and a lot of innocent bystanders in turf wars because of the war on drugs. They're killing police, going into hospitals and terrorizing doctors, even kidnapping them. It's horrible."

"Jesus. I had no idea it had gotten that bad."

"It makes you wonder whether more people are dying because of the war on drugs or the drugs themselves," he added, shaking his head.

Just then, my phone rang. It was John calling, and sure enough, Kirkpatrick had been reported missing. Clearly, he was not in that prison by choice. John also confirmed that there was no official prison anywhere near that location, but an abandoned military encampment was reported to be in that area.

"That must be it," I said to Jesse as I hung up. "They've taken over the old military camp and set it up as a factory."

"I wonder whether they're doing this with the blessing of the Mexican government or are flying under their radar."

"Based on the canopies covering the cars, I'm guessing the latter. But you never know. They might have paid the local officials to look the other way and are just making sure they're keeping a low profile."

He nodded. "That's the most likely scenario. No matter how careful they are, someone has to notice that trucks full of cars are driving through, even in the middle of the night."

We grabbed our backpacks and headed out the door. Jesse stopped at the front desk to check out of the hotel and get directions to the bus depot. We caught a bus going south and spent the next couple of hours hardly speaking at all as we thought about what lay ahead of us. I was not looking forward to going back there, and my brain kept screaming to turn around as I remembered the hideous conditions the prisoners were living in and the overwhelming despair emanating from them. Finally, we disembarked at a tiny town near the turnoff we'd taken on our last trip. Doing our best to look like a couple of tourists, we hiked up the road until we were sure we were alone, then disappeared and flew into the air.

It wasn't long before we arrived at the edge of the prison's property. We started flying around the full perimeter, taking pictures as we went, searching for vantage points and any other useful information about the terrain. There was only one entrance: the gate we'd gone through on the trucks. But there was a more heavily forested area on the south side of the prison, which might make a good place for the units to rendezvous and launch missions. Plus, there were several trees that were close to the perimeter, which the Warriors and Sentries could easily climb and use as access points for getting into the compound. Getting out again would be another story, though, and Jesse and I concentrated on trying to find escape routes. We stashed our backpacks in the trees and continued our search.

After we'd scouted the outer perimeter, we carefully flew in over the fence and looked around on the inside. This time, we looked for cameras and tried to figure out what kind of security they had. As far as we could tell, there were just armed guards, barbed wire, and a handful of dogs. It might as well have been a scene from a hundred years ago. It was incredible that so few guards and such low-tech security could keep that many prisoners under control. They had to be completely without hope. I wondered how long prisoners survived there, and I tried not to think about what happened to those who became too weak or ill to work.

Our next task was to figure out exactly how many guards there were, their schedules, and their locations. This was more challenging, because it was hard to be everywhere at once, and also because it was just really boring and hot in the sun. We took turns sitting in the shade by the backpacks while the other person scouted. We'd decided that we needed to stay on patrol all night so that we could get a full twenty-four hours of information and hopefully figure out the time when the fewest guards were on duty.

The most significant event was when the prisoners changed shifts. They were divided into three groups. There were always two groups of prisoners working at a time, and each group worked sixteen hours in the factory. The other eight hours was spent eating their one paltry meal at the end of their shift and then sleeping. It was sickening to see them shuffling listlessly between the factory and the mess hall, the mess hall and the barracks, and back to the factory again, all without struggle or complaint of any kind.

During these shift rotations, we flew down among the prisoners, getting as close as we dared, and rapidly took pictures, trying to get photos of as many people's faces as possible. We also shot video, which we hoped would help provide the evidence needed to shut the place down. If the factory was on the take by the government, it was going to be very difficult to get through the red tape and stop them. But Rebecca's parents worked for a human rights organization, which would at least have a better shot at it than we would alone. Meanwhile, we really had to get these people out of here, and it was not going to be easy.

By nightfall, we were already exhausted from being invisible and flying all day, and we took turns taking naps and eating while the other person patrolled, always being careful to stay clear of the dogs. So far, they hadn't detected us, and we guessed that our scents simply didn't stand out among the strong odors of all the prisoners. But it wasn't worth the risk, and we continued to give them a wide berth.

At three in the morning, I was awakened by a piercing scream. I bolted into the air, searching for Jesse, but he was nowhere to be seen. I forced down the panic that was rising in my stomach as I shot over the fence and into the compound. I looked around, but I couldn't see anything at first except the light seeping through the cracks in the walls of the factory. I flew desperately from building to building, trying to hear something, when suddenly I spotted a light coming from the building with the showers. I flew up to the door and listened. To my horror, I heard Jesse's voice inside. It sounded ragged, and I could feel terror emanating from him.

It only took a moment to realize he was being tortured.

"I told you," he said in Spanish, "I'm a tourist. I hiked and got lost, and then some bad men on the road stole my backpack. I came here to find a phone."

"How did you get into the compound?" a man's voice demanded.

"I yelled at the gate, but nobody came, so I climbed it."

"Again," the man said. I heard two sickening thuds, and Jesse cried out.

"You climbed, you say? Over the barbed wire?" the man nearly shouted.

"I'm very . . . how do you say it . . . agile," Jesse said, his voice nearly hysterical. "I can climb things easily. I wandered around but saw nobody. I was so tired from hiking that I lay down and went to sleep."

"Liar," the voice growled. "Hit him again."

I nearly vomited as I heard the sound of bone breaking followed by Jesse screaming. I couldn't waste one more second. I felt rage build up in my core, and I shot a fireball at the small building next to the one where Jesse was being held. The dry wooden wall went up in flames immediately, and within seconds there were shouts coming from inside. Four men ran outside, still in their underwear, coughing from the acrid black smoke that was streaming into the sky. "Fire!" they yelled, and the whole compound started stirring.

"Damn it!" Jesse's tormentor cursed. "Stay here!" I heard steps running toward the entrance, and a moment later the door swung open and a man ran out. I shot into the building just as the door was closing behind him. I flew down a short hallway and then turned a corner, where I almost ran right into a guard. Jesse's hands were over his head and bound by a rope that was secured to a shower head. His face was covered in blood, and his eyes were nearly swollen shut. His jaw hung from his face at a weird angle. Again I fought the urge to vomit and focused instead on the guard, the sound of my heart thumping so loudly in my ears that I could barely hear anything else.

He was standing with his rifle trained on Jesse but was looking in the opposite direction toward the door, alarm written across his face. He was clearly not happy about being stuck in this building while there was a fire going on somewhere out there. I felt his irritation with the man who had ordered him here. Information seemed to flood out of the guard and into my brain in a split second . . . the captain was not at all liked . . . there was a plot brewing to overthrow his authority.

I glanced around quickly, desperate to rescue Jesse as fast as I could. There were no windows, but there was a vent leading to the outside, meaning that if the gun went off, it would be heard. I would have to take out the guard quickly and quietly, and I had to make it look like Jesse had done it without the help of any special powers.

I flew behind the guard and kicked the rifle up toward his face. As it flew upward, I grabbed its muzzle, pulling it out of his hands, and in one smooth motion swung it around like a baseball bat and hit him across the back of the head. He crumpled to the ground. I reached down and felt his pulse, which was slowing. I gave him a few seconds of healing until his pulse felt stronger, taking my hand away before he regained consciousness.

I raced over to Jesse and sliced through the ropes with my knife. I put my hands gently on either side of his face, sending all the healing energy into him that I could. I saw the swelling start to go down, and I heard a crunch as his jaw popped back into alignment. His rapid breathing calmed. He blinked a couple of times and focused on me, and I felt a surge of relief when I realized he could see. But it was obvious that he didn't have a lot of strength left. I put a finger to my lips to keep him quiet and then turned to the guard. I studied his clothing for a second and then turned to Jesse and covered him in illusion so that he looked like the guard.

"Let's go," I whispered, handing him the rifle. "You're going to need to walk and stay visible to preserve your strength." Jesse nodded, and we headed out the door. There was a crowd of guards around the burning building, yelling and throwing buckets of water on it. I turned to Jesse.

"Go to the rendezvous. I'll meet you there in a few minutes. I'm not sure how long I can keep the illusion going, so stick to the shadows. And only disappear if you have to. Save your strength for flying home." He nodded wearily and for once didn't argue. Seeing him without his usual swagger was almost as disturbing as seeing him covered in blood.

My stomach churning, I headed for the main building. The guard on duty was busy watching the fire, but there was a dog at his side. As I shot past him and through the open door behind him, the dog started barking wildly, but the guard just yanked his chain and told him to shut up. I flew wildly around the factory, my heart hammering in my chest.

Finally, I spotted Kirkpatrick. As I flew over to him, I grabbed an empty sack that was lying on the ground. I quickly put it over his head and put my hand over his mouth. He immediately became invisible, but the other workers didn't seem to notice. They all had that same dull look in their eyes and just continued doing their work in their lifeless way. Kirkpatrick only struggled slightly, and in his weakened state, he was no match for me at all. With my hand still over his covered mouth, I hoisted him under my other arm and flew past the guard, the dog barking wildly again, and shot into the night.

Chapter Fourteen: Escape

"I'm sorry about the hood," I said quietly. "We're here to rescue you, and I had to make sure you didn't give us away as we escaped. I'm going to take my hand away from your mouth now and remove the hood. Do you promise to stay quiet?"

Kirkpatrick nodded, and I pulled the hood off. He blinked a few times and looked back and forth between us. We were back at the rendezvous spot. Jesse was sitting on the ground with his back against a tree. I had never seen him so passive, but I didn't have time to worry about that right then. I had to deal with Kirkpatrick first.

I handed Kirkpatrick a bottle of water, an apple, and an energy bar. He took them and started eating slowly, as if the muscles in his jaws weren't working quite right.

"My name is Ashlyn, and this is Jesse. We're here to help you. How long have you been here?"

He chewed a moment and swallowed with some difficulty before he spoke. His voice was flat and thick. "'bout a month, I think."

"What do you remember?"

"'s all hazy," he slurred.

"He's been drugged," Jesse said. I'd begun to suspect as much, but Kirkpatrick's speech confirmed it. That sugar they were mixing into the punch probably wasn't sugar at all.

"What is your full name?" I asked.

"Anthony Kirkpatrick," he answered hoarsely before taking a long drink of water. "I go by Tony."

"What's your occupation?"

"Attorney."

"Good. We've been monitoring this compound for the last few days, and I thought it was you, but I wanted to make sure. We're planning a rescue operation, but now that I've kind of jumped the gun and busted you out, we're going to have to make some adjustments to our plans." I glanced at Jesse, who was watching me with a hard expression. "I'm sorry, Jesse. I know this makes things more complicated, but I just couldn't leave him in there one more minute. And besides," I said, turning back to Tony, "I suspect you might have some information that will help us shut this place down."

I stood up. "We have to get out of here. As soon as they realize he's missing, they'll send the dogs out." At the mention of the dogs, Tony looked anxious. "Don't worry. We have a special mode of transport that will get us out of here safely. I'm afraid I'm going to have to put the hood on you again, and then you'll have to climb onto my back. Please trust me." He nodded dully, and I put the hood over his head. Jesse put on both of our backpacks, and I hoisted Tony onto my back. We sped away into the night. Tony quickly fell asleep, and his soft snores were the only sound aside from the night wind rushing past us.

As we flew, Jesse was very quiet, and I left him to his thoughts. I wanted to give him space after what he'd just been through. Finally, he spoke in a small voice.

"Thank you for coming and getting me," he said.

"Well, of course," I replied. "What did you think, I was just going to leave you there?"

"It would have been the sensible thing to do."

"You can't be serious. How would I ever face Paul again?"

"This has nothing to do with Paul. This has to do with the mission, which has now been compromised. Leaving me in there to gather more information probably would have been the better strategy."

"Assuming they didn't kill you first."

"Yes, assuming that."

I sighed. "Jesse, your being tortured wasn't going to help us. I'm so sorry you had to go through that. How are you feeling now? Is your jaw okay?"

"Completely normal. Your healing is getting a lot stronger."

"All my extra powers are stronger during times of crisis, and then they fade again. It's weird."

He was quiet again for a minute. "I'm sorry I've been such a smart ass with you. I totally blew it in there, and, well, now I know how it feels to be the one who screwed up. I appreciate your not rubbing it in my face."

"What do you mean you blew it? How?"

"I fell asleep and got captured," he spat.

"An occupational hazard. We'd been invisible for longer than we'd ever been before. It could have happened to either one of us."

"But it happened to *me*."

I suppressed a smile. "Well, I can't pretend that knocking your bravado down a few notches isn't a good thing, but for the record, I don't think any less of you for it. I thought you handled yourself brilliantly in there. That story you came up with was a perfect cover. And hopefully we've made it look like you somehow managed to get free, knocked the guard down, and escaped in all the confusion. You'd already told them you could climb over barbed wire, so there's nothing that will lead them to believe you were anything other than what you said you were."

"Except that now Tony is gone."

"Yes, but the way I see it, they'll probably think he got away during the confusion as well. The guards were all distracted. Hell, he could have started the fire for all they know." I shifted Tony slightly on my back, and he continued snoring.

"He's still drugged," Jesse pointed out, "but we won't be able to fly with him for much longer before he figures out that he's not in a 'special vehicle' or whatever you told him this was."

"I said 'special mode of transport,' which is true. But you're right. We have to get him back before he wakes up. And for good measure, I'd like to drop him off across the border. I don't want him to have to tangle with the Mexican authorities at all in case any of them are on the lookout for him. So if you're up to it, I think we need to fly as fast as we possibly can to the other side of the border, and then we can crash in San Ysidro for a few hours before driving home. You with me?"

"I don't see any other option."

We sped up and burned as hard as we could toward the border. I was already exhausted, but I didn't want to say anything to Jesse. He was undoubtedly a lot worse off than I was after what he just went through.

The sky began to lighten to a dull grey, and then hints of blues and pinks started appearing as thin fingers of color caressing the night sky. In my exhausted state, it seemed like a swarm of angels, chasing away the darkness. It gave me strength and hope, and I flew even faster.

Finally, the red and orange of the sun began bursting over the horizon. We saw Tijuana spreading before us, and I could feel the end in sight. We were almost there!

At that moment, Tony gave a loud snore and started stirring. I put on an extra burst of speed and shot past the grimy streets below, past the factory off on the left where only half the cars were made, past the parks and discos and hotels. I flew over the border and touched down in a grassy field just on the other side of the parking lot. I fell to the ground, and Tony rolled off my back. A few seconds later, Jesse landed next to me.

"Tony," I said, panting from the effort. My vision was getting dim, and I felt like I was about to black out. "How are you feeling?"

"Where am I?" he asked. His voice had become stronger, more like it had been in Minnesota. He started to take the hood off, but I stopped him.

"Please, don't take it off yet. I need you to listen carefully to me. You're on the U.S. side of the border, in a park. There's a pay phone on the building across the field. Go over there and call the police. Tell them that you're a missing person who has just been rescued by a secret group and—"

"I know what to do," he interrupted. "Let me take off this hood."

"No, you have to hear me out," I said firmly, holding his wrist. "You'll be getting a phone call from two men, Paul and Kai. They're going to ask you to give them as much information about the prison camp as possible, and you need to cooperate with them and tell them everything you can so we can shut that place down. But this is very important: you *cannot* tell anyone about any of us. We're working in secret. We risked a lot getting you out of there, and all we ask in return is that you tell us everything you know so we can defeat those bastards who were holding you in there."

"I will. I promise. Now please let me take this off!" I could feel his panic rising.

"Okay, count to five and take it off. You won't see us again."

I released his hand, and he took the hood off after a few seconds. He looked wildly around, trying to spot us, but we were still invisible. He wobbled to his feet and walked stiffly to the pay phone. With the last of our strength, we followed him and listened to him call the police, and after a brief conversation, he called his associate, Ellie. I could hear her shrieking through the phone in shock and glee.

Within a couple of minutes, a squad car pulled up, and two officers got out. They talked with Tony briefly, then helped him into the car and drove away. I just managed to get the officers' names before my vision started to blur.

At that moment, completely exhausted, we reappeared. Jesse had double layers of bags under his eyes, and I could tell from the way he gaped at me that I didn't look much better. We staggered over to a couple of trees, fell down on the grass, and passed out.

When I next awoke, the sun was high in the sky, and I was hot and very thirsty. I called Kai to let him know I was okay and to tell him everything that had happened, but all I could do was murmur a few slurred words of explanation. I could hear the anxiety in his voice, but he told me to go back to sleep and call him later. He said he'd call Paul and the others since Jesse was still out cold, and he said he'd check up on the officers to make sure they were real police. I rummaged around in my backpack for a bottle of water, chugged it down, and then fell asleep again.

In my dream, I saw Jesse tied to a large grey rock under a threatening orange sky. The guard was whipping him over and over as he screamed. Waves of nausea coursed through my stomach as I tried to fly forward to help him, but I couldn't move. I looked down and saw that I was also tied to a rock, and next to me was Tony.

"I told you," Tony said, his eyes dull and lifeless again. "We'll never defeat him. Never." The guard turned around, and I saw that it was Deimos, wearing his immaculate suit as he always did in my dreams, his hair slicked back, his beetle-black eyes burning with flames as he pulled back the whip and lashed it at Jesse again with a loud crack.

I jolted awake, the smell of warm grass and dirt filling my nose. A group of boys were playing baseball in the field next to where we lay, and they were all shouting as a boy ran around the bases. "Home run!" they screamed. A moment later, another boy hit the ball with a crack that made me shudder as the images from the nightmare came flooding back to me. I nudged Jesse.

"Jesse, Jesse wake up."

"Mmm mmmmmm," he groaned.

"I know, but we need to get going. What do you say to us getting lunch and then hitting the road? Some food and caffeine and I'll be ready to drive. You can sleep in the car."

"Fooood . . ." He opened his eyes. "Okay," he said thickly as I handed him a bottle of water. "As long as it's not Mexican food."

We ate the last of our provisions as we wandered slowly to our car, which was in the long-term parking lot next to the park. We drove to downtown San Ysidro, the town closest to the border, where we found a sandwich shop. I got a foot-long sandwich with tons of veggies, cheese, and avocado on a whole wheat roll and a large root beer. Jesse got a large turkey sandwich with everything on it and six more bottles of water. We got in the car, turned up the music, and ate as we drove north. I was so happy to be going home, I could barely sit still. I bounced and sang until Jesse told me to shut up so he could sleep.

When we approached Anaheim, I saw signs for Disneyland. "So Jesse, you still up for Disneyland?" His only response was a loud snore. I laughed and kept driving, so anxious to get home I wished I could pick up the car and fly.

We finally pulled into Isla Vista around six o'clock. I was exhausted again and needed a shower badly. Jesse and I dragged ourselves up the stairs to my apartment. When we walked in, Rebecca jumped off the couch.

"Ashlyn! Jesse! You're safe!" she cried as she darted toward us. But her face changed as she read our feelings, and she started talking rapidly as she sprang into action. "Jesse, come lie down on the couch. Good idea, Ashlyn, a shower is definitely going to help. Go do that and then take a nap. I'll order pizzas later when you wake up, okay? Oh God, you're about to pass out. Here, I'll help you."

She bustled me into the bathroom and helped me get into the shower. The hot water felt so good that I never wanted to get out. But I was so tired, I was afraid I'd fall down in the shower. Grudgingly, I dried off and went straight to bed, falling unconscious the moment I felt Rebecca pull the blanket up over me.

When I awoke again, I felt much better, but I was desperately hungry. It was dark outside, and I guessed we'd slept through dinner time. I wandered out into the living room, where Jesse was already up, happily stuffing a slice of pizza into his mouth. The smell of garlic and onions made my stomach growl angrily. I grabbed a slice and sat down next to Rebecca.

"There's plenty of veggie pizza here for you and some cheese, too," she said. I smiled as I saw that there were four large boxes of Woodstock's Pizza, my favorite place in Isla Vista.

"Rebecca, I can't tell you how amazing it is to be home. Thank you so much for all of this."

She beamed at me. "I'm so glad you're home safe. Which reminds me," she continued, picking up her phone and dialing, "Kai is dying to see you but didn't want to risk waking you, so he asked me to call him as soon as you woke up. Hello Kai? Yeah, she's up. Come on over."

Kai! I couldn't wait one more second to see him. I walked to the door and saw him jogging toward me. I ran out to meet him and threw myself into his arms. He hugged me so tightly that it would have broken my ribs if I hadn't developed Sentry powers.

"Ashlyn," he whispered, his face buried in my hair. "You're okay."

I squeezed him back as tightly as I dared. "I missed you so damn much." I leaned up and pressed my lips to his, kissing him deeply. I nuzzled into him and held him, his warmth and his very presence making me feel all glowing and happy inside.

"Come on," he said at last, "you need to eat." He took my hand and walked me back in to the apartment.

Over the next hour, we told Kai and Rebecca everything that had happened. We had already told them about the prison when we called, but they were appalled to learn that the prisoners were kept drugged, and Rebecca nearly burst into tears when we told them about Jesse's capture. I tried to keep that part short to avoid upsetting Jesse, but he seemed to need to talk about it. Rebecca went over and inspected his jaw and ribs, but Jesse said he felt fine. Rebecca looked at me approvingly.

"Your healing has come along nicely. I can't even find any scar tissue to heal."

"It comes and goes," I explained. "All my powers seem supercharged in a crisis, but then they fade again. I could understand everything they were saying in Spanish when Jesse was captured, while earlier that afternoon I couldn't understand a word."

"It's great that it's there for you when you need it," she said. "Although it must be hard not to be able to harness it on command, especially for someone who likes to have things under her control." She gave me a wink.

"I can't imagine who you could possibly mean," I snorted in mock surprise.

"Knock knock," Jesse said suddenly.

"Who's there?" I asked, bewildered.

"Control freak. Now you say 'control freak who?'"

"Control fre—oh, very funny." Jesse burst out laughing at his own joke, and I shook my head. Only Jesse could tell a knock-knock joke after what he'd just been through.

He looked at Rebecca and his face fell. "Don't you get it? I was being a control freak by telling her what to say next! It was self-referential humor."

"Yes, Jesse, I got it," she said with a smile. "I just didn't think it was that funny."

I snorted. "Besides, everyone's so used to you being bossy, who could tell you were joking?" He flung an olive at my head and went back to devouring his pizza.

After that, Jesse started acting like his old self again. He told me that he had already called Paul and checked in, and that Paul and Kai would be calling Tony the next day. Tony had been taken to a hospital and was staying overnight for observation. This seemed like a good idea, since he was malnourished, dehydrated, and detoxing from the drugs. But I was really sad when I thought about all the other prisoners in the camp. Of the hundred and fifty we'd counted, how many would still be alive the next time we went back?

Next time . . . I was so happy to be home that I'd forgotten I had to go back there. The whole episode was already starting to fade away like a bad dream, one I certainly didn't want to revisit. I felt my stomach churn as I thought about it.

Rebecca reached over and put a hand on me. "We'll take it one step at a time, okay? By the time we're ready to make our move, you'll be ready, too."

I nodded, not at all convinced I'd ever be ready to go back there, but I knew I had no choice.

That night, I let Jesse have my bed, and I stayed at Kai's. Sleeping next to him—his arms wrapped tightly around me, the warmth of his body melting away all the tension I'd built up over the last week—was absolute bliss. I could swear that he had healing powers of his own. By morning, I felt completely like myself again.

After breakfast, we went to John's to have a conference call with the San Francisco unit, who was gathered at Theresa's penthouse. This was my first visit to John's house, and I was very curious about what we'd find as we headed down the path from the dojo. The path was lined with bamboo trees and opened up into a clearing where his house stood. It was surrounded by avocado trees that were heavy with large fruit hanging high up in the branches.

The house was two stories high and covered with dark brown shingles. To the left was a patio set up as an outdoor dining room, and beyond that, up a gravel path, stood a shingled outbuilding that looked like a large gardening shed. There was a beautiful round window in the front of the house, and recessed into a covered entryway was the front door. The whole place had the pure, serene air of a Zen monastery. I loved it.

We walked up to the front door and knocked. John opened the door wearing jeans and a T-shirt. I thought to myself yet again that even in casual clothes, he had a grace and elegance about him that I could never hope to imitate.

"Good morning," he said. "Please, come in." We walked into an open room with white walls and rich dark wood floors.

A thick wooden beam ran across the ceiling and marked the entrance to the kitchen, which had wooden counters with Mexican tiles in blues, yellows, and white along the backsplash. The round window I'd seen from the front of the house was just above the kitchen sink, providing a beautiful view of the garden. The living room was furnished very simply, with a sofa and a chair, and a wall of built-in bookshelves on the right. I noticed there wasn't a television.

"John, your house is gorgeous," Rebecca remarked.

"Thank you. I bought it in the eighties, when an avocado farmer needed to sell off some of his land. I left as many of the trees as I could. They'll be coming to the end of their fruit-bearing years soon but can live on for many more years."

"It's so peaceful," I said. "It must be a nice retreat for you."

"It is. I was lucky to get it when I did. I could never afford it with today's real estate prices, and having my dojo on the same property is very convenient."

We sat down and called the San Francisco unit, going over all the details of what we'd learned so far and what information was still missing. When we were all ready, Paul and Kai added Tony to the call. Kai took the phone off the speaker so it wouldn't be as obvious that people were listening in the background. Thanks to our acute hearing, Jesse and I were able to hear the whole conversation clearly from across the room. John, Michael, Christoph, and Rebecca listened quietly on extensions.

"Tony? This is Paul, and I have Kai on the line as well. We work with Ashlyn and Jesse, who helped you yesterday. How are you feeling?"

There was a pause, and then Tony spoke. "I'm okay now. I'm trying to remember everything, as much as I'd like to forget it."

"If this isn't a good time," Kai said, "we can call back, but we'd like to get as much information as we can."

"No, this is fine. I've already told the police everything I know, but I'll tell you, too. First of all, can you please tell the two people who rescued me that I'm very grateful to them. I'm still not sure how they managed it."

"We'd like to keep it that way," Paul said. "The less you know about us, the better. That's why it's very important that you don't tell anyone about us."

"What did you say to the police about your rescue?" Kai asked.

"Just that some people managed to break me out of there, but I was too drugged to know how they did it, and I'm guessing it was an inside job. I said that they dropped me off at a park on the U.S. side of the border, but I have no idea how I got there because my face was covered."

"Anything else?"

"No. I remembered . . . Ashlyn, you said her name was? I remembered that she asked me to keep them a secret, so I told them I never saw my rescuers. The truth is that I was so out of it, and it was very dark, so I don't remember what they looked like anyway."

I breathed a sigh of relief. I glanced at Jesse, who also looked more at ease.

"Tony, what can you tell us about how you ended up in the prison?" Kai asked. "Did it have anything to do with the layoffs at the factory?"

"Yes. After our so-called negotiations went south, along with the jobs, I spent time digging into the details of the merger and the new factory. I went to the Tijuana factory and looked around, and I quickly realized that the numbers weren't adding up. Fewer cars were coming off the assembly line than they were putting on the ships."

I smiled at Jesse, who had so quickly reached the same conclusion. I tried not to be disappointed in myself that I hadn't noticed the discrepancy, too.

Tony continued his story. "I hired a car and followed the trucks to the prison, but when I got out and tried to do some more looking around, I was captured. And after that, things get very hazy. They beat me and questioned me, and when they saw my name on my passport, they made me drink some of that juice that they gave us every day, which must have been laced with drugs, and then they put me on the assembly line. And from that point forward, everything is a blur. I was there for three weeks, but it could have been a few days or twenty years. It's just lost time." His voice had taken on a rough tone. It had to be horrible to have to think back on such an awful ordeal.

"Did your captors say anything to you? Or did they just question you?" Paul asked.

"I speak very little Spanish, so I have no idea."

"Did they ever mention anyone's name that sounded familiar?

"No. I never heard them mention anyone I recognized."

Suddenly, something came back to me. I remembered Jesse's guard, and how I'd picked up information about his captain. I tapped Kai on the shoulder and whispered in his ear. He nodded.

"Tony, did you get the sense that any of the guards were unhappy with the leadership in the camp? Possibly planning a coup?"

Tony took a deep breath. "Hmm . . . I have vague memories of some of the guards sometimes whispering to each other and then pulling apart when the captain walked in."

"What was the captain's name?"

"I don't know. I just remember them addressing him as 'Capitan'. But you know, now that you mention it, I do think there was some unrest with the guards. It must have been unbelievably dull, sitting in a stinking hot factory, with nothing to do but watch a horde of drugged prisoners on an assembly line. I'm surprised they didn't start shooting just to relieve the boredom."

"And you think they might have been plotting something?" Paul asked.

"I just don't know," Tony said, sounding frustrated.

"It's okay, this is very helpful information," Kai said. "Maybe as you rest over the next several days, more things will come back to you. If you remember anything at all, can you please let us know?" Kai gave him an email address he'd set up with an anonymous name.

"I'll do that. And if I might ask a favor of you . . . if you find out anything incriminating about the executives of Drake or Magnum, I would appreciate you sharing it with me. If I can prove they had anything to do with it, I'll be able to file a lawsuit on behalf of the shareholders."

"Do you think the merger could be invalidated and the factory in Minnesota re-opened?" Kai asked.

"It's too early to say, but that's certainly my goal."

Paul and Kai thanked Tony and wished him a fast recovery. When Tony hung up, Kai put the other unit on speakerphone again, and everyone weighed in on what we'd just heard. I also filled them in on the information I'd picked up while rescuing Jesse.

"The guard was really angry," I explained. "And there were definitely plans in the works to get rid of the captain."

"Can we use that to our advantage?" asked Christoph.

"Yeah, we could go in there and pay them each a hundred bucks to take out the captain and his buddies," Michael suggested. "Then we could just stand back and watch."

I laughed. "As if you'd stand back and watch when there's a fight going on."

"But one thing I'm still wondering is whether we're sure we can trust Tony," Claire said over the speaker phone. "Maybe I'm just paranoid after what happened with McIntyre, but I think we should check him out before we give him any more information."

"You're right to be cautious when it comes to anything related to Deimos," John said. "His strength lies in his subtle abilities to play on people's fears, and he can turn even the strongest people to evil."

"Well, we know Kirkpatrick lives in San Francisco, so Ashlyn and I can check up on him and make sure he's legit," Jesse suggested. I nodded, even though all I wanted right then was a break from being a Soterian.

Rebecca shook her head. "I think you both need some down time to recharge. There are other ways to check up on Tony."

"Right," Kenji chimed in. "Like tapping his phone and breaking into his email."

"Can you do that?" I asked.

"Sure, piece of cake."

"When did you start learning how to be a criminal?" Raina asked in the background.

"When I figured one of us better learn some high-tech surveillance techniques instead of having to rely on Jesse and Ashlyn all the time," Kenji retorted.

"Very good plan," Theresa said briskly. "We need all the help we can get. Kenji, tap his line. My suspicion is that it's already tapped, and if so, see if you can figure out who's tapping it."

"You bet," Kenji said eagerly.

"Jesse," Theresa continued, "you should come home and rest. I want you in top form for our next mission, which will likely be in just a couple of weeks."

"I'm heading out this afternoon," he replied.

"Good. I expect you'll go straight to Paul's, but I'd like everyone to come to my place tomorrow for breakfast, and we'll do some more brainstorming, look at photos of the compound, and see if we can figure out a plan."

Back at the apartment, Kai and I helped Jesse load up his car. I gave Jesse an extra-long hug and a kiss on the cheek. We'd been through a lot together this last week, and it was hard to see him go.

"Take care of yourself, hon," he said.

"You too. I won't be there to watch over you, so please try to be careful."

He smirked. "You still owe me a trip to Disneyland."

"Sure thing, if you're not passed out again next time." I gave him one last hug and then waved until he'd driven out of sight.

Chapter Fifteen: Complications

"It feels like I haven't seen you in a year," I said, snuggling into Kai.

We were lying on our beach towels, enjoying the sun and the light breeze that was blowing off the ocean. Seagulls were circling overhead, and I watched a large pelican dive into the water. Kai had the day off, so we'd headed to the beach as soon as Jesse left. A day of swimming and lying on the sand, just being together, was exactly what I needed to drive the horrible memories of the last week out of my head. It was so peaceful and relaxing, lying there with Kai. It was hard to believe that just yesterday Jesse and I were breaking Tony out of an illegal prison and flying across the border.

"It wasn't an easy week," he said. "I was worried about you."

"You don't have to worry about me. It's becoming pretty clear that I can take care of myself. Anyway, enough about that. How is your band going?"

"Not bad. Since Toby went home for the rest of the summer, Ryan has fewer distractions, so we've been jamming a lot. We're taking a break from auditioning singers, though. Too many people are gone right now. We're going to start up again at the end of the month."

"That makes sense. Are you writing any new songs?"

"Yeah, we're working on a new one that has a pretty cool funk groove behind it. But we're finding it harder and harder to write without knowing what the vocals are going to sound like."

"It just doesn't seem like it should be so hard to find someone," I mused. "I wonder why it's been so difficult."

"It's always difficult. I was really lucky to hook up with Max and Ryan. There are plenty of good musicians out there, but not everyone understands how to collaborate. You can't make a band out of a bunch of soloists."

"Hmm, sounds a lot like what John has been teaching us."

"Exactly. You all have these powerful skills, but you have to be able to work together. If you tried to all get out there and do your own thing, your unit would fall apart."

I brushed some sand off Kai's cheek. "I'm really starting to get that. Michael's the one I was most concerned about. I was seriously worried that he was going to go renegade a few times. But so far he's been great."

Kai was silent, and I felt anxiety churning in him. "You're worried about him, aren't you?" I asked.

"Yeah, I am."

"Because of his drinking?"

He nodded. "It's getting worse. It's going to be a problem, Ashlyn."

I looked out at the frothy waves of the ocean, enjoying the salty breeze that was blowing gently over us. I didn't want to think about Michael or Tony or Deimos or anything else right then. I got to my feet and walked slowly in the surf, feeling the soft wet sand ooze between my toes. I needed a break from all the worry, the constant fretting over everything. But it was so hard to compartmentalize it all.

Behind me, I heard Kai's phone ring, and I turned and headed back toward him when I heard the tension in his voice. "Hey Dad . . . what? Oh man, when did this happen?" I watched as concern spread across Kai's face. "You're kidding!

Well, all that matters is that she's alright. Give her my love, okay? Right . . . thanks for letting me know . . . I love you too, Dad." He hung up just as I reached him. "Angie was in a car accident."

I felt a sickening jolt in my stomach. "Oh my God, is she alright?"

"She's okay, but the car is totaled. And get this: it was a brand new car he'd bought her for her birthday."

"No way! Oh poor Angie . . . "

"Wait, it gets better. It was one of the new Magnum-Drake cars, and the accident happened because the whole front left wheel just flew off while she was driving. I guess that's what happens when you have drugged prisoners building your cars."

"Are you serious?! Kai, this is insane! We have to stop them!" I was suddenly so angry, I wanted to take off into the air and fly to the factory right then.

"Stop who?" asked a nasty voice.

Kelly was standing two feet from us. I felt sick to my stomach, wondering how much of the conversation she had overheard.

"Hey, Kelly," Kai said, his voice even. "What's up?"

"I'm just out for a walk and I saw you over here, so I thought I'd say hello." She turned to me. "I left my sweatshirt at your place last time I was over. I'm going to stop by later and pick it up."

"Sure, no problem," I said cautiously.

She got a strange smile on her face and walked away. I bit my lip as I watched her go.

"Now do you believe me?" Kai asked.

"Yeah, I'm beginning to. I just wish I knew what she was up to." She was obviously plotting something; the smugness was practically dripping from her. But what could she possibly do to us?

Later that day, I called my mom to tell her about my trip. She didn't like me travelling at all and had been worried sick about me going to Tijuana the first time. She was beside herself when she heard that I was going back.

"Honey, I don't understand you. I thought you were trying to be so careful with money, and now you're going back to Tijuana after you just got home? They're killing people right and left down there! Don't you watch the news?"

"I know, Mom. I promise you I'll be careful. How is Laurel?" I asked, skillfully changing the subject. "Is she excited about coming home?"

"Just like your father, always changing the subject," she grumbled. Okay, maybe it wasn't so skillful. "Yes, I can't wait for her to be home. I don't know why you girls want to go running all over the globe like that."

"Says the woman who was in the Peace Corps," I laughed. "What day is she coming home?"

"September fifth. She's flying into San Francisco and is going to stay here for a few days before heading down to Santa Barbara. She and Jason are moving into a unit in your dad's apartment building downtown."

I was stunned by this news. And hurt. I had just assumed Laurel would live in Isla Vista, and I had been so excited to be within walking distance of her. But I was also annoyed that she was moving into Dad's apartment building when he hadn't bothered to tell me that there was an open unit. I guessed he wouldn't be giving her much of a discount, and maybe he knew I had already committed to staying in my current apartment for the next school year, but it still bothered me.

My thoughts were interrupted by a knock on our front door. I heard Rebecca open the door and begin talking.

"You still there?" my mom asked.

"Yeah, sorry. Just got distracted for a second. I'll give you a call when I get back."

"I'll be keeping you surrounded in white light." She always visualized me in a protective white light when I traveled. I usually scoffed, but considering what we were up against, I welcomed whatever help she could give me, no matter how esoteric.

As I hung up the phone, Rebecca came into the room. "Kelly just came by," she announced. "She said she left her sweatshirt here, but she didn't find it."

"She's up to something, Rebecca! Did you happen to get a read on her feelings?"

She nodded. "She was definitely planning something. But I couldn't figure out what. She was searching Tracy's room for her sweatshirt, but it seemed like she was looking for something else, too."

"Well, as you said before, we're just going to have to deal with her crap as it comes. We have way too much to worry about without adding Kelly to the mix right now."

The next week flew by as our unit worked out the details of our strategy. Kenji had checked out Tony's home phone line, and sure enough, it had been tapped. More importantly, he was able to trace the tap to a line on Prescott's property. We decided that we had to trust Tony and treat him as an ally, so Paul and Kai sent him all the data they'd collected so far, including copies of the photos and video we'd taken at the prison as well as the statistics on the production volume, payroll, and extra payments to people who were not on the list of employees. Tony was ecstatic to receive this information and felt sure he could use it as the basis for an investigation and lawsuit.

With Tony taking over the legal angle, we decided that we had to take action to rescue the prisoners immediately. If we could break into the camp and disarm the guards, we could get the prisoners to safety and stop the production of the cars, which would quickly make it obvious that the Tijuana factory wasn't producing the cars on their records. If we timed this right, we could hit the company with a one-two punch that would make it impossible for the board and the shareholders to ignore what was happening.

Tony told us that all of the prisoners he met had been kidnapped and brought there against their will. None of them had been through a trial. One man had failed to pay protection money to a Mexican drug cartel. Another had been an accountant for Magnum-Drake and had refused to participate in shady accounting. Since none of the prisoners seemed to be dangerous criminals, we decided that releasing them would not spread any further evil. A mass breakout was our best strategy.

Meanwhile, I was getting very concerned about school. I had signed up for my classes for the fall, but I had no real interest in going anymore. I felt like my life had become all about fighting fires, responding to each crisis Deimos created. It seemed so trivial to be studying the geography of Europe and urban planning when there were lives at stake. I tried to tell myself that I just needed a break, and that as soon as my classes started again I'd get back into the swing of things, but I wasn't so sure.

The one thing that helped was getting back into triathlon training. I dusted off my bike and went for a ride, and I nearly shouted with joy when I stepped on the pedals and felt myself rocket forward. Flying was wonderful, but it didn't use any muscles, and it felt so good to have the feeling of speed along with the workout. I felt all my stress and worries come to the surface and then slip away as the miles rolled by.

After coming home from a ride one afternoon, I found Rebecca sitting on her bed. She looked positively bubbly.

"Hey, Bec, what's up?"

"I just had 'the talk' with Christoph," she said, her face breaking into a huge smile.

"No way! What happened?" I ran and sat next to her.

"Well, I finally got my courage up and sat him down and told him everything I'd been feeling. He was so great about it! He told me that he was in love with me, but that he had been afraid to tell me because he was terrified it would freak me out." She looked like she was going to burst with joy. "He said that he'd never met anyone like me before, and that I'm everything he's always wanted."

"Yes!" I said and gave her a big hug. "See? Aren't you glad you finally talked to him?"

"It gets better."

"Better than he's madly in love with you?"

She giggled. "He said that New York is one of the cities he wants to check out as a place to settle. And he has no strong feelings about religion and has no problem with his children being raised Jewish. He made it really clear that marriage and children are part of what he wants in his future."

"Marriage and children in general, or with someone specific?" I teased.

Rebecca blushed. "He didn't say so explicitly, but yes, it was clear that he was talking about me. Not that I'm sure whether that's what I want," she added. "But I'm just so happy that Christoph feels that way about me."

"Rebecca, you are such a rock star for having that conversation with him. It can't have been easy, but what a fantastic outcome!"

"I know. I'm so happy, Ashlyn." She grinned and gave a little bounce. I was ecstatic for both of them. The next time I saw them together, it was obvious that there had been a very positive shift in their relationship, and he looked even more in love with her than ever, if that were possible. It was great timing, since her parents would be coming to visit in just a few days. I just knew that they were going to love Christoph, especially with Rebecca looking so happy.

The day before Rebecca's parents were due to arrive, I was busy reviewing the latest plans for our mission when I heard a knock at the door. It was Morgan from the apartment management office.

"Hi, Morgan. How's it going?"

"Okay," she said, but there was tension in her voice. "May I come in?"

"Sure." I stepped out of the way and gestured to the couch as I closed the door. "Have a seat. Can I get you some tea?"

"No, thanks, I'll only be a minute. I'm here on official business. We've received an anonymous tip that you have drugs in your apartment, and we have to follow up on it."

I was flabbergasted. "Drugs? Are you serious?" Then the light dawned, and I smiled bitterly. "Ah, I get it. The 'anonymous' tip came from someone who's not too happy that I'm going out with her ex, right? Morgan, I assure you, there's absolutely no truth to it at all. You're welcome to search the apartment, and Rebecca and I will happily submit to drug tests if necessary."

She shook her head. "That's what I thought. You've always been good tenants, and aside from one particularly loud party," she said with a smirk, referring to Candace's graduation party, "you've been quiet and haven't caused any complaints. I'll make a note that the tip was a hoax and leave it at that."

"Thanks, Morgan. Let me know if you need any further information or anything at all."

I showed her out and closed the door, and my smile faded to a frown. I looked behind the couch, looked carefully through its cushions, and got down on the floor and peered underneath it. Nothing. I inspected the other furniture in the room and found nothing there, either. Finally, I went into Tracy's room and took a quick look around. I didn't think Kelly would have had the opportunity to plant anything while Rebecca was watching her, but she might have just let something drop on the bed or dresser. Nothing was there.

I sighed with relief as I walked back into the living room. I was overreacting. Kelly wasn't stupid enough to plant drugs in our apartment. She wanted to stir up trouble, but she wouldn't go so far as to frame us.

Rebecca came out into the living room. "Who was that?" I told her about what had just happened, and she went pale. "What if Kelly pulls something when my parents are here?" she asked nervously.

"Don't worry. Tracy won't be back for another two weeks. I think we'll be okay until then."

She twisted her hair nervously around her finger. "I'm freaking out, Ashlyn. I'm so worried my parents are going to hate Christoph."

I smiled at her. "Of course you're worried. Christoph and your family are what matter most to you in the world, so it's very important to you that they get along. I'm kind of feeling the same way, actually, about my sister meeting Kai. You and Laurel are my very best friends in the world, and if either of you didn't like him, I don't know what I'd do."

"But who wouldn't like Kai?" she asked in surprise. "He's so perfect for you."

"I could say the same thing about you and Christoph. He's smart, funny, gorgeous, very kind, and completely in love with you. Hard to find fault there."

"He just looks so . . . intimidating," she said, searching for the right word. "I hope he doesn't wear his leather pants to meet them."

I laughed. "He *is* intimidating when you first meet him. But the second he opens his mouth, it's obvious that he's just a big pussy cat. Trust me, it's going to go great. Now, let's get to the dojo, and when we get home we can make this place spotless for your parents' arrival."

We met up with Michael and Christoph and headed to the dojo. When we pulled into the parking lot, there was a beautiful new Ducati motorcycle parked by the door.

"Oh man, it's the Monster eleven hundred," Michael said in awe. "These things are crazy fast."

"The mufflers look like cannons," Rebecca remarked.

We spent a couple of minutes admiring its shiny black paint job, the sleek design, and its cool trellis frame. I'd always been too scared to learn to ride a motorcycle, and my mom would probably disown me if I ever did get the nerve to do it, so I always just admired them from afar. But deep in my heart, I wanted to have a Ducati one day. Maybe after my flying power faded, that would be the thing that would get me through the transition. Riding a Ducati had to be about as close to flying as you could get.

After our warm-up run, we entered the dojo to find John on the phone. He said good-bye quickly and hung up when we came in. "Is that your bike?" Michael asked.

"Yes," he smiled. "I've wanted that model ever since it came out, and I finally just took the plunge."

"Excellent choice," Michael said.

"Very nice!" Christoph agreed. "I prefer Harleys, but the Ducati is a beautiful machine."

"You're welcome to ride it later," John offered, and Christoph and Michael gave each other a high five. "But first, we've got a lot to do today, so let's get started." We went through our series of stretches and then ran through our kicks and punches. After that, we practiced rolling and falling. I was getting more and more comfortable with falling, and Rebecca could finally do a perfect shoulder roll. The training was definitely paying off.

Next, John had us gather in the center of the room. "Today we're going to learn knife defense," he said. "This is a critical defense for us, because a Sentry's shield cannot stop a knife. What do you think is the best way to avoid getting cut?"

"Don't be there," Michael said.

"Right. Your first defense is to get out of the way of the knife. But perhaps more important is to recognize that nine times out of ten, you will end up getting cut. The key is to minimize the damage. Getting your hand sliced open is far better than letting your enemy plunge it through your heart." I saw Rebecca wince, and Christoph moved slightly closer to her. "But obviously, our first goal is to learn how to get out of the way."

John showed us how to jump backward, grabbing the attacker's wrist, and disarming him if he stabbed forward with the knife. We also learned how to avoid an overhand attack by stepping to the side and guiding the knife into the attacker's own body. I had used this same technique when Kai and I were attacked in San Francisco, but it had been with a crowbar instead of a knife. I knew first-hand how effective it could be if you moved fast enough.

After knife defense, John asked Michael and Christoph to spar in the corner. Rebecca went back to the mats to work on a series of high falls she was having some trouble with. John motioned for me to follow him to the other side of the room.

"I want to work with you on stealth," he began. "You're relying a lot on your invisibility, which is fine for a few hours at a time. But as you saw in Mexico, it can wear you down. I want you to learn to be stealthy while visible so you can conserve your energy if needed."

I nodded. "That's a really good idea. Flying and being invisible at the same time burns up energy way too fast."

John rolled out a large sheet of butcher paper and asked me to walk along the paper as quietly as possible. The first time, I made a loud crinkling sound as I walked. I did a few more passes and soon was able to go almost noiselessly. I looked proudly at John, who had a small smile on his face.

"Very good. Now, put your shoes on and try again."

My heart sank. "Shoes on?"

"You usually wear shoes on missions, yes?"

"True." I went over and put on my shoes, my dismay growing as I noticed for the first time just how many ridges and bumps there are on the bottom of a running shoe. They were going to chew right through the paper, but at least he wasn't making me try it in spiked heels or something. I went back over to the paper and walked as gingerly as I could. A roar of crinkling filled the room, and I started walking even lighter. Miraculously, the noise stopped, and I was about to get excited by my progress when I was stopped by the frown on John's face.

"Ashlyn, you're airborne," he said. I looked down and saw that I was indeed floating an inch above the paper. Whoops. I touched down and tried to focus on not hovering as I walked, but it was awful to hear the paper crinkling so loudly.

"Try to imagine your feet melting into the paper, their molecules blending together. When you no longer fight the paper, you can merge with it."

I sighed. Sometimes his teaching was just too esoteric for me to understand, but I tried not to get frustrated and just do the best I could. I imagined the rubber soles of my shoes melting into the paper, making a smooth rubber strip down the center. I walked along the imaginary strip, and the crinkling became quieter.

"That's good," he said, looking pleased. "I want you to practice that every day. Okay, everyone, that's it for today." We lined up and bowed to John before heading out the door.

"What was with the paper?" Michael asked on our way home.

"Trying to learn to walk silently so I don't have to rely on flight and invisibility."

"That sounds difficult," Christoph said.

"It is. I don't know if I'll ever get it."

"Of course you will. It might take a while, but you'll get it eventually," Rebecca said encouragingly.

"Hey, do you want to join our poker game at The Manor tonight?" Michael asked.

"No, we have to clean the apartment tonight to get ready for Rebecca's parents' visit."

"What, all night? Come on, it can't take that long."

"The way you guys clean, I'm sure it doesn't, but we have slightly higher standards," I said. Rebecca grinned.

"Suit yourselves, but we'll be playing late in case you change your minds."

"A nice game of cards might be just the thing to help you relax," Christoph said to Rebecca, reaching forward from the back seat and touching her gently on the shoulder. "I could help you clean to make it go faster."

"You'd help me clean?" she asked, her eyes wide. I laughed at the memory of having said the same thing to Kai when we first met. Willingness to clean seemed to be our litmus test of a guy's true awesomeness.

"Yes, of course," he laughed. "I will even wash the windows."

"Okay," I agreed. "You help us clean, and you'll have two more for your poker game."

"Michael will help, too," Christoph announced, looking straight at Michael. I laughed out loud as I saw the expressions on their faces in the rear-view mirror.

"Yeah, all right," he grumbled. "Only because it'll make me feel better about taking your money when I kick your asses at poker."

I pulled into our complex and saw that Kai's car was in the lot. I looked at the clock on the dashboard. It was early for him to be home from work, and I wondered what was going on. "Bec, I'll meet you at the apartment. I want to go check in with Kai first." I walked to The Manor with Michael and Christoph. Kai was sitting on the couch, playing the guitar.

"Hey," he said when we walked in. He put his guitar down and came over to hug me. "How was training?"

"Ashlyn has to learn to walk silently on paper," Christoph said.

"How did that go?"

I sighed. "Not great, but I'll get there eventually. How come you're home early?"

He had a twinkle in his eye, but there was also a strange apprehension in him that I couldn't put my finger on. "Power went out at the clinic, so we had to cancel our last clients and went home early. But I'm glad, because I got an idea for a tune that I want to work on. What are you doing tonight?"

"I'm going to help Rebecca clean the apartment and get ready for her parents' visit tomorrow. Christoph and Michael are going to help, and then we're all going to play poker."

"That sounds like fun," Kai said. I could tell he was torn between wanting to hang out with us and wanting to work on his music. Maybe that was the apprehension I felt coming from him: he had extra time in his day, and he wasn't sure if he should spend it with me or playing music.

"Tell you what," I suggested. "If you're still working on your song by the time we start playing poker, you can go work at our apartment where it's nice and quiet. And if you finish up, you can come join the game."

He smiled in relief. "You're very sweet to me." He held my chin and looked into my eyes. "Sometimes I wonder what I did to deserve you."

"Please don't make me puke," Michael growled, walking out of the room. Kai chuckled.

"We need to find Michael a girlfriend," Kai said.

I snorted. "I can just see the personals ad. 'Cranky college student with a big ego and lousy communication skills seeks gorgeous woman who will put up with mood swings and drinking binges.' That should get a lot of phone calls."

"Seriously, he'd be a lot happier with a girlfriend."

"I agree. He has a big heart. He just doesn't know how to apply it." Michael walked back into the room looking irritated.

"So are we going to clean or what?"

"Yes," Christoph said. "And don't be so annoyed. Think of it as training."

"Training for what?"

"For being in a relationship," I said. "Come on." I kissed Kai quickly and we headed back to my apartment to help Rebecca get ready for her big day.

Chapter Sixteen: Meltdown

"What a lovely place!"

Rebecca's mom, Susan, was looking out the window, the sun bouncing off the copper highlights in her black hair. Rebecca's parents had invited Christoph and me to join them for lunch, and we had chosen a nice Japanese restaurant in Santa Barbara. Rebecca was definitely nervous, but she was also happy. It was clear that she and her parents were very close.

"Is it this nice all year round?" Susan asked.

Rebecca nodded. "Most of the time. It does get a bit colder in the winter, but not by much."

"It must be strange not to have any real seasons," her father said. Bob had dark brown hair that was thinning on top. Above the bridge of his wire-rimmed glasses was a permanent crinkle, as if he were always deep in thought, but his face was friendly.

"It was a bit strange to get used to," Rebecca agreed. "I feel like I missed winter last year altogether, and now we're a month away from fall again."

"What's it like in your home town?" Susan asked Christoph.

"It snows some in the winter, and it gets hot in the summer. The autumn is quite beautiful," he replied. He was wearing a nice charcoal grey sweater over his jeans, which gave him a softer, more approachable air than usual. Rebecca clearly approved, her eyes sparkling as she looked at him.

"You should see autumn in New York," she told him. "It's spectacular."

He beamed back at her. "I would like that." He turned to Bob and Susan. "New York is one of the cities I am considering as my new home, so I plan to visit."

"Rebecca tells us you're majoring in education, is that right?" Susan asked.

"Yes, early childhood education," he clarified. I saw Rebecca flinch ever so slightly, and I realized that she hadn't told them the whole story. I didn't see why she was so worried, but then again, if the expectation was that she would be a doctor, they might expect her to marry someone in a similar profession.

"Really?" Bob asked. "Is there a demand for professors in that field?"

"Oh, I'm not planning to teach the subject, I'm planning to use it," he laughed. "I want to open a preschool."

"Oh, how sweet," Susan said. Bob was quiet, his eyebrow raised slightly. Rebecca had gone pale, and I reached out under the table and touched her gently on the wrist, sending as much calming energy into her as I could. She relaxed a bit and sat back in her seat.

"Christoph is going to be an awesome preschool teacher," I said enthusiastically. "If I were to have children, I couldn't imagine a better person to leave them with than Christoph. He'll be able to charge outrageous fees and people will still be lining up to enroll their kids." Christoph smiled widely at me.

"Rebecca has told us a lot about you, Ashlyn," Susan remarked. "I'm glad she's met such a nice friend."

"Aren't you the marathoner?" Bob asked.

"Triathlons, actually. Just the short distance."

"And you girls are doing karate together?" Susan asked. "That sounds pretty exciting."

"It's great exercise, and it's really good for learning to defend yourself," I explained. Something about the look on Rebecca's face made me want to burst out laughing. She looked like she was sitting on a tack.

"I hope you don't need to use self-defense very often," Bob said, the crinkle turning to a furrow.

"No, it's pretty safe here," I assured him. "And Rebecca doesn't actually need it with Christoph hanging around. Not too many people are dumb enough to try to get past him."

"Rebecca, honey, are you okay? You look pale," Susan said with concern.

Bob laughed. "I think she's a little embarrassed by us."

Rebecca looked aghast. "No! Not at all. It's just . . . kind of weird."

Susan chuckled. "I remember feeling that way when your grandparents came to visit me at Stanford."

"Your mother was a wreck," Bob clarified, taking a sip of tea.

"You met at Stanford?" I leaned in closer. I loved hearing stories of how couples met. It always fascinated me that of all the billions of people in the world, you could actually meet the one perfect person for you. I still couldn't believe that Kai and I had found each other.

"We were both majoring in pre-law," Bob explained. "We didn't talk much the first semester, but we saw each other at the airport on our way home for the holidays, and that's when we found out we were both from New York."

"That seemed to be the nail in the coffin, so to speak," Susan added.

"Nice choice of words, dear."

"I had no intention of getting involved with anyone," Susan insisted. "I had exactly one purpose in going to Stanford: to become the best lawyer in America. I had no interest in falling in love."

"But you learned to work around it?" I asked.

She nodded. "It didn't take long to figure out that Bob wasn't taking anything away from my life." She reached out and took his hand.

"Funny, I seem to remember having a similar conversation with a friend recently," I mused, giving Rebecca a wry smile.

"That's a wonderful story," Christoph said. Just then the waiter came and took our order, and while Rebecca's parents consulted their menus and talked to the waiter, Christoph and Rebecca beamed at each other. I could hear both of their hearts racing, which was sickening and adorable at the same time.

After lunch, Bob and Susan went to meet a real estate agent who was going to show them some vacation properties, while Rebecca, Christoph, and I headed back to Isla Vista. Rebecca looked much more relaxed.

"Rebecca, your parents are awesome!" I gushed. "I don't know why you were so freaked out."

"I know, it was just weird. I'm glad you both met them. Thanks for coming along."

"You look a lot like your mother," Christoph commented. "You got your beautiful hair from her."

"So when are you going to meet Christoph's parents?" I asked teasingly.

Rebecca groaned. "I'm not sure I'm ready for that. Besides, they don't speak English." I felt a faint twinge of emotion from Christoph that I couldn't identify, but a moment later it had passed.

"You should take your parents to The Palace for dinner," he suggested. The Palace Grill was a fantastic Cajun restaurant in downtown Santa Barbara.

"Oh, good idea. I love those muffins they serve. I bet my parents will love it."

"Don't forget to order the whisky bread pudding," I said. "It takes a while to make, so you have to remember to order it at the beginning of the meal."

As we talked about all the delicious things they could have at The Palace, I noticed that Christoph was rather quiet in the back seat, but he had just met his girlfriend's parents for the first time. For someone who looked like he was made of solid rock, Christoph really was a sensitive guy.

When we got back, Kai and Ryan were just walking up to the apartment. "Great news!" Ryan said. "I think we found a singer!"

Kai looked slightly uncomfortable, a strange tension emanating from him. That was twice in one day I hadn't been able to identify what someone was feeling. Was something wrong with my Empath powers? I pushed the thought away and focused on their news.

"That's awesome!" I said. "Oh guys, I'm so happy for you! Where did you find him?"

"Oh, it's not a him, it's a her! Her name is Marlowe, and she's amazing. She's sexy as hell and has the most incredible voice. Kai met her at the vet clinic, and she auditioned today. And she's perfect! She's exactly what we need. She improvised over our tunes and came up with some awesome melodies. She's seriously got star potential." Ryan was on fire, happier than I'd seen him in a long time.

I felt numb. Deep inside me, I felt the first twinges of insecurity gathering steam, getting ready to launch a full-blown assault. *No. Do NOT give in to this!*

"That's great!" I said a little too loudly, forcing myself to act cheerful. Emotions were swirling all around me. I could feel concern coming from Rebecca as she felt my insecurity rising. I could feel Kai's discomfort and worry. I could feel Ryan's excitement and his attraction to Marlowe. It was too much to deal with all at once, and I became light-headed.

"Ashlyn, are you okay?" Kai asked.

"Fine, just a little dizzy. I think I'm going to go lie down. I'll see you guys later." I headed up the stairs, desperate to be alone with my thoughts, but Kai was right next to me.

"You're not okay," he said in a low voice. "What's wrong?"

I walked more quickly. "I need a little alone time, okay?"

"Okay," he said after a pause. "I love you," he added as I charged ahead. I barreled through the front door and into the bedroom, where I started pacing.

"Calm down," I said out loud as I walked back and forth. "Just calm down. It's just an oversight. He didn't tell you about her because he just met her. It was a fluke. They didn't want a female singer, but then they met her, and she's got the voice and the image they want . . . "

And that's when I melted down. The panic rose in me like a hungry demon, consuming all the joy and love in my heart as it went. I lay down on my bed and curled up into a ball. I was completely freaking out. Slowly, I started realizing that I'd been getting very worried over the last few months but kept talking myself out of it. Kai had been spending less and less time with me, and when we were together, he was getting more distant, more preoccupied. And when Ryan let it slip that Kai had met this . . . this *Marlowe* at the vet clinic, Kai just stood there looking busted.

Oh my God, why didn't I see it before? He probably met her months ago and was seeing her whenever I was training. Maybe he was with her the whole time I was in Mexico! While I was risking my life for the Soterians, he was off with someone else. *Of course she's got a fantastic voice*, I thought bitterly. Certainly better than mine could ever be. Not that he ever let me audition. He said he wanted a male singer, but he was probably trying to find a female singer the whole time and just told me that so I wouldn't bug him. And Ryan made it sound like she was drop-dead gorgeous. Oh my God, how could I be so stupid?

I felt sick and ran to the bathroom. Rebecca came in and put a hand gently on my back as I kneeled over the toilet.

"Ashlyn, what on earth are you doing? You've worked yourself up into a total frenzy. Take a few breaths and try to come back to reality."

"I can't believe I didn't see it before," I choked as I began to sob. All I could see was a dim, grey future stretching before me with no love, no happiness—no Kai. What had I expected when I was such a loser? He and Marlowe would go on tour together, write music together . . .

I threw up. Rebecca put both hands on my back, and I could feel her warmth spreading through me. "Ashlyn, you have to stop it. I know what you're feeling seems very real, but it's all a lie. You're letting evil get the upper hand, and you have to fight it."

"It's not a lie. I'm seeing things clearly for the first time in a long time." I was trembling uncontrollably.

"No, you're not!" she shouted, sending a jolt of surprise through me. "Ashlyn, this is your worst demon, and you have to fight it! You cannot let it win like this! Now concentrate," she said, grabbing my face firmly in her hands. "I've felt what's in Kai's heart, and all he feels is tremendous love and concern for you. You need to give him a chance to explain things. And you need to pull yourself together *right now*."

I was completely taken aback. I'd never seen Rebecca act so assertive, and it shocked me out of my nightmare. Slowly, I felt the wall start to come down that I'd put up around myself, and surges of calming energy flowed into me from Rebecca's hands.

I took a few deep breaths, trying to ease the panic. I was hyperventilating, and my heart was pounding like it would explode.

Finally, after what felt like an hour, I was able to catch my breath.

"That's better," Rebecca said. She cocked her head and looked at me. "You put on a good act of having it all under control, don't you?"

"Most of the time," I said weakly.

She searched my face. "You have to deal with this ridiculous fear of abandonment. And the one person who can help you do that is Kai, if you'll let him."

"I can't let him see me like this!" I shrieked. "He already feels like he can't tell me the truth because he worries that I'm going to freak out. I can't give him proof that he's right."

"He *absolutely* has to see you like this, to see what happens when he keeps things from you," she insisted. "You can't keep your feelings from him because you're afraid of scaring him off, and he can't try to protect your feelings by keeping you in the dark. Come on, stand up." She took my hand and pulled me to my feet. "Get cleaned up, and I'm going to call him in." I started to protest, but her face was like stone. "You can do this, Ashlyn," she said flatly and strode out of the room.

I stared blankly at the door for a moment and then turned and looked in the mirror. My eyes were red, puffy, and filled with fear. Holy crap, what just happened? One minute everything was fine, the next minute my entire world was upside down and Rebecca was acting like a drill sergeant. What was wrong with me?

I did as she told me and washed my face and brushed my teeth. I went and sat on my bed and took some steadying breaths. A moment later, Kai came in, his face so full of worry that I nearly burst into tears again.

"Ashlyn? What happened?" He came over and put his arms around me, and I collapsed into him.

"I'm sorry, Kai. I'm so sorry."

"It's okay, just tell me what's going on."

I held him for a moment longer before I spoke. "It took me by surprise that you chose a female singer, and that it was someone you met at work that you never said anything about, and, well, I just kind of freaked out."

Kai smoothed his lips across my hair, his warm breath sending tingles across my scalp. "I'm sorry," he said. "I should have told you. I've been taking my guitar to work so I can practice on my breaks, and I was sitting outside practicing when she came to the clinic one day. When she heard me playing, she asked if I was in a band, and I told her that we're looking for a singer." My stomach clenched, and I fought to keep it under control. "It turns out we know some of the same people in L.A., and I thought what the hell, I'll have her audition. I just felt a little weird about it, since she approached me, and I didn't want to upset you if it ended up not working out anyway."

I pulled back and looked into his face. "You can't keep things from me, Kai. I thought we went over this already. You have to understand that no matter how hard it might be to tell me something, no matter how much you think I'm going to freak out, hiding it from me is always going to make it a hundred times worse. It really hurt to hear about her from Ryan instead of from you."

Kai looked down. "I'm sorry. I just didn't want to worry you, and I know it backfired."

"Swear to me you'll be honest with me from now on."

"I will."

"No matter what it is, you have to tell me."

"Okay. I'm so sorry I hurt you." He stroked my hair again, and I felt my heart start to melt.

"I'm sorry I'm still such a train wreck," I muttered.

Kai paused. "You don't think I chose Marlowe because I'm interested in her, do you?"

"Honestly, Kai, you don't want to hear where my brain went. When I go into nuclear insecurity mode like that, I imagine all kinds of horrible things. The rational part of me knows that you're far too serious about your music to choose a singer based on looks alone, and that if you chose her, she must be fantastic. I promise to try to keep an open mind."

He sighed and shook his head. "Ashlyn, what is it going to take for you to trust me?"

"It's just going to take time. And that reminds me: we have got to spend more time together. I know we've both been busy, but I feel like you've been more distant lately, and it hurts like hell."

"I haven't meant to be distant." He pulled me to him again and held me tightly. "Don't you know that you mean more to me than anything else in the world?"

"I do, but it's hard when I only see you for five minutes as you're running to work or to band practice. And, truthfully, it just seems like you're not feeling as intensely about me as you used to." I choked slightly on these words. It made me feel slightly panicky again, and I fought hard to stay in control.

He looked thoughtfully at me. "We had a very intense start to our relationship. It's only natural that that's going to calm down some. But I don't feel like my feelings for you are lessening—they're just deepening, if that makes sense. It's not as crazy a high as it used to be, but it's a much stronger, deeper love. Do you know what I mean?"

"I guess so." If I were completely honest with myself, I could see that he was right. I still got butterflies in my stomach when he looked at me with that beautifully intense gaze of his, but it wasn't as overwhelming as it used to be. I didn't feel dizzy as often when he kissed me. I just felt deeply in love with him, and completely right. It was a saner feeling, one that didn't interfere with my sleeping or eating but was completely satisfying.

As if he were reading my thoughts, he lifted my chin and looked into my eyes with such intensity, I felt my stomach flutter. He kissed me, gently at first, and then more passionately and urgently until the world disappeared and there were just the two of us, merged into one.

Chapter Seventeen: Slur

"Well?" I asked Rebecca, who had just returned from taking her parents to the airport.

"They said that Christoph is a 'sweet boy', and they asked me to tell you both that you're welcome to come visit any time."

"That's great!" I said. "They wouldn't have said that if they hated him, right?"

"True," she conceded. "I'm going to take it as a good sign. Oh, I'm exhausted." She let out a huge sigh and flopped back on her bed. I thought about how lucky I was that Kai's parents liked me and that my mom liked him so much. My dad and step-mother were another story, but whatever. Three out of four sets of parents wasn't bad.

"You know, I've never been to New York," I said. "What do you say to taking a trip back there, maybe over spring break?"

"Are you kidding? That would be fantastic!" Rebecca beamed. "I can't wait to show you around. Just wait 'til you see the Met. And the pizza is to die for." Rebecca talked happily about New York, and I started getting very excited about the prospect of finally visiting there.

That night, I got an email from Laurel, who was coming home in a couple of weeks. She wrote about all the things she wanted to do when she got back. First on her agenda was the Hartford, a swanky hotel that had an outrageously lavish brunch that we went to on special occasions. Second was getting an authentic burrito, and third was going to the beach. I imagined us walking around Santa Barbara together, which was now my home just as much as it was hers, comparing notes on our favorite places and going for coffee. It was going to be so great to see her again, and I couldn't wait to hear all about her time in Japan.

But I wondered what our relationship would be like when she got back. I was so busy, and I couldn't ever tell her about the Soterians, which was going to be really tricky. I thought a lot about the kinds of things I could tell her: that I was studying martial arts, that I was spending a lot of time with Kai and Rebecca, and that I was going on field trips with my martial arts school. Maybe she'd be so wrapped up in her own life she wouldn't pay much attention to the details. But it was bound to cause some awkward moments.

The following day, Kai and I were hanging out in his room when his phone rang.

"It's Tony," he said as he answered it. "Hi, Tony. How are you doing?"

"Very well," I heard Tony reply. "I'm calling to let you know that I've collected enough evidence to file a lawsuit on behalf of the shareholders. And better yet, the SEC is investigating the executive team at Magnum-Drake."

"That's fantastic news. I'll pass this along to the rest of our organization. They'll be very glad to hear that there's progress. What are the next steps?"

"The Commission will file a complaint with the court. Magnum-Drake is still hemorrhaging money, and the stock price has dropped by forty percent, so I suspect prosecutors will try to move quickly. There's a great deal of pressure from the shareholders and the union. How are things going on your end?"

"Really well. We're planning the mission and will keep you posted once we've locked everything down. Thanks for the good news, Tony."

That night, we all met at John's to finalize our plans. Everyone was encouraged by Tony's report, but there was a lot of general anxiety about whether we'd be able to pull off the mission. Disarming a handful of bombs on the Golden Gate Bridge had been one thing; breaking hundreds of prisoners out of an illegal prison in Mexico was quite another.

Once again, Kai would stay behind, and I dreaded being away from him. I was really ashamed to admit it to myself, but a big reason was this constant, nagging fear that he was going to cheat on me. I hated myself for even letting those thoughts into my head, but I couldn't help it. I had done a great job of keeping it under control for the last several months and had thought I was finally outgrowing my insecurity, but ever since Marlowe came onto the scene, it felt like I was right back where I started. Every time I found myself imagining Kai with Marlowe, I pinched my arm to snap myself out of it. I hadn't met her yet, which was fine. I needed to concentrate on the mission, and I couldn't risk introducing her face into my mind, which would make it easier for my twisted imagination to picture her and Kai together.

The night before the others arrived, Kai and I went out to dinner at a Thai restaurant downtown. I decided to dress up a bit and wore a black skirt and a soft purple blouse. Kai wore his cute khaki pants and a black dress shirt. His hair curled softly, and his eyes were an especially deep green. He looked gorgeous. It was nice to do something special with him, but the mood was definitely overshadowed by the fact that I'd be leaving in two days for what could very well be our most dangerous mission yet.

"Here, try some of my tea," he offered. I had just ordered water, but he insisted that I would love Thai iced tea. I sipped it hesitantly and then smiled. It was sweet and earthy, with a slightly woody taste.

"Mmm," I said. "You were right. This is awesome."

"Excuse me," he called, flagging down the waiter. "We'd like another one, please."

I took another sip and then handed it back to him. "I can't wait to try the spicy basil tofu. And the pad thai."

"Both great choices. Thai food is the best. I can't believe you haven't had it before. I've obviously been neglecting you."

"Hardly," I laughed. "Besides, the last thing I need is more food to fall in love with." The waiter arrived with an appetizer of crispy fried tofu that we dipped in a sweet and sour sauce. It was incredible.

"So how are you feeling about school?" I asked, happily munching the tofu. "Are you stoked to start at UCSB next month?"

"Yeah, I think it's going to be good. The music program looks pretty cool."

I swirled the ice in my glass, watching the drips of condensation roll down the outside and stick to the paper table cloth. "I'm so excited for you, Kai. If Marlowe is as good as you say she is, I think you've got a good shot at making something happen."

"We'll see." He was always so humble about his music. But there was a gleam in his eye, and I could tell he was excited about the band. "We've got some good tunes. We're going to record our demo this weekend, so hopefully we can start getting some gigs soon. Marlowe is fairly well-connected and knows some club owners in L.A., so we think we might be able to get a gig as early as next month if we can get our demo done."

"Next month! I had no idea you were so close to finishing. That's awesome!"

"Yeah, it should be pretty cool."

"Maybe you guys should play at our birthday party," I suggested.

"That would be fun. I'm glad you're into the idea."

"Of course I am. Why wouldn't I be?"

He looked down at his fork, which he was absent-mindedly twirling in his hand. "I just wasn't sure how you would feel about having Marlowe at our party."

I felt a stab of pain. "Kai, don't worry, you don't have to walk on eggshells with me. I'll get over this. I want to meet her when I get back from Mexico. It'll be good to take the next step and put this stupid jealousy behind me."

He looked intently into my eyes. "I'm sorry this is so hard for you. I wish there were something I could do to make it easier."

I reached out and took his hand. "Just be patient, and keep talking to me. As long as I know you're not hiding anything from me, I'll trust you more and more."

Our main course arrived, and we spent the rest of dinner talking about the classes we were taking in the fall, about martial arts training—everything except my trip. It was too upsetting to think about, and I'd finally learned my lesson about discussing Soterian business in public.

When the check arrived, Kai gave his credit card to the waiter.

"You don't have to pay for everything, you know," I said. "We're both on a tight budget."

"I want to buy you dinner. It's the least I can do the night before you leave."

A moment later, the waiter returned. "I'm sorry," he said in a low voice. "Your card was declined."

Kai dug another credit card out of his wallet. "Sorry about that. Try this one."

"What happened?" I asked as the waiter walked away.

"It was declined. I must be over my limit."

I looked at him in concern. "How did that happen?"

"I had to buy a new amp," he said simply. The waiter returned, and Kai signed the slip.

"And?"

"And what?"

I cocked my head to the side. "Do you usually go over your credit limit?"

"No, not usually. It's happened a few times. What's wrong?"

I took a deep breath. He was a lot more relaxed about it than I would have been if my card had been declined, and I thought again about what his dad had said. But I reminded myself that it wasn't my business, and besides, Kai couldn't just go without an amp. I was also a lot more uptight about money than most people I knew. I always felt like my dad was looking over my shoulder whenever I bought anything, which was usually enough to keep my spending in check.

"It's nothing. Forget it. I'm just anxious about the mission. Let's get going."

When we got back to the apartment complex, Kai pulled me into his arms. "Stay with me tonight," he murmured.

"Well, if you're going to twist my arm." I kissed him slowly, savoring the feeling of his soft lips on mine and his wonderfully strong arms around me. A moment later, I pulled away. "But I can't hang out in the morning. I have a lot of packing and preparation to do before the others arrive tomorrow."

"That's fine. I just want to be with you tonight. I don't know how long it's going to be until I see you again." He stroked my hair, his breath warm on my neck.

"You really do miss me when I'm gone, don't you?"

"I'm not even going to answer that," he said. I wrapped my arms around him and hugged him tightly again, then took his hand as we walked slowly to the apartment. I sighed as peace washed over me. These days, my head was such a jumble of insecurity, intense love for Kai, anxiety about our mission, and worry about my future. But at moments like these when I was close to him, everything suddenly seemed very simple.

* * *

The next day the San Francisco unit rolled into town in the late afternoon. Claire and Raina were staying with us, Jesse and Kenji were staying at The Manor, and Theresa was staying at John's. Once again, I wondered if there was something more between John and Theresa than just collaboration as Soterians, but if they had feelings for each other, they kept them well concealed. Paul stayed behind in San Francisco, but he and Kai would be available to provide any support we needed via the satellite phone Theresa had brought. I felt much better knowing that we'd be able to contact them whenever we needed to instead of having to wait until we were in range of a cell phone signal.

We all gathered at John's place that night for dinner. John made a large vat of spaghetti and marinara sauce, and Rebecca and I brought salad. Christoph and Michael arrived with French bread and drinks, while Kai brought a batch of homemade cookies for dessert. It wasn't quite as fancy as the meals we'd been having when Theresa was hosting, but it felt really special and nice, all of us having a home-cooked meal together. It was really like we had become one big family.

After we'd finished eating, and Christoph and Kenji had finished everything that was left over, we sat down in the living room to review our plans. Kai took notes as we talked so that he could brief Paul later. We talked through all the scenarios, went over our strategies and contingency plans, and double-checked our reservations.

After a couple of hours, we decided we'd done everything possible and had pretty much talked it all to death, so we took the night off. John and Theresa were driving down to L.A. that night to go to a concert and would stay at a hotel down there. Jesse and I would drive everyone else down in the morning in our cars. I was bummed out that Jesse and I wouldn't be driving together this time, but we were just going as far as the border again and then were catching the trolley into Tijuana, where we'd spend one night before heading off to the prison.

It was going to be a very different trip this time, with a much clearer mission, thanks to all the reconnaissance Jesse and I had done. I was beginning to see just how valuable it was to be a Scout. It wasn't as exciting as being a Warrior, as impressive as a Sentry, or as glamorous as an Empath, but our work was the critical first step that enabled everyone else to do their job.

We had to get up early so we could hit the road by seven, so we decided just to hang out and play poker at The Manor. Raina and Michael went to the liquor store, returning with beer and a bottle of whiskey, which they started going through at an alarming pace.

"Guys, you might want to slow down on the shots," I cautioned. "It's a long way to TJ, and we're hitting the road early . . ."

"Shut up and deal," Michael slurred. I glared at him, trying to keep my anger in check. I was glad Christoph, Kenji, and Raina were there to keep him under control, but it was just so annoying that he had to go and get hammered all the time. It was going to make the next day even more stressful.

"Maybe tomorrow we should divide up by sex," I suggested, trying to sound cheerful. "I'll drive the girls, and you guys can go in Jesse's car."

"As if," Jesse said, rolling his eyes. "I'm not going to be stuck with that fool and his hangover all the way to Mexico."

Michael's face turned red. "Who are you calling a fool, you little faggot?" he barked.

The room erupted in chaos. Jesse flew over the table and attacked Michael, who was caught completely by surprise, knocking him flat. Before Michael could react, Jesse was sitting on his chest, punching him in the face with all of his strength. I'd never seen a fury like that in him.

Raina leaped to her feet and pulled Jesse off of Michael, and Michael jumped up. But he was so drunk that he lost his balance, fell on the table, and knocked it over. The poker chips, cards, and drinks went flying everywhere, the glass shattering on the floor. Claire jumped back and shrieked as she stepped in broken glass. Kenji lifted her up and carried her to the couch, where blood streamed from her foot all over the cushions.

Without a word, Christoph went to get stuff to clean up the mess, and Rebecca walked carefully over to the couch and started healing Claire as she picked glass out of her foot. As I watched the chaos in disbelief, I was grateful that Ryan and Kai were at band practice and not in the middle of this.

Raina was standing over Michael looking furious, ready to smack him down if he tried to get up again. Jesse was standing back with his fists raised, panting. I went over to him and laid a hand on his shoulder.

"Easy, Jesse. He's just being an asshole. You don't have to take his bait." I poured healing into him, and it took nearly thirty seconds before he finally took a deep breath and closed his eyes.

"I'm sorry," he said hoarsely. "I can't believe I reacted like that."

"He definitely had it coming. And we're all on edge because of tomorrow. But yeah, not your finest moment."

I patted him on the shoulder and then leaned over Michael. He was lying on the ground, massaging his jaw.

"Who knew he had that in him?" Michael said, looking completely perplexed.

"I guess that's the last time you'll underestimate Jesse. And the last time you say something so bigoted and stupid! Honestly, Michael, what in the hell got into you?"

"The same thing that always gets into him," Rebecca called angrily from the couch. "A toxic blend of alcohol and testosterone."

I leaned down and put a hand on Michael's head. He tried to brush it away, but I persisted and healed him. His eyes slowly cleared, and the swelling on his face where Jesse had pummeled him went down.

"Up you get," I said, helping him stand.

"Thanks." He looked at me with a strange expression. "Why did you do that?"

"You mean why did I heal you? Simple. I wanted to make sure you were sober and could enunciate clearly when you apologize to every single person in this room. Starting with Jesse, of course." I crossed my arms and glared at him, but I couldn't help feeling compassion for him, too. I had my way of freaking out, and he had his. It must have shown in my face, because he nodded at me and then turned to Jesse.

"I'm sorry, man. That was way out of line." He looked around. "And I'm sorry about the mess. Claire, are you bleeding?" He sounded genuinely concerned.

"Not anymore," she said quietly.

"Here, Christoph, let me do that." Michael took the rag from Christoph and started scrubbing the blood off the couch. We all just stood there, watching sadly, and I felt a tear roll down my cheek. That this incredibly powerful man, this Warrior, could have such a terrible weakness was both humbling and frightening all at once. I looked around and wondered if we were all thinking about our own weaknesses— our demons, as John called them—and how Deimos would exploit them.

Chapter Eighteen: The Mission

"Disneyland!" Rebecca cried as we drove through Anaheim. "Ooh, I've always wanted to go."

"Jesse will be thrilled to hear that," I said. "I promised him last time that we'd go."

"Really? That's great! I think that would be a perfect way to celebrate. After the mission, I mean."

Raina snorted from the back seat. "Count me out. I'll go surfing instead."

"I would have thought you'd like Space Mountain at least," Claire said. "A roller coaster in almost total darkness is about as scary as it gets."

"Snore. Not much of a ride if you're strapped down. Besides, I'm not into standing in lines."

"Jesse was trying to talk me into flying over the walls and going exploring behind the scenes," I said. "I put my foot down there, but I promised him we'd go if we paid and went in like normal people."

"I'm in," Claire said. "I absolutely love Disneyland."

"Yeah, well, we have to survive the mission first," Raina pointed out. We were all silent as we thought about what was coming. Could we really pull this off? I shook the question out of my head. I couldn't afford to doubt. Our plan just had to work.

We continued south, watching the beaches get whiter and more beautiful the farther we drove. We parked in the lot near the border and caught the trolley. It had only been three weeks since I last saw that parking lot, but it seemed like months ago. I felt anxiety growing in the pit of my stomach as we rode into Tijuana.

When we got to the hotel, Jesse and the guys had already arrived, and we went to find them in their suite.

"Nice room," I said. The main room of their suite was large but looked like it was last decorated in the seventies. "How'd you guys get here so fast?"

"We didn't stop to use the bathroom every five minutes like you girls do," Michael answered.

"How's your jaw, Michael?" Raina asked pointedly. He gave her an icy expression and turned away. I heard Claire stifle a snort.

I pointed at a large cardboard box in the middle of the floor. "Is that . . . ?"

"Yeah," Jesse said. "We had no trouble finding a supplier. You can get anything in TJ."

I fidgeted. "I really hope this works."

"It will," Christoph said, sounding completely confident. "It's a very good plan."

We went back to our room and started unpacking and organizing our things. Like the guys' suite, ours also had two rooms, with two single beds in each room. I went into one of the bedrooms and called Kai to let him know that we'd arrived.

"How are you doing?" he asked.

"I'm nervous. Is everything all set on your end?"

"Yep. Don't worry. It's all going to work out fine. Just stick to the plan, improvise if you need to, and you'll be great."

"It's just that there are so many different pieces in play. So many things that can go wrong."

"Which is why you're so valuable. Your ability to tap universal knowledge at key moments has been huge."

"No pressure," I muttered. "God, I wish you were here."

"Me too. I miss you already," he said softly.

"When this is all over, can we go camping for a weekend or something and just get away?"

"That's the best idea I've heard in a long time." He paused. "I love you, Ashlyn. Be safe, okay?"

"I will."

We hung up, and I lay back on the bed, my mind racing. I closed my eyes and visualized the plan over and over again until Raina tapped me.

"Dinner time. Gotta fuel up before the big day."

Grudgingly, I got up and followed her out the door and into the street below, where Theresa and John were waiting with the guys. I walked over to Jesse.

"Kind of a different vibe this time, wouldn't you say?" I asked.

"You can say that again. I'm kind of freaking out." He looked it. I'm sure the memory of what he went through last time was haunting him in a big way.

"I'm glad it's not just me," I said. He smiled and put his arm around me. Claire snapped a picture of us. "Hey," I protested. I hated having my picture taken.

"We're supposed to look like tourists," she said. "Might as well act the part. Besides, that's going to be a great picture. I'll send you a copy."

We walked several blocks to a restaurant where Theresa had made us a reservation. She spoke rapidly in Spanish to the waiter, and we were seated at a large table in a corner with windows overlooking the plaza. Theresa had a knack for doing everything with style. Clearly, she had loads of money, but she didn't flash it the way people like the Prescotts did. She knew how to do things in a low-key but very classy way. I watched her as she sat perusing the menu, looking as if the world was at her fingertips, and to my surprise, I found myself wishing I were more like her.

"What are you thinking?" Rebecca was looking at me quizzically.

"I just had a weird revelation. About Theresa. She's kind of my hero."

"Why is that weird?"

"I don't usually look up to people," I explained. "I'm kind of cynical that way. The last time I had an idol was when I was in grade school and was reading the Greek myths, and I learned about Artemis. She was who I wanted to be when I grew up."

"Goddess of the hunt, right? Kind of funny for a vegetarian," Rebecca said with a smile.

"She used painless arrows, which I thought was so cool. And she was super independent and ran through the forests at night, totally free. She was actually kind of a loner."

"Kind of like Theresa," Rebecca said, gazing at Theresa as she spoke to the waiter. "Or at least, that's how it would appear on the surface. In any case, you're independent, but you're not a loner at all, and I think you're happier for it."

Just then, a musician strolled over to our table, playing the guitar and singing in Spanish. I didn't know the words, but I was suddenly very sad. I thought about Kai, playing guitar alone in his room. I hoped so much that he would make it as a musician and wondered what would happen to him if he didn't.

I thought about Marlowe and how much faith he had in her talent, and I decided right then that no matter how threatened I might feel by her, I was going to do everything I could to support the whole band and encourage harmony among them.

The last thing Kai needed was for me to turn into the typical controlling girlfriend who causes political turmoil in the band.

Happy that I'd reached a place of peace about Marlowe's role in Kai's life, at least for the time being, I turned my attentions back to the present and my amazing companions. It was hard to believe that a year ago I still lived in Berkeley and hadn't met Rebecca or Jesse, or even Kai. It was incredible what a difference a year could make in your life.

The next morning, a jolt of adrenaline shot through me the second I opened my eyes, and I nearly sprang out of bed. It was only four in the morning, and we didn't have to be up for another hour. I sat up and calmed my breathing. I was going to need all my self control and every ounce of concentration to make it through the day.

After meditating for twenty minutes, I got up and showered, being careful not to get any water in my mouth. I dried my hair and went back into the bedroom to get dressed. Rebecca was up and moving around.

"How are you doing?" I asked. I felt a wave of emotion come from her, and I laughed. "Ah, about the same as I am."

"We're going to be fine," she said in a shaky voice. "I'll just feel better when we're on the road."

There was a knock on the door, and Theresa appeared with a basket of pastries and fruit and four cups of coffee. "Brewed it with bottled water in my room," she said. "I'll see you in the parking lot in half an hour." She turned and strode off, all business as usual. Today was a good day for that, I thought, as I brought the pastries and coffee into the suite. Immediately, I heard Raina call out from the other room, "Is that coffee I smell?"

Soon we were all fed and caffeinated and ready for action. With our backpacks hoisted over our shoulders, we gathered in the parking lot, where a bus was waiting for us. We got on board and settled into the cushy seats.

"Slightly more comfortable than last time," I remarked to Jesse.

He snorted. "I hate these motor coaches. They always smell like cherry air freshener."

"Keep complaining and you'll be walking," Theresa snapped as she stepped on board. She took a seat next to John, where they sat in silence, both deep in thought. There was a highly charged mixture of excitement, anticipation, and worry in the air.

About two hours later, we turned onto the side road that led up into the mountains. Theresa had told the driver that we were planning to hike and camp in the mountains and had arranged to have him drop us off at a location a few miles northeast of the prison. If he thought our choice of location was odd, he didn't say a word about it. He was probably very used to Americans coming up with all kinds of wacky vacation schemes.

When we arrived at the drop-off point, Theresa paid the driver, and we got off and started hiking south. Jesse and I occasionally took to the air and scouted ahead to make sure the way was clear. The trees got thicker, and finally we reached the spot where we had decided to make our camp. We spent the next hour setting up our tents and unpacking the huge packs that Kenji and Christoph carried. When everything was organized, Jesse, Kenji, John, and I turned to the west and hiked to the rendezvous spot.

Noiselessly, John and Kenji set up the gear while Jesse and I stretched our hearing to make sure nobody came our way. Even from outside of the property, we could hear the sounds of the prisoners working in the factory, and it turned my stomach.

I watched as Kenji took two plastic containers from the large box that the guys had procured the day before. Jesse and I loaded the containers into our backpacks and then disappeared and sailed over the fence. We went straight to the mess hall. We knew that the next shift of prisoners wasn't due to eat for another two hours, and the kitchen crew would be on a break.

Silently, we crept into the kitchen and began looking around, opening the cupboards as quietly as we could while constantly keeping an ear out for guards. Finally, Jesse gestured to me, and I hurried over to him. There, at the bottom of a pantry, was the plastic bin full of white powder I had seen the first time we were there. Working together, we carefully lifted the bin and poured its contents into two garbage bags. Next, we took the plastic containers out of our backpacks and emptied them into the bin. The powder we brought looked almost identical, and I was confident that the cooks wouldn't notice the switch. We closed the lid and put the bin back in the pantry, stuffing one of the garbage bags of drugs up on the top shelf where it wasn't likely to be spotted by the kitchen crew but would be found easily in a search. We shoved the other bag in my backpack and flew back to the rendezvous point.

"Done," Jesse said quietly as we handed our packs to Kenji. "A couple of days of drinking that vitamin C powder, and the prisoners will probably do our work for us."

"Excellent work," John said. "Time for recon. Kenji and I will head back to camp now. As soon as you find out anything, meet us back there to report."

Jesse and I headed back to the prison. This time, we flew around the perimeter, listening and watching for the head guards. We flew past the small building with the showers, shuddering as it brought back memories of Jesse's capture all too vividly.

On what seemed like the twentieth pass, we finally spotted the captain who had interrogated Jesse. I saw Jesse stiffen, and I reached out and gently laid my hand on his arm.

"Don't worry," I whispered. "He'll get his. Just be patient."

"Let's find out what he's up to," Jesse growled. The captain walked into one of the smaller buildings, where we could hear a few other people moving around inside.

"Capitán," a man said and proceeded to speak quickly in Spanish. He talked for a few moments while the others murmured in what sounded like agreement. The captain asked questions occasionally but was mostly quiet. My Spanish was gone again, and I couldn't understand anything they said, so I watched Jesse's reaction. His eyes were narrowed in deep concentration, and I saw him nod a couple of times to himself. Finally, he motioned for me to follow him, and we flew up higher into the sky where we could still see the compound but wouldn't be overheard.

"Okay, here's the deal," Jesse whispered. "The captain has an inner posse of guards who are loyal to him, and his top men are in there with him now. They've heard rumors that there are guards in the compound who want more money and shorter hours, and they're afraid of a coup. The captain told them to find out everyone who is involved in the plot, and they'll make them into prisoners."

"Crap. This could complicate things significantly. We really need to wait a couple of days for the drugs to wear off. What if we have to move sooner?"

"We'll improvise," Jesse said. "Right now we need to find out when the other guards are planning their revolt."

"But how will we find out who those guards are?"

"The most likely people to want out of this dump would be the factory guards. So let's start with them."

"Good plan, but let's report back first. Also, I think we should bring Claire and Rebecca back here with us. They might be able to detect who's on which side."

Just then, the captain and four guards left the building. Two of them headed to the warehouse while the other two headed to the showers. Jesse and I snapped some pictures of their faces before we flew back to camp, where we told the others what we'd learned.

"This changes everything," Theresa said. "We're going to have to go in there sooner than planned."

John frowned. "I'll make the call and get everyone on high alert." He quickly called Paul and Kai on the satellite phone.

With Rebecca and Claire settled onto our backs, Jesse and I flew back to the prison. We patrolled the compound, straining to hear conversations, trying to identify which guards would be involved in the uprising. Finally, we heard a couple of guards whispering as they stood outside the main building. Jesse strained to listen to them while Rebecca took pictures.

"It sounds like a guy named Alvarez is the leader," Jesse said quietly.

"We need to find him," Rebecca whispered. "Let's go inside the factory." It was a very hot day, and the doors were open wide in a vain attempt to let in a breeze. We carefully flew past the guards and went inside the factory, where it was stifling hot and smelled almost as bad as the barracks. I felt the shock and horror coming from Rebecca and Claire, and I wished they didn't have to witness this. As we slowly drifted along the assembly line, the prisoners toiled away, looking even more pathetic than last time. I stifled a gasp as one man crumpled to the floor, clearly overcome by exhaustion. I felt all of our anger rising as a guard walked casually over and dragged him into a corner, dumping him there like a broken piece of machinery.

Finally, after what seemed an eternity, Rebecca tapped me on the shoulder and pointed to a far corner. Claire was looking in the same direction, and I knew they'd found Alvarez. I felt terrible for Claire and Rebecca, having to read the feelings of all these people. It was bad enough for me with my weak Empath powers. For powerful Empaths like Claire and Rebecca, it must have been unbearable.

We flew toward the corner to find three men huddled together, talking in low voices. Jesse cocked his ear toward them, listening intently. After a few moments, the men broke up and went their separate ways, and we flew back toward the entrance. When we were almost at the doors, we saw to our dismay that there was a new set of guards in front, each with a dog at his side. The dogs sniffed the air anxiously, and one of them started barking directly at us.

We immediately dropped to the ground, where our scents would mingle with the prisoners. The dogs looked around, their noses pointed in the air working frantically. The guards seemed bored and paid no attention to the dogs at all. They obviously relied on the drugs to keep the prisoners under control.

We stood pressed up to the wall, holding our breath every time someone went by. The dogs continued to bark at us, and the guards started becoming more interested. A very large guard snapped a command at the dogs and then walked slowly toward us. He stopped a couple of feet from us, glancing around lazily, mopping his forehead with a filthy handkerchief in the suffocating heat. We breathed a sigh of relief as he turned and started to walk back the other way. Suddenly, he spun back toward us again and stepped right on Jesse's foot.

Jesse let out a tiny gasp, and the guard jumped back in alarm. Wide-eyed, he shouted out. We were all frozen, not daring to breathe. The guard yelled something again and was just pulling out his gun when there was a sudden commotion at the door. The guards were shouting and running away from the building, the dogs barking madly. The large guard hurried toward the entrance, and Claire and Rebecca gave us the signal to go ahead.

We flew out of the building and saw the guards trying to catch two wild turkeys, which were racing around in circles. I had to fight the urge to laugh at the ridiculous sight. As we flew away toward the camp, the phantom turkeys took flight and soared into the air, disappearing over the tree tops. The frantic barking of the dogs continued to fill the air behind us.

I patted Rebecca on the arm. "Nice one, you guys."

"Theresa's idea," Claire said. "She suggested it yesterday as a possible diversion. And she was right, they really went for it. Those turkeys must have looked delicious."

I turned to Jesse. "How's your foot?"

"It's fine, thank you," was his arch reply. "Let's get back."

When we got back to the camp, Jesse reported what we'd overheard.

"They're planning to start the uprising in two days. But if the captain's men already have suspicions about it, my guess is that it's all going to go down earlier than that."

Theresa snapped her notebook shut. "We can't wait to find out. We move in at midnight tonight."

"But what if the captain's men capture Alvarez today? It could trigger an early revolt and blow our plans," Claire pointed out.

"That's true," John mused. "I think we should take down the captain's men immediately. We might even be able to get a confession out of them. We should all move to the rendezvous point now, and let's send in a small unit."

Once we'd all reached the rendezvous, Jesse and I flew Kenji, Michael, Raina, and Claire over the fence one-by-one.

Claire had created an illusion that made them all look like guards so they could walk around freely, allowing Jesse and me to focus on scouting instead of having to keep them invisible.

We went to the warehouse, a huge, dusty room with tall shelves stacked with boxes and parts. We crept up the aisles until we found two of the captain's men doing inventory. Michael and Raina immediately crouched down like panthers, slipped up behind them, and took them down in seconds. Kenji rushed in to help bind their hands and feet and slip gags over their mouths before taking them to a far corner of the warehouse.

"Great!" Jesse whispered to Kenji. "We'll get Theresa in here later to question them. Keep a close watch on them in the meantime."

We headed toward the showers. Claire, Michael, and Raina were on foot, still disguised as guards, while Jesse and I flew along next to them, whispering directions as we went. When we reached the building, we went inside and looked around, but it was empty.

"They've probably gone to their bunks," Raina said. "Claire, can you figure out where they are?"

"No need, I can hear the snores from here," Jesse said. "One sec and we'll check it out."

We flew over to a window of the small building and peered through a gap in the curtains. In the dim room, we saw several men sleeping. Sure enough, two of them were from the group we'd seen coming out of the captain's quarters. We went back to tell the others which beds they were in. Raina and Michael stole quietly into the room, the sound of the snores drowning out all other noises. They approached the beds, looked at each other and nodded, and then sprang into action. They quickly tied gags over their mouths, and before the men even had a chance to fully awaken, they had slipped bags over their heads so they couldn't see. The men kicked and thrashed, and Jesse and I helped to carry them out so that we were all invisible, while Claire stayed visible but disguised as a guard so she could open the doors for us. We made our way to the warehouse and left them in Kenji's care with the others.

"That's all four down," Michael said. "Time to get Theresa."

Theresa was raised in Brazil, but her mother was from Guatemala, so she was a native speaker of both Portuguese and Spanish. She could be very determined and persuasive, and knowing her, I thought, she'd probably not only get a confession out of the guards but would convert them to our cause by the end of the conversation. As we arrived at the rendezvous, an idea occurred to me.

"Theresa, what if we try to recruit Alvarez? If he's already got many of the guards on his side, he could convince them to stay out of our way when we take out the captain."

Theresa's mouth formed a thin line. "I don't like it. Too much risk of exposure."

"Not if you pretend to be one of the captain's guards," Jesse said, catching on to my idea. "You could warn Alvarez that the captain knows about his plan but that you're sympathetic to the uprising. You could tell him that outside forces are being recruited and to keep his men out of the way at midnight."

"That might work," John said. "Theresa, do you think you're up to it?"

She gave him a withering look and cursed at him in Spanish in a low voice just as Rebecca cast an illusion over her that made her look like one of the captain's guards.

"Never mind," John said with a smile. "You're perfect." Theresa looked only slightly appeased.

Jesse and I flew Claire, Rebecca, and Theresa over the fence, while Christoph simply ran up a tree and jumped over. John stayed behind with the satellite phone. Once back in the compound, Claire, Jesse, and Theresa waited in the warehouse. I followed Rebecca and Christoph, who were disguised as two of the captain's men, to the factory. I could hear Rebecca's heart pounding in her chest and feel her intense concentration as she maintained the illusions for herself and Christoph.

When we got to the front of the factory, she and Christoph strode through the front door. The guards asked them something in Spanish, but Christoph just waved them off and walked more quickly. They went all the way back to where Alvarez was stationed, and I followed closely, hovering just above their heads.

Alvarez looked up at them, an expression of surprise crossing his face. Christoph quickly grabbed him and secured a gag over his mouth while Rebecca tied his hands behind his back. She slipped a bag over his head, and once he was fully restrained, she disguised him as a prisoner. They marched him out of the factory. The guards at the door started to question them once more, but Christoph just waved them off again. They looked irritated, obviously unhappy that they'd missed out on the excitement.

We took Alvarez to the warehouse, where Theresa was still disguised as one of the captain's men. Rebecca dropped the illusion from Alvarez and removed his hood. Alvarez looked terrified as Theresa immediately started speaking to him in a very low voice, her deep, rich tones sounding just like a man's. Jesse translated for us in whispers.

"She's telling him that the captain knows about the coup, that his guards are rounding up, um, dissenters I guess is the word, and that their only hope for escape is to set the prisoners free and escape in a mass breakout . . . now she's telling him that two of the captain's men are on their side and will help. Look at Alvarez—I think he's going to puke." Alvarez was listening carefully, but he looked panicked. After Theresa had finished, he nodded quickly and spoke in very rapid Spanish. She nodded to Christoph, who untied him. Alvarez glanced nervously between Theresa and Christoph. He spoke quickly again and left.

"Done," Theresa said quietly. "He's going to spread the word that the breakout will happen at midnight during the shift change and to stay away from the captain's quarters. That gives us six hours." Her eyes became fierce, much more like a Warrior than a Mentor. "Time to get some evidence."

Chapter Nineteen: Breakout

"This is the part where he finally confessed," Theresa said in a low voice. We were back at the rendezvous point, and she was showing us the video Jesse had taken as she interrogated the guards one-by-one. "This guy was a tough nut to crack, but he eventually saw reason when Jesse partially reappeared a couple of times. I think he wet his pants. These men are very superstitious."

She fast-forwarded the video. "Here," she said. "He's giving the name of the captain and each of his men." She grabbed a pen and quickly scrawled the names as he rattled them off. "The captain is named Perez. Well, Señor Perez," she said with a cold gleam in her eye, "we look forward to making your acquaintance."

She set down the camera. "There's more, but we can analyze the rest later. He confirmed that they'd kept the prisoners drugged to make them more compliant, and that he didn't know what the drug was but that it was a white powder that was mixed into their juice every day."

"Did he say where it came from?" John asked.

"It was delivered with the rest of the supplies. That's all he knew."

Theresa got up and stretched. She'd played her part brilliantly. I wondered if John was envious of the active role she'd gotten to take. But he seemed to be in his element running the rendezvous point, keeping in contact with Kai and Paul by satellite phone and poring over the photos we'd taken on our earlier recon mission.

Kenji and Claire were still in the warehouse, keeping the first watch over the captain's men. There was nothing else we could do but sit and wait. Jesse and I had gotten used to waiting around during our scouting duties, but it was much more difficult for Raina and Michael, who paced like caged animals.

At nine o'clock, Christoph and Rebecca relieved Kenji and Claire. She was exhausted from maintaining the illusions that kept them disguised for so long, and she immediately fell asleep. I gently laid a hand on her while she slept, sending her what little healing I had. I knew all too well how it felt to be wiped out from using your powers for hours on end.

Finally, it was eleven-thirty: time to get into position. Jesse and I helped everyone over the fence except Theresa and John, who were staying behind. Claire had her hands full again, keeping everyone in disguise, but as we got closer to the breakout time, I found that my Alchemist powers were getting stronger, and I was able to help her with maintaining the illusions. The timing was perfect, as I was beginning to understand the whisperings I heard coming from the large building where the prisoners were just waking up. Since they were fed at the end of their shift, this group had eaten at four o'clock, just after Jesse and I had replaced the drugs with the vitamin C powder. That meant that they hadn't had the drugs in over thirty hours, and the extra boost from the vitamin C was helping them to wake up more alert.

"What's happening?" I heard a voice whisper.

"A guard told me that we're breaking out at midnight," another voice said.

"My God, can it be true?"

"My head feels strangely clearer, but my body is so weak. I don't think I can fight."

"How long have we been here . . . ?"

" . . . must pray for help . . . "

The whispers faded as we continued to the warehouse, where we joined Christoph and Rebecca. Invisible, I flew in and whispered in Rebecca's ear. "It's time." She nodded and motioned to Christoph. They left the warehouse to join the group waiting outside.

"Where are you going?" one of the men shouted. "We've been trapped in here for hours!"

"You'll soon be free," I said in Spanish. The men looked wildly around for the source of my disembodied voice. "But you must atone for the evil you have done. Cooperate with the authorities when they arrive."

The men looked terrified, and I knew the message would stick. I flew out and joined the others. Alvarez must have been true to his word, because other than a few shadowy figures darting among the buildings, we didn't see a soul on our way through the compound.

When we arrived at the captain's quarters, I suddenly knew he wasn't alone.

"He found out about tonight," I said in a low voice. "He's got his remaining loyal men holed up in there with him."

"How many?" Michael asked.

I flew up to a crack in the wall and quickly counted. "Eleven, in addition to the captain," I said.

"Twelve," Jesse corrected me. "You missed the guy whimpering in the bathroom."

"Twelve, possibly more," I said.

Raina looked at our Empaths. "Ready?"

"Ready," Claire and Rebecca said in unison. They both focused intently, and a moment later screams swelled from the building.

"Ai! Serpientes!" The door flew open, revealing the horrifying image of a floor covered in long, slithering black snakes. The captain was standing on a chair, shouting at the men to hold their position, but they were scrambling and shoving to get through the door.

Once outside, they pulled out their guns and started firing. Despite my faith in our Sentries' shields, I recoiled at the terrifying sight of a group of men firing their guns directly at us, but the bullets hit the shields and fell to the ground. One man dropped to his knees in fear, and Kenji immediately tied him up. The other men ran around him, and Michael and Raina took out four apiece, hitting them with lightning-fast strikes. Claire and Jesse darted from guard to guard, tying their hands and feet with zip ties as they were knocked down or thrown to the ground.

I was flying overhead, keeping an eye on the guards to make sure none escaped. Suddenly I saw Jesse stand up very straight, and to my astonishment, he charged at one of the guards and started hitting him like he'd gone completely insane. I raced over and saw that it was the guard who had been torturing him when he was captured. The guard looked terrified as he tried to defend himself against his invisible assailant.

"You . . . stupid . . . bloodthirsty . . . dick weasel!" Jesse yelled as he hit him over and over. I grabbed Jesse's arms and held them back.

"Our job is to apprehend, not to punish. Remember?" I hissed in his ear.

"Let me go so I can kill him!" Jesse screamed, struggling against me, but my Sentry powers made him no match for my grip.

"Christoph!" I yelled. "Come get this guy!"

Christoph scooped up the bloody guard, and he and Kenji ran around grabbing the remaining men as they tried to run away. One of the men got past Christoph and took a swing at Rebecca, but she stepped nimbly out of the way and threw him to the ground, where I grabbed him and tied his hands and feet.

I was about to congratulate Rebecca when suddenly the captain appeared at the door. In slow motion, I saw him draw back his arm and hurl a large knife, which spun through the air straight at Claire. Kenji and Christoph looked like blurs as the three of us raced to jump in front of her, but we were too late. Claire turned just in time for the knife to plunge deep into her belly. She screamed as she doubled over in agony, her eyes bulging wide, and crumpled to the ground.

"No!" Rebecca shouted and ran to Claire, where Kenji was already cradling her in his arms, his face twisted into an expression of acute pain. Michael and Raina rushed the captain, hitting him so hard he was knocked out as soon as he hit the ground.

"Lay her down," Rebecca ordered, and Kenji immediately obeyed. Rebecca kneeled next to Claire, carefully examining the knife sticking out of her belly. Rebecca looked focused but was breathing very fast, and I could feel that she was near panic.

"Claire!" Jesse said, but she didn't answer. He looked on the verge of hysteria. "Rebecca, is she going to be okay?"

"We need to heal her fast. Ashlyn, help me!" We both put our hands on Claire and started pouring healing energy into her.

I noticed the others were standing around watching. Kenji now looked like he was near tears.

"What are you doing!" I shouted. "Get back to the mission!" They looked dazed for a moment and then sprang into action, herding the guards to the warehouse.

"Go, Jesse," I said gently. "We've got this." Grudgingly, he got up and followed the others.

Rebecca grasped the handle of the knife, and Claire screamed as Rebecca pulled it out of her belly and tossed it aside. We kept pouring the healing into her. "Come on, Claire, help us out," Rebecca murmured.

After what seemed like an eternity, Claire finally opened her eyes just as the wound slowly closed up. Moments later, the skin was smooth again.

"Are you okay?" I asked, pulling my hands away. I was dizzy and seeing spots. Rebecca looked thoroughly worked as well.

"I . . . I think so," Claire said, her voice trembling.

"We have to go right now," Rebecca said. We helped Claire up and ran as fast as we could toward the back of the compound. I heard Claire choke back a sob, and out of the corner of my eye I saw tears streaming down her face.

Suddenly, lights appeared in the distance followed by the sound of helicopters. "They're coming!" I shouted.

We hurried to the fence, and everyone ran back over to the rendezvous point, where Theresa and John were anxiously waiting.

"Well?" Theresa asked.

"Mission accomplished," Raina said. "The captain and his men are all secured in the warehouse."

"We just heard from Tony," John said. "They're pulling up to the gates now."

"And does he have the chairman with him?" Kenji asked.

"Yes, plus two other members of the board who wanted to see this first-hand. They're going to do the press conference live from the factory floor for maximum impact." John's eyes blazed with intensity.

"It's time for us to go," Theresa said. "Jesse, Ashlyn, stay behind and look for snipers in case we missed anyone. We'll wait for you at the camp site." They all hoisted their packs on their backs and immediately headed east.

When Jesse and I arrived back at the factory, a very different scene lay before us. There were several jeeps and a helicopter on the grounds, and headlights illuminated the interior of the factory. Tony Kirkpatrick was standing in front of a camera, talking into a microphone, with three men in suits by his side. As he talked about his capture and hellish life in the illegal factory, the camera zoomed in on the prisoners being led outside. Their haunted faces spoke volumes, and I knew every news channel in the Unites States as well as abroad would be playing these images over and over to a shocked audience.

Tony handed the microphone to the chairman of the board of Magnum-Drake, who read from a prepared statement. "In light of the discovery of this illegal factory and the lawsuit that was filed today on behalf of the shareholders, the board of directors at Magnum-Drake has acted swiftly and taken the necessary steps to correct course. As of today, we have fired the entire executive staff at Magnum-Drake, and the board will take over the day-to-day operations of the business until a new staff is hired. We will actively participate in helping with the criminal investigations that are now underway. Additionally, we are in negotiations with the labor union and are revisiting our strategy for taking Magnum-Drake forward."

The chairman looked very tired and anxious as he spoke. I didn't get the sense that he had any idea that this factory existed, and I felt his horror over the fact that the executive team had been engaging in such atrocious illegal activities right under his nose.

Tony took the microphone back and started fielding questions from reporters. All of a sudden, a round of shots rang out, the sound ricocheting around the building, and everyone dived to the ground.

"Jesse!" I shouted.

"Where is it coming from?" We looked desperately around. At the back of the room was the large guard who had stepped on Jesse's foot earlier. He had a rifle and was shooting wildly into the middle of the room, but my shield was protecting us. He ran out of ammunition and dropped the rifle in disgust. But instead of running, he stood his ground and pulled a canister out of his pocket.

"No!" I shouted as Jesse and I both charged him at once. We knocked him flat, the tear gas canister flying out of his hand. It hit Jesse squarely in the face before bouncing back down and landing on the guard's chest. It was already spraying gas, and the guard started coughing violently.

"Everybody clear the hall!" I yelled. The guard was rolling on the ground vomiting, having received a face full of the spray.

My shield protected Jesse and me from the gas, but it hadn't protected Jesse from the canister itself when it hit him in the face. Blood was flowing freely from his nose, and tears were streaming from his eyes. I put my hands over his face and focused all my energy on healing him.

"Goddamnit, that sucked!" he said shakily. "That stupid bastard!"

"Why the hell can't Sentry powers include protection against stuff being thrown at us?!" I said in dismay. "Oh well, that crime carried its own punishment. Look at him." The guard was still where we'd left him, writhing on the ground in agony.

"Not punishment enough," Jesse said. "Cover me." I covered him in illusion so that he looked like one of Alvarez's guards, and he reappeared. He ran over, grabbed the guard, and dragged him out of the hall.

"Here's the shooter!" Jesse said in Spanish and threw him at the feet of the guards, who pounced on him. Jesse walked quickly back inside and disappeared, and we flew out over their heads, escaping into the night air.

We headed to the mess hall, where the prisoners were crammed inside getting food. The guards were opening every can and box they had available. Police came out of the kitchen carrying the garbage bag full of the drug powder that we'd stashed in the back of the closet.

The prisoners ate with terrible urgency. The drugs were wearing off, and the dead expression in their eyes had been replaced by fear and pain. I shook my head in disgust. How could people treat other human beings like animals? Come to think of it, how could people treat animals like this? The wisdom of being a vegetarian really hit home. At that thought, I was suddenly filled with longing to talk to Kai and to let him know that I was okay.

We left the mess hall, and I heard the showers going. Some prisoners must already be in there, I guessed. I could only imagine what it must feel like to shower for the first time after being filthy for so long.

We headed over to the warehouse, where the police were handcuffing the captain and his men and taking them into custody. I saw Alvarez talking with the police and giving them the full story about how he and his crew had been hired to guard what they were told was a prison. They had soon realized it was not legitimate and wanted out, but the captain had threatened their families if they tried to leave, and one guard had even been murdered. As he was describing how he and his men were planning to overthrow the captain and his men, I found it more and more difficult to comprehend what he was saying, until finally all I heard was a string of Spanish words that I could no longer understand.

Satisfied that everything was under control and that the crisis had passed, Jesse and I flew over the fence. The stars were very bright, and the moon cast serene blue-grey shadows from the trees onto the ground. A faint breeze was blowing, cooling the night, and there was a slightly sweet smell in the air. A wave of peace washed over me, and suddenly I felt completely exhausted. Jesse and I flew in silence all the way back to the camp site.

Chapter Twenty: R & R

On the bus ride back to Tijuana, we talked in low, tired voices. Jesse and I had risen early to do some more scouting and found that some of the prisoners were already gone. The police had worked all night to process the prisoners, taking their names and statements, having medical staff check them out, and giving them all some cash to get home. Kai, Paul, and John had matched many of the photos we'd taken with the names of missing people and then sent the information to Tony. I saw several copies of Tony's printouts on the tables where the police were working, and I was glad that it was helping them expedite the process for those who were still too out of it to give their information.

For those who were able to leave right away, Tony and the chairman simply handed over the keys to all the cars on the lot so that they could get out of there as quickly as possible. Rebecca had thought that was a gesture of good will on the company's part, but I couldn't help being cynical about it, since the cars were undoubtedly worthless and the company would write them off anyway. My faith in executives had become about as weak as my faith in politicians.

Most of the prisoners had to stay behind to receive additional medical attention. They would be boarding a bus that morning to Ensenada, where the hospital was ready to receive them. Some were in terrible shape, with a long recovery ahead of them.

"They're all going to need a lot of counseling to get over this," Claire said sadly.

"I hope the physical detox from the drugs isn't all that bad," Rebecca added. "It only took Tony a few days to recover."

"I wonder what drug they were giving them," I mused.

"We'll find out in about a week," Kenji said. "I'm going to drop off the sample you got me at a lab in Tijuana before we go."

"Just don't try to take any across the border," John warned. "If you get caught trying to bring it into the States, you'll be in prison for the rest of your life."

We rode in silence for a while, and I noted how different we felt after completing this mission compared to the mission last December. Back then, our work was still kind of new and exciting. This time, it was just sickening to know the things people were willing to do to make more money. Greed appeared to be a bottomless source of evil, and I wondered what other ways it would manifest itself. The experience had left a bitter taste in all of our mouths.

Christoph was the first to break the mood. "You know," he said in his cheerful voice. "We should all be very proud." He turned to Rebecca. "The way you and Ashlyn saved Claire was brilliant." He reached out and took her hand.

"How are you feeling, Claire?" Rebecca asked.

"I'm okay now. But . . . that was just horrible." Her face looked haunted by the memory.

"I think we should celebrate that it's over, that we succeeded," Christoph continued. Nobody felt much in the mood for celebrating, but John nodded.

"Christoph is right. As we saw so clearly from the prisoners, one simple way to spread evil is to take away hope. It's important that we celebrate our victories and not give in to despair."

"Very true," Theresa agreed. "When we get back to the hotel, let's get cleaned up and go out."

I still didn't feel like it, but I saw their point, and I tried to feel happy. I was glad the prisoners were going home, and that they would be reunited with their families and could go on with their lives. I wished I knew what would happen to the workers in Minnesota, though. I didn't see how our victory in Mexico would help the situation in Cooke, but I knew Tony was actively working on a solution there. I had done my job, and all I could do was trust that others would do theirs.

We arrived at the hotel and took turns taking showers and getting ready to go out. John had already called Kai and Paul from the satellite phone the night before, but I hadn't had a chance to call Kai yet, and I was dying to talk to him. As soon as I found a moment, I called him from my cell phone.

"Are you sure you're okay?" Kai asked. "You don't sound so great."

"I'm just tired. And yeah, it was a really bad scene. I mean, the mission went incredibly well. But I just don't know what it's going to take for those poor people to put their lives back together after this."

"You've done all you can, and you've given them back their futures. I'm so proud of you, Ashlyn."

"Thanks. You did an incredible job, too. The way you guys coordinated with Tony and the Mexican police and the reporters and everything . . . well, it was amazing. I can't believe how smoothly it all went down."

"We got lucky with Tony. He's been a great ally. By the way, he said he wants to meet us, and I thought we could get together when we go up to San Francisco next week to pick up Laurel at the airport."

I felt a flutter of excitement. Laurel was finally coming home! It was going to be so great to see her again. For the first time, I wasn't worried about Kai meeting her. I just knew now that they would get along great.

My thoughts were interrupted when I heard a knock on the door on Kai's end of the line.

"Oops, I'm sorry, I have to go. My lesson is here."

"Lesson?"

"I'm giving guitar lessons to one of my co-worker's kids."

"What a great idea! That's a perfect way to make some extra money."

"Actually, she's a single parent and doesn't have much money, so I'm doing it for free. Her son is apparently really excited to learn guitar."

"I think that's a fantastic idea. But how are you going to find the time?"

"It's only an hour a week. I'll make it work. Anyway, I have to go. I love you, Ashlyn."

"I love you, Kai. I'll see you soon."

I hung up and shook my head in amazement. Kai was the most giving person I had ever met. With everything he had going on, he probably didn't think twice about donating his valuable time to help someone out. And when I thought about it, was it really that big of a sacrifice? It was one hour a week, and who knew what a difference it would make in that kid's life? I wondered if I should start teaching kids to swim or to fix their bikes or something. I knew I was already giving back plenty, being a Soterian, but ironically, fighting evil on a grand scale didn't have the same feeling of reward as working one-on-one with an individual. We'd just broken hundreds of prisoners out of hell, and I didn't really feel all that fulfilled.

The restaurant was a much wilder place than the first one Theresa had taken us to, with piñatas and decorations all over the walls and loud music playing. We had a great dinner, and then Jesse and I lead the way to the dance floor. It really did feel good to blow off steam and have some fun. Christoph was right, we needed to celebrate our victories. Even Theresa and John danced. Michael and Raina stayed at the table drinking beer and talking, but I noticed that Michael was taking it easier than usual and that no tequila was involved. Was it possible that he was actually getting his shit together? It seemed like too much to hope for.

The next day, we headed north again. Raina, Michael, Theresa, and John went to Huntington Beach to spend the day at the ocean, while the rest of us went to Disneyland. Jesse was bouncing all the way to the entrance, and we were all excited to run around the park like a bunch of kids, going on the rides and getting photos with the Disney characters.

Waiting in line for Space Mountain, I felt my phone vibrate. It was Kai.

"Hey, how's it going?" he asked.

"Great! We just went on the Matterhorn and now we're in line for Space Mountain. It's going to be about an hour wait."

"That's too bad. But it's worth it. It's a fun ride." He sounded odd.

"Where are you? You sound like you're outside."

"Yeah, I'm at the park," he said in a weird distracted voice.

"The park?"

"You know, the park." There was definitely ˙something strange going on.

"Kai, where *are* you?" I asked again, getting worried.

"Turn around." I spun around, and there he was, a big smile on his face. I threw my arms around him, and the joy that had left my heart over the last couple of days came rushing back all at once. I started babbling like an idiot.

"Kai! Where did you come from? Oh my God, I'm so happy you're here! We already went on the Haunted Mansion ride, but it's my favorite, so I'll gladly go on it again if you want. And we haven't been on the Wild Ride of Mr. Toad yet . . . or do you not go in for the little kid rides?"

"Ashlyn, shhhh," he said. He put his finger to my lips and then kissed me. "It's okay. We have all day."

"I can't believe you're here. It's so good to see you!" I said, squeezing him tighter.

Rebecca grinned. "Hi, Kai. Glad you found us."

"Did you orchestrate this?" I asked her in surprise.

"Of course, silly. I texted him our location."

"This doesn't count as hiding information from you, does it?" Kai asked with a trace of concern on his face.

"No," I laughed. "I don't like surprises, as you know, but this was a good one." I pulled him closer. I didn't care if we had to stand in line all day as long as I was with him.

At nine o'clock, we gathered by Sleeping Beauty Castle to watch the fireworks show. The music started, and explosions of color bloomed across the night sky. Christoph was standing behind Rebecca with his arms around her as they both looked up in wonder. Jesse was forcing Claire to dance with him to the music, making her laugh, while Kenji regarded the fireworks with a look of fascination on his face. I looked at Kai, the reflections of the lights dancing in his beautiful eyes. I still found him so breathtakingly gorgeous, even after almost a year.

Suddenly, someone shouted "Look behind you!" and we saw Tinkerbell shoot across the sky, drawing enormous applause. I pointed at her and tugged on Jesse's sleeve.

"Jesse!" I shouted. "I think I just figured out what I can do after I graduate!" He howled with laughter, and Kai pulled me close to him.

"I have a better idea," he said. "Come on the road with me."

"As your groupie?" I teased.

"As my wife."

I felt a jolt of electricity course through my body. "I like the sound of that." We walked slowly through the immaculate streets of Disneyland, hearing the shrieks of people riding on the Matterhorn, and I realized I could no longer remember what it was like to have a normal life.

Chapter Twenty-one: Confessions

"Tony, it's a pleasure to meet you at last," Paul said. He and Kai took turns shaking Tony's hand, and then they all sat down at a table outside a small café in San Francisco. Jesse and I were invisible, perched on the roof just above them where we could hear their conversation. We were also keeping an eye out in case Tony had been followed. I still didn't quite trust him, as helpful as he'd been. I got the impression that he was hiding something, and I didn't like it.

"Thank you for meeting me," he said, looking at them curiously. "I must say I'm surprised. I assumed you were much older."

Paul winked. "All part of the cover."

"What's happening with Magnum-Drake?" Kai asked. "Is there any news on the factory in Cooke?"

"Yes, I have some very good news to report," Tony replied. "We worked closely with the board on a new strategy for the company, and we've decided to re-open the factory in Cooke but to retool it for hybrid and electric cars. And, we're going to devote part of the factory to research and development of renewable energy."

Kai's eyes lit up. "That is good news."

"I'm surprised the board went for that idea," Paul said with a slight frown. "That doesn't sound like a strategy that's going to turn a profit any time soon."

"You're right," Tony said. "The Cooke factory is part of our long-term strategy for growth, and we're getting government subsidies because of its work toward clean energy. For the short-term, we're also keeping the factory in Tijuana as well as Magnum's factory in Detroit. The Tijuana factory is a first-rate facility and more than capable of meeting demand. The prison wasn't necessary at all . . . it was just a way for executives to make extra money for themselves."

"So we were right? Those extra employees didn't exist?" Paul asked.

Tony nodded. "Purely fictitious. There were hundreds of phony employees on the books, and their paychecks went straight into accounts owned by the executives. They were also cutting extra checks to vendors and then changing the names on the checks to the executives. And then there was the money they were taking from the drug cartels in Mexico in exchange for imprisoning their enemies. All of those schemes together added up to a lot of money."

"The thing I don't understand is how they thought they would actually get away with it," Kai said. "I mean, the quality of the cars coming out of the prison was terrible. Did they honestly think nobody would notice?"

"They were blinded by greed, or in some cases, fear. Which brings me to another topic. It's the main reason I wanted to meet with you, actually." The waiter arrived with their coffees, and they waited for him to walk away before continuing to speak.

"There was one piece of the puzzle that allowed the merger to go through the way it did," he said in a low voice. "Did you ever wonder how the labor union had allowed the contract to expire?"

"Yes, of course," Kai said. "But I just assumed you thought you were in a stronger position than you were."

"It was more insidious than that. Nine months ago, I sold some stock in Magnum right before its price went down. I made a good chunk of money off the transaction. But about a month before the merger, I got a call from Gary Prescott. He said he had evidence that I had participated in insider trading and that he was going to report me unless I worked with him on the merger."

"Did you have inside information?" Paul asked, his eyebrows raised.

"I had heard rumors about a merger, but nothing official. In hindsight, it was very stupid of me to sell stock when there was any hint that something might be going on. I'm the attorney for the labor union, after all. But I didn't do it intentionally, and I was suddenly stuck."

Kai sighed. "So on Prescott's order, you found a way to let the contract expire. Because you were afraid of going to prison."

"Yes," Tony admitted. "Quite ironic, since it happened anyway." He took a sip of coffee, shuddering slightly at the memory. "After the merger and the layoffs, I was wracked with guilt. I had no idea they were going to shut down the entire plant. They had assured me that there would be a small layoff that wouldn't impact the majority of the workers. I think I wanted to believe it more than anything else, but I must have known on some level that they were lying. So when the plant shut down, I started investigating the Tijuana factory, determined to find a way to invalidate the merger and get the Cooke factory re-opened. I had no idea how much corruption was actually at play until I found the prison. I don't know what I thought I was going to do, going there completely unprepared. It's not surprising I was caught." He looked pensively over his cup at Kai and Paul.

"That clears up a lot of questions," Paul said. "But why are you telling us this? You could have gotten away with no one knowing anything about it. People think of you as a hero now."

"That's the problem. I don't want to live a lie anymore. I'm not a hero. I was a coward, and because of me, thousands of people have suffered. You've been working in secret to resolve this crisis, which means that you must have everyone's best interest in mind. So I wanted to get your advice before I go public with this information."

Paul and Kai looked at each other. Finally, Paul spoke. "Tony, I don't think it would be the wisest course of action to go public with this. The company is balanced on the edge of a knife as it is. One more blow to the public trust could sink the company, which would mean many more people out of work. The best thing you can do is keep silent."

"My guess is that's what you were planning to do anyway," Kai said, looking hard at Tony. "But you wanted us to know the truth so you could unburden your conscience."

Tony looked down at his coffee again. "You're probably right. I know that it would be a useless gesture to come forward with this. I was sort of hoping for forgiveness, I guess."

"Forgiveness doesn't come from someone else. It comes through your own actions," Kai said, an impatient edge to his voice. "You'll find forgiveness if you don't give in to the temptation to take the easy road again. Hopefully it should be less tempting now that you know where it leads."

"Believe me, nobody knows that better than I do. An eighteen-month sentence in a white-collar prison would have been a vacation compared to the month I spent in that hell hole."

"Then the next step is to devote yourself to nailing those guys to the wall," Paul said. "Is there anything else we can provide you with? You have our videos and all the evidence we collected."

"No. The only other thing is that I want to thank you. If there's ever anything I can do to help you out, please let me know."

"I'm sure we'll take you up on that," Kai said. He looked somewhat placated, but I could tell he was going to have a hard time ever trusting Tony again.

Later that day, we went to Theresa's to meet John, who had come up to San Francisco for a martial arts tournament with several of his students. Theresa was in a particularly foul mood.

"That woman is driving me crazy," she said walking into the living room, snapping her phone shut.

"Who?" John asked.

"Helen Prescott. Suddenly I'm her confidante, and she keeps calling me to talk about her personal life. If she weren't such a good customer, I'd tell her to go to hell."

"What's happening with her?" I asked.

"She's leaving Gary. She said she feels she has to divorce him to 'protect their assets,' which of course simply means she no longer wants to be married to someone who's about to be imprisoned, and she wants to make sure she gets her take of their estate before it's confiscated."

"I'm sure it's already too late for that," John said. "Their assets would have been frozen as soon as the criminal investigation began."

"Yes, but Helen seemed to sense that something was wrong and had already liquidated several of their larger assets a few months ago, putting the money into offshore accounts. Her own personal accounts, mind you. She might be a brainless twit in most respects, but she definitely has some sense when it comes to money."

"I think she deserves our compassion," John said. "She must be going through a terrible time."

Theresa stared at him like he was from another planet. "John, for a man of your years, you are unbelievably naïve sometimes."

Kai and I quickly said good-bye, leaving Theresa and John to seethe at each other. As we walked to the car, we passed a health club where we could see several televisions tuned to news stations that were broadcasting stories about the merger and the illegal prison. The bizarre contrast of people on exercise machines watching images of the starving prisoners turned my stomach, and I quickly looked away. "Do you think Helen knew anything about the illegal stuff Gary was doing?" I asked Kai.

"I wouldn't be surprised. As Theresa said, she knows money. Some people just seem to be able to sniff it out. I meet a lot of women like her at the vet clinic. The irony is that it's always the people who are dripping with money who argue most about their vet bills."

"I guess if money is your primary love, you'll do whatever you can to avoid parting with it."

He nodded. "I understand the impulse, just not the object. I'm certainly motivated to do whatever it takes to avoid parting with you." He put his arm around me and held me close to him as we walked.

When we got to the car, I stopped and faced him.

"Kai, when we get back, I want to meet Marlowe."

"You sure?"

"Yeah, I'm sure. I'm ready to meet her. Who knows . . . maybe we'll even become friends. No matter what, I want to support you however I can, and I never want you to restrict what you're doing with your band because you're worried about my reaction. I want to be a help to you guys, not an obstacle."

Kai slipped his arms around me. "Thank you," he said, relief written clearly across his face. It made me feel terrible that I'd caused him so much stress over my stupid insecurity. "Please believe me, you have nothing to worry about. And I do think you and Marlowe will like each other. She's going to be great for our band, but you always come first, okay?"

I nodded, and we got into the car to drive back to Berkeley. As we drove over the Bay Bridge, I looked out at the water and saw the Golden Gate Bridge in the distance. I had a special appreciation for that bridge ever since it had almost been destroyed. Between terrorists and corrupt executives, stolen elections and illegal prisons, I was really getting a crash course in the negative side of life. Part of me wished that I could go back to the innocence of a year ago, when all I cared about was meeting some fun people in school and training for triathlons.

But there was no going back. I was a Soterian, and my life was centered on restoring the balance of good and evil. And as an Alchemist, my power came from merging the powers of light and dark to achieve that balance. Life was not about avoiding hardship and having fun all the time. What had Kai said about Puccini all those months ago . . . that his music was like a meal of whipped cream? While I didn't agree with that, I saw his point in the greater scheme of things: that challenges and difficult times were what made life interesting.

I took Kai's hand and let his warmth flow into me. His love really was the key to my strength, and I knew that as long as I had him in my life, I could do anything. We drove to Berkeley, completely content in each other's presence, ready to face whatever challenge life threw at us next.

Acknowledgements

Since I published *Rising Shadow*, I have been overwhelmed by the many people who have come forward to offer me guidance, assistance, and support, have followed my blog or become fans of The Soterians on Facebook, and have written reviews and interviewed me on their blogs. To all of you I offer my most heartfelt thanks and sincere appreciation. Special thanks go to the following people:

Drew and Holly, for your constant support and allowing me to bring the Soterians into our daily lives as extended family members.

Mom and Betsy, for continuing to listen to me obsess on a daily basis.

Dad, for reminding me so wisely of one of my favorite Shakespeare quotes: "This above all, to thine own self be true."

Elizabeth, for sage advice from your many years of writing.

Charlotte, Jim, Gloria, Rick, Laurie, Jake, and the rest of Drew's family, for welcoming me so warmly into your lives.

Rachel Tennenbaum and Barbara Wright, for your incredible devotion to editing my books and making them so much better.

Christi Weidling, Marlene Romaine, and Marilyn Hilton, for your outstanding guidance on marketing and publicity right when it was most needed.

Marianne Schwerdtfeger, Ginny Gelczis, Mary James, Lauren James, Anna Durr, Niko Durr, Ilene Goldberg, Jill Honodel, Barb Levanfisher, and Matt Rodriguez for being such strong supporters of my books.

Meghan Ward, Aaron Maurer, Jennifer Sprague, Jami Slack, Mishel Zabala, Eleni Xekardakis, and all the other great bloggers I've met out there in the blogosphere.

Kenneth Wilson, for being so generous with timely and helpful advice.

The incredible kids at The Crowden School and the Virtuoso Program at San Domenico. Your music is a gift to all of us.

To the rest of my family, my friends, and everyone who has felt the pull, I thank you for taking this amazing journey with me.

About the Author

Jacquelyn has worked as a professional writer since 1991. She has received numerous awards for her technical writing, but creative writing has always been her passion. After writing poetry, children's stories, and screenplays, Jacquelyn embarked on The Soterians series for young adults. You can read the first novel in the series, *Rising Shadow*, for free on her web site (www.soterians.com), or purchase the paperback. As an advocate for volunteerism and service, Jacquelyn donates 20% of her royalties to the charities listed on her site.

In her spare time, Jacquelyn practices martial arts, trains for triathlons, skis, plays music, and volunteers. She lives in the San Francisco Bay Area with her husband and their daughter.